Secrets that
Created Wishes

ORLA
KELLY
PUBLISHING

Siobhan Clancy

Best Wishes

Siobhan Clancy

Feb 2021

978-1-912328-88-8

Published in Ireland by Orla Kelly Publishing.
Proofread by Red Pen Edits.

This book is dedicated to Marie, my best friend.

I didn't get to write a poem for you, but I hope a book will do.

Always missed and loved.

About The Author

I was born in Clonmel, County Tipperary, in the shadow of Slievenamon. One of eight children, I have four sisters and three brothers. I started writing poetry and short stories in my twenties. I have always wanted to write a book and it has been on my bucket list for many years. Finally, I found the time and opportunity to write this story. Most of which was written while wintering with my partner in our campervan, in the south of Spain, in a small town called Castell de Ferro. Where the peace and tranquil surroundings were of great inspiration.

After losing my close friend, I took a good long look at life. This helped me decide to write my bucket list and do all in my power to achieve my life's ambitions. Gladly, I have gone many miles down that road. As activities on my bucket list span a wide range, between learning to ride a motorcycle, skydiving and backpacking around Asia, writing this book was one of the safer aspirations.

Contents

Start at The Start

Pete

"Look at the excitement in her little face, her big blue eyes are all aglow. How lucky am I to have such a precious daughter?" These were the words Pete used to describe his little Angela that Christmas morning when she saw the presents under the tree. The excitement was just too much for her. She was seven now and not a sound had she ever heard.

Pete remembered the day the doctor told them. The memory never left him. A pain like no other. That was the day he was to truly learn a lot about his strengths and weaknesses.

Charlotte had taken it very badly, blaming herself. This he could never understand, no matter how hard he tried.

Pete had stood there and listened intently. His beautiful little girl would probably never hear any of the sounds, be they good or bad, that the world contained.

Somewhere deep down, they both knew something was not right. Angela had never reacted much to the sound of their voices, even when she was in the womb. She had cried like all babies do on their arrival into the world. But to be honest she had hardly ever cried much since then. She was just a quiet baby, their families and friends would say, how lucky they were to have such a quiet little girl. What a beautiful, gentle soul. Who knew what lay ahead…

Three days after the birth of their beautiful 7lbs 5oz baby girl, was to be the day that would change everything.

The paediatrician had stood at the end of Charlotte's bed as she fed our little Angela. Mr McSharry was his name. His solemn face and words are forever embedded in my mind.

"Mr and Mrs Williams, it was brought to my attention that there have been some concerns about Angela's sensory developments. After observing your daughter's reaction to sounds and her low communication on my last visit, I feel she is not responding with the reactions expected of a newborn. I regret to say the diagnosis is not a good one. We feel that Angela has some hearing issues. We suspect congenital sensorineural hearing loss. There will, of course, be more tests to confirm this diagnosis as she develops. There are always so many new developments out there now, and that gives us hope. We should keep our minds open and be as positive as possible…"

I am sure Mr McSharry said a lot more, but I have to admit I missed most of it at the time. As I was so focused on the expression on Charlotte's face. Pure devastation. Mr McSharry left, giving us some time to privately digest the information. I held Charlotte and we both wept as the news sunk in. I told Charlotte everything would be fine. Sure, it just made our baby a little bit more special.

Later I was to think how, at least at that moment, Charlotte was present and reacting. Within a few hours, her face became devoid of any emotion or expression.

She seemed to slowly distance herself, unable to take the news onboard.

Let me explain about the lady I married. Charlotte's childhood was not easy. Her home life was dysfunctional, to say the least.

When we decided to have children, she told me how terrified she was. It took me a long time to convince her that she would make an amazing mother. Eventually, she had started to dream of the moment she would become a mother.

Their baby was going to be perfect. She was going to be the perfect mother, so different from her own. She would do everything in her power to make this happen.

But now this had changed everything. "It wasn't meant to be this way…"

I tried to tell her how we needed to be realistic. It would be hard, but she's our beautiful little girl and we will cope. We will pull together. Charlotte agreed with me. I felt as long as she had some time to recover from the birth and got some sleep, she would see things in a better light. Things would get better with time. They just had to, I thought in desperation.

After a week in hospital, the day arrived to bring our Angela home. I arrived at the room with her lovely new going-home outfit, that Charlotte had chosen. Charlotte asked me would I get the baby dressed as she was still sore. She packed the bags, and we were ready to go. There was not that air of excitement I imagined there would be bringing our little lady home. When I went to the nurses' station to collect the prescription, the nurse on duty, asked if she could speak to me for a moment.

"Mr Williams, it might be no harm to get Charlotte to speak to somebody when you are settled home. Baby blues are quite normal you know, a lot of women suffer, a bit of counselling would really help."

I smiled and said thank you for the advice. This was advice I should have taken, but I wanted to believe we would be alright.

I tried not to notice how Charlotte was having less and less contact with Angela. I suppose I thought things would change with time. She was bound to be feeling low. It was a lot to take in. She had been through a lot. She had only given birth seven days ago and it had been a long, painful labour.

I would never have predicted what was ahead of us. I don't think anybody could have if I am truly honest.

Things were to become a lot harder when we arrived home. There was no button to press, no nurse to help, to tell us what we needed to do.

Angela cried a lot. It was so difficult to judge what her needs were and that they were being met. Charlotte had no real input in any of this.

I had taken two weeks holiday leave to be at home to help Charlotte but had now found myself to be in full care of Angela. It did start to get easier, as I learned to recognise Angela's expressions and cries. When she was hungry, her already big blue eyes just seemed to grow massive. When she had a pain, her little face would scrunch up and it was like her eyes were pleading with me to help her. Of course, a required nappy change became very obvious. When I would tell Charlotte these things, she would just shrug and say, "Oh ok."

She was only rising for a few hours in the day and had stopped looking at Angela. Family and friends told me this would change, just give her time. Her maternal instincts would kick in soon.

My sister suggested postnatal depression, and to give her space and time. I did just that and took the full responsibility of Angela. She was such a good baby and I felt she was teaching me all I needed to know.

It was coming near the end of the two weeks and I was really starting to worry. I had to return to work, but how was Charlotte going to cope with caring for Angela.

That Friday before I was due to return, I told Charlotte I had to go into work to get organised for Monday. At first, it was as if she had not even heard me. Then she asked if I had organised somebody to mind 'The Baby'. It was so hard holding my patience and keeping a calm voice when I told her I felt she was the best person to care for Angela. Come Monday she would be on her own. I could see the look of panic on her face, so I told her that my mother would be there to help her. "So today can be a practice run, ok? I will only be a few hours."

Two slow agonising hours passed. It just didn't feel right. I had this terrible feeling in the pit of my stomach. I kept seeing Angela's little face with tears running down it. Then the strangest thing happened – it was if I could hear her crying. It was heart-breaking. It was at that moment I knew something was wrong. I knew I should not have left Charlotte alone with Angela. What had I been thinking?

Jumping into the car, I headed straight for home. As I pulled into the drive, I got a sense that something was terribly wrong. I turned off the engine, grabbed the keys and ran for the front door. This all seemed to take a lifetime. I struggled to get the key into the lock, panic had set in and I did not know why. Eventually the door opened, I ran to the kitchen, there was no sign or sound to be heard. Taking two steps at a time I arrived in Angela's room, she was in her crib, eyes were wide, as large tears ran down her tiny red cheeks. I took her in my arms. She snuggled into my neck. I held her close until she calmed down.

It took a few moments, but then I noticed that Angela had not even been changed and had been sick on herself. How could Charlotte have left her like this? I went looking for her trying hard to suppress my anger but having had enough of this. I called her name but there was no answer, no noise. I entered our room then it became obvious why.

The wardrobes were thrown open, random items belonging to Charlotte gone. There, stuck in the mirror, was a note. I decided to take care of Angela first and then I would deal with the note. I bathed her and put fresh clothes on her, fed her and settled her to sleep, kissing her forehead as I slipped her into her crib. I was working on automatic pilot, not able to think about anything but Angela.

When Angela was settled, I returned to the bedroom and took the note from the mirror. I unfolded it. I thought how blind I had been, not to see this coming, Charlotte was gone and now her note told why.

Secrets That Created Wishes

Pete,

I am so, so sorry. You have been amazing taking care of Angela and I know you will do a better job than me. I just can't do it. Nothing is as I expected. I can't hold her without feeling blame. I look at everything I did every day of my pregnancy. When I look at her, I think of how much I wanted her to be perfect and she isn't, Pete. Maybe it was the time I fell down the stairs and nearly lost her. Maybe I should be grateful, as she is here but I just can't shake the guilt. And maybe, I was right. Maybe I am just not mother material.

I don't know what it is. I just know I have to leave. Angela is so lucky to have you as her dad. She will be so loved and cared for, just as she deserves.

I hope that one day you will be able to forgive me for this. I know I never will forgive myself.

Tell Angela I love her but I was just not strong or good enough to give her what she needs most – A Mother.

I know you will think me weak and a coward. I am so sorry.

Love you always,
Charlotte xx

I sat on the bed with the note in my hand. The first I knew I was crying was seeing the large drops hitting the paper. How was I going to cope? Where was Charlotte gone? Question after question ran through my head and none of this made any sense to me.

Eventually I got up. I phoned my mother. I should have gone looking for Charlotte, but I didn't know where to start. I suppose, hindsight is a great thing. All I felt for a long time was anger towards Charlotte, blind to the real cause of her going.

Charlotte

Angela is seven now. I wonder what she looks like. It is Christmas and as much as I try to forget these occasions, the milestones in her life, it is impossible. The image of her face is always in my mind. Nothing works, no matter what I do to distract myself.

My mind always wanders back to that time. I could never have imagined how everything would change. Questioning every day why I did not turn back, go home, talk to Pete. Reliving that time over and over in my mind, unable to comprehend what happened.

There are no words that can describe the excitement and terror that enveloped me when I discovered I was expecting our baby.

Questions filled my head. Would I be good enough to be a mother? Could I do it? Could I be the mother my mother never was?

At the four-month stage, I had a bad fall down the stairs. I was terrified something was after happening to my baby. I insisted on having lots of tests done, to be sure. The gynaecologist said, as far as she could tell, everything seemed fine. That I should try to relax and enjoy my pregnancy. Even asking if I wanted to know whether it was a boy or a girl, but Pete wanted to wait, not knowing being part of the excitement...

Pete was absolutely amazing throughout the pregnancy. There was nothing he wouldn't have done to make sure I was happy and at ease. I did wonder if my mother had that kind of support and love, would she have been different? Made a better mother maybe? My dad was next to useless, a real Jack the lad. Street angel, house devil, is probably the best way to describe him. Everyone's friend, especially those in the local pub, Kenny's. Sure, he was a great man to buy you a pint...

It was a relatively easy pregnancy, and everybody told me how I glowed. How pregnancy really suited me.

I loved the feeling more and more as my bump grew and I could feel the baby move inside me.

I was so excited, but still worried too much. I feel now that maybe I made the worst happen, as my thoughts were always, 'What if...'

Pete would always ease my mind with a positive response. All would be fine. I would be terrific. Always so reassuring.

The nearer it got to my due date, despite everything, my anxiety grew...

The morning my waters broke at six o'clock, I woke Pete when the pains got stronger and wow, were they full-on! I thought this will be a fast labour, as surely the pains shouldn't be this strong so early. Oh, my naivety! We arrived at the hospital at half past nine and it would be another twelve long hard hours before my beautiful little girl was laid across my chest by the midwife. A head of black hair and the biggest blue eyes. Her loud cry reassured me all was fine. We fell in love immediately. This truly was a precious moment. I counted her fingers and toes. Everything was in place. I was so overwhelmed that I don't even remember being stitched. Pete and I were just besotted. No matter what words you use, there are none that can truly express that moment.

We had decided on Angela for a girl from the beginning, and she truly was an angel.

The next few days passed in a blur of hospital routine and lots of visitors. But something wasn't right with me. I couldn't put my finger on it, but when I spoke to Pete, he would always calm me. The nurses, family and friends, all told us how lucky we were to have such a sweet, quiet little angel. Nobody seemed to notice that I wasn't myself. I suppose it was all the excitement, but I later learned the real reason…

The day the paediatrician, Mr McSharry, stood at the end of my bed and spoke about his worries for Angela, to tell the truth – I was in complete shock. All my fears had become a reality.

This was all my fault. Truthfully, I hardly heard the doctor's words after that. My mind was a million miles away. Every drink I had taken, the times in my twenties when I experimented with drugs, then the fall down the stairs. It was all my fault. I knew I would mess up – that was all I could think.

To others, it must seem so selfish, but I couldn't think of anything other than I was a bad mother already. I will only make things worse...

I suppose looking back now, the final straw had to be when Pete's mother came to visit me in hospital. Strangely, she had come on her own.

She sat on the edge of the bed and looked at me. "Hello Charlotte, how are you getting on? Pete told me you are finding things quite hard. I do understand, dear. I am sure you are looking at all the things you did wrong during your pregnancy."

How could she know? "I am, Joan. I can't help blaming myself."

"Yes, that is understandable. Not everyone is cut out for motherhood. Baby comes first, Charlotte. At least Pete sees that. He takes after his mother, you understand. Has your mother visited you yet? Parenting wasn't really her thing either. It is a skill you either have or you don't. It's in the genes, you see. I don't blame you, dear. It is not your fault. I will help in any way. You can always rely on me."

"Thank you, Joan. You are being very good."

"Well, I want to make sure my granddaughter is cared for in the correct way, you understand?"

I never replied or even tried to defend myself. I knew she was right. Never did I speak of this conversation with anyone, not even Pete, but I knew what had to be done.

For the days that followed, I had to distance myself from Pete and Angela. If I didn't bond, then she would not miss me when I was gone. I would be no great loss. As Joan said, motherhood is not for everyone.

I had to find a way to get away before I did any more damage to this beautiful child.

Pete would never understand. I couldn't explain it to him.

I really wasn't in my right mind. If I had been, I would never have left that day, never left the sweet baby alone. That is all I can say in my defence. My mind was not my own, panic and fear were running the show.

That morning when Pete said he was going into work to prepare for his return to work on Monday, I completely panicked.

Could he not see how bad things were, was he so blind and unaware? Or was he still hoping, things would improve, with his 'this would pass' attitude? I just knew I could not do this. No matter what, this would not pass. It would only get worse.

When I heard the car drive away, I leapt from the bed. I started throwing things randomly into a suitcase.

Then I stopped. I took a breath. I started to think about what I was doing, hesitating even.

The phone rang.

I wasn't sure I should answer it. What if it was Pete? But it wouldn't stop. It was Joan. She confirmed my thoughts and finalised my decision. It was her words that sent me on my way.

"Best decision, dear. But do keep in touch with me. I will help in any way possible."

Before I left, I decided to write a note to explain and apologise to Pete and Angela. What words can you use that might make any of this sound right or understandable? But I tried my best.

I loved Pete so much and this was the hardest thing I would ever do, but I knew it was for the best. They would be better off without me here, making things harder for everyone.

When I showered and dressed, I put my case at the top of the stairs. I had to see Angela one more time. When I entered the room, she wasn't asleep. I walked over to the crib and looked in at my sweet little beauty. I did not expect to see her as she was – her big blue eyes staring straight at me, as if she knew what I was about to do. I couldn't bear it, the pain was indescribable, so I ran. I ran down the stairs and out the front door.

There was no turning back now. The words in my head were telling me to just keep going, don't look back. Our neighbour, Mrs Hewitt, said hello as I passed her. I waved and kept going.

I got to the bus stop and jumped on the first bus that came. Not even knowing where it would bring me. I just knew it was further away from that house and all that came with it.

I sat on the bus like a zombie. I am sure I looked like a crazy woman, which looking back now, is what I truly was. Not even seeing where we were going until the bus driver announced, "Last stop!" and "For the third time, last stop!"

We were in the main bus terminal. I could go anywhere from here.

I needed time to think. I got a coffee and sat down.

Where to from here, Charlotte?

It had to be somewhere far away, where nobody would find me. I had plenty of money in the bank. The only good thing my dad did was he left us all fairly wealthy. Nobody knew he had an obsession with insurance policies, so we all did well out of them when he passed away.

I remembered the only happy holiday my family had when I was a teenager.

And that is how I ended up working at Cafe de Rosa in Los Cristianos on the island of Tenerife. A place I thought I could forget everything, move on and let Pete and Angela be happy. I really was not thinking straight. That was for definite.

Angela

Christmas morning. Yippee! I am so excited! Did Santa bring her? Would she be under the tree?

My baby doll. I saw her in the toy shop window – oh, she's so lovely. She comes with a pink and white stroller. I am seven now and Daddy says I am getting all grown up. I still love Christmas. I think I will always love Christmas.

I know it's very early, but I have to see. I run into Daddy's room and start to jump on him and pull him by the arm, not able to get down the stairs fast enough. When we get into the sitting room, I get such a surprise. I cannot believe that all these presents are for me. I can see Daddy looking at me, but I just can't move. My eyes search for Baby Doll. Then I see her! She is sitting in the pink and white stroller. I pick her up and dance around. Oh, she is so lovely! I name her Amelia.

It takes me some time before I start to open my other presents. A lovely watch with a butterfly face and the most beautiful butterfly on a chain from my grandparents. They are always so good to me. There is an art set from Nana Anne. She always gets me something special for birthdays and Christmas. She knows how much I love to draw and colour in pictures.

We always have a lovely Christmas day. We go to Granny Joan and Grandad Frank's house for Christmas dinner, eat too much and then I get to play with my presents and watch the Christmas Disney movie with Granny Joan.

Granny Joan is always good to me and Daddy. She loves to mind me or bring me to school. I spend a lot of time with her and Grandad. Grandad Frank is very funny and he gives the best hugs. I think Granny is too bossy to Grandad and that makes me sad.

Nana Anne calls for an hour after mass on Christmas morning. She wants to see what Santa brought me. I give her lots of cuddles. I know she loves me lots and loves my hugs. She smiles lots when I do. Daddy says I am the only person who can make her smile. I think she is kind of sad.

Daddy says he doesn't know how he would have coped without all the support he had from family and friends. Sometimes I read their lips. They don't know I can do this. That is how I know they talk about my mother sometimes. When they do, I can see Daddy looks really sad, but I don't know why. One day Daddy and Nana Anne were talking. I watched as they spoke. They seemed to be very cross but Daddy mostly. I think he blames Nana Anne for something. I don't know what it is, but I think it is something to do with my mammy.

Sometimes, I think I do remember her. It is a strange memory of a pretty face with blue eyes like mine, looking down on me, she looks really sad. This is something I have only told my friend Emma, not anyone else, not even my Daddy. I was only a newborn when she left, but I think I remember her face. I have never seen a photo of her and Daddy has never really spoken about her. He just says she left us.

As soon as I could learn, Daddy taught me sign language. When other children were learning to say their ABC's, I was learning to sign mine. As long as I can remember, I could communicate with Daddy in our own special way. Daddy says it is our bond. It has always been there.

I know I am not meant to think about her, but I do sometimes. I wonder if she remembers me? Does she have any photos? Does she wonder how I look? Will she ever come home? Lots of questions are in my head. I never even get a birthday card from her. I said this to Granny Joan once and she sat me on her lap and told me I was probably better off and sure, don't I have a wonderful family who love me loads?

When I started my new school, I noticed most kids arrived with both their mammy and daddy, but it was just Daddy and me. I like school. It is a special school for children like me. My teacher is so kind and makes school fun.

I still go for check-ups with Mr McSharry. He is our friend and lets me call him Richard. He keeps checks on me and says he is keeping up with any new treatments that might suit me. He told us at my last appointment that he is talking with a friend of his in America. We have tried hearing aids, but they didn't suit my problem. He makes me laugh when we visit. The tests can be hard sometimes.

My bestest friend is Emma. She can hear and talk but knows sign. She is the daughter of Daddy's friend Andrew. They have been friends since they were kids. We do a lot together, go to the zoo and have picnics. Emma's mother died when she was only small, so we both don't have a mammy.

We know we will be friends forever. We love going looking for fairies when we are in the woods behind our house. Daddy has brought us to the fairy tree in the woods. Emma and I make wishes when we go there. We hope to see a fairy one day. My first wish is to be able to hear. My second one is to meet my mother one day and get her to come home. Emma has wished for a new mammy, to make her daddy happy. We make the same wishes every time we go there. Daddy seems to really like it there too.

Joan

Looking back, I know I should regret what I did, have some remorse but I don't. You see, she not only my took son away from me, but my confidante and friend. He was meant to meet a girl of my choosing, someone who wouldn't question my words. But he met her, she was too common for him. Her family were from different breeding.

Of course, I would never let anyone know that was how I felt. I was always polite and nice to her. Deep down I was hoping Pete would get sense and the relationship would end. Or even better, she would leave Pete. I just needed to be patient. Even after the wedding, I knew it would just be a question of time. My chance would come.

When Charlotte and Pete told us they were expecting a baby, I was crushed. This changed everything. I knew

Pete would be as dedicated a father as he was a husband. Just like his father. But his father was a weak man, letting me run the show all these years, never questioning me, never guessing my true feelings about him or our world.

When Angela was born, things changed. During the pregnancy, I could see how anxious Charlotte was becoming. How that strong girl would now question herself and trust more in my words and advice. As her time came nearer, I would say things to her – not to help but to make her doubt herself more and more. "Do you really think that is a good idea?" or the day she fell down the stairs; now that was an ideal time. "Oh my goodness! Charlotte, you have to be more careful, a good mother wouldn't be so careless!" It is funny how you can do this to someone without them even noticing. This is where being nice to her all the years stood to me and my plan.

I knew I had to get to Charlotte before she went home with the baby. I had to get her on her own. This was the chance, the one I had hoped for all these years. When I arrived in to see her, she was just staring into space. Thankfully, Angela was fast asleep. It would have been harder if she were awake. Such a beautiful little baby. She made me so happy to be a grandmother.

I sat on the edge of the bed and looked at Charlotte, smiling of course. "Hello Charlotte, how are you getting on? Pete told me you are finding things quite hard. I do understand, dear. I am sure you are looking at all the things you did wrong during your pregnancy."

I could see the disbelief on her face.

"I am, Joan. I can't help blaming myself."

"Yes, that is understandable. Not everyone is cut out for motherhood, you know dear. Baby comes first, Charlotte. At least Pete sees that. Takes after his mother, you understand. Has your mother visited you yet?" The woman just sat there not saying a word, such a weak person. "Parenting wasn't really her thing either. It is a skill you either have or you don't. It's in the genes, you see. I don't blame you, dear, it is not your fault. I will help in any way. You can always rely on me."

"Thank you, Joan. You are being very good."

"Well, I want to make sure my granddaughter is cared for in the correct way, you understand."

It might take time, but I had her at her most vulnerable, and without knowing it, she had let me know her weaknesses and greatest fear over the past months. These would now help me to get my son back. Pete would need me again and now, I would have his beautiful baby daughter dependent on me too.

She never said a word to defend herself, just sat there with tears rolling down her face.

I did doubt it at times, especially when they had gone home from the hospital. Pete was doing everything in his power to help her. Even her selfish mother was pulling her weight, trying to encourage her to bond with her baby. But that woman is such a cold woman herself, I felt Charlotte didn't even listen to her.

I rang her that morning, knowing Pete had left the house. He had told me what he intended to do. The phone rang a few times before she answered in a weak, pathetic voice. Charlotte told me what she intended to do. I couldn't miss my opportunity.

"Best decision, dear. But do keep in touch with me. I will help in any way possible."

The line went dead, and I could only hope I had gotten through to her.

I had to wait and see.

Then when my phone rang that afternoon and it was Pete, I just knew it was with the news I wanted to hear.

"She's gone. Left us just a note. I just can't believe it. What am I going to do?" I knew by his voice that he had been crying. My heart broke for him. I didn't want him to hurt but it had to be done.

"I will be there as quick as I can. We will try find her and talk to her," I lied.

I called Frank from his shed. Thankfully, he spent most of his life down there or playing bridge. He came into the kitchen and asked me what was going on. I told him what had happened. It's funny, but he gave me a strange look and didn't seem surprised by this news.

"We must go over to him and be as much support as we can. That poor girl! What was she thinking? We must try find her!" he said, ever the concerned father.

I agreed with Frank out loud but if he could get inside my head, he would know differently.

Pete was a lot calmer when we arrived. He was feeding Angela. I put on the kettle and waited for him to start talking.

He was very distant and there was sadness and anger in his voice when he spoke. "I phoned the Gardaí, but she is not seen as a missing person until she's been gone twenty-four hours. I suppose we will have to wait until the morning and phone again."

Franks words startled us both. "We will have to find her. Where do you think she would go, Pete? She must be in an awful state to have left like that."

"We will look for her, but right at this moment, I'm not sure if I care how she is feeling, Dad. She left Angela alone. She was covered in sick with a full nappy, her clothes and cot were soaked through. What kind of mother would do that, Dad? How could she have done that?"

"Pete, I think she is ill. Depressed after having the baby. I know it must have been terrible to find Angela alone and in such a condition, but really, Charlotte needs help. We need to find her and help her."

"Frank, what would you know about these things? For God sake, let the boy be. He's upset."

"There is nothing we can do until the morning. I am to phone if she doesn't show up before then. I have no idea where she could have gone. I phoned Anne and she was as stunned as the rest of us. I just don't know what to do," at this, Pete just breaks down again, his father put his arm around his shoulders, patting him on the arm.

Charlotte was gone and I should be happy, but I was worried about Pete. Had I gone too far? This was not my son – I had never seen him in such a state.

Time will help. Things will ease, I thought to myself. He is in shock and upset.

There was no sign of Charlotte. She could not be found. With a little help from myself, of course. I still see that Mrs Hewitt woman giving me strange looks.

Now Pete and Angela depended on me. We had some lovely times together, but Pete seems lost. His life revolves around Angela and work. He hardly ever goes out, and if he does, it's with his friend Andrew. He shows no interest in meeting another woman, and I have introduced him to many suitable ladies.

He never speaks of Charlotte, not to me or Angela. This I encourage. It is for the best. No need to be bringing up the past.

I will do all I can to keep them apart. No matter what that takes.

Frank

The day we got the call that my granddaughter was born, I was over the moon and even when we received the news of her hearing difficulties, it did not take from the joy of seeing that little beauty.

I know it was hard on Pete and Charlotte, but I thought given time, they would get through this. God knows they had survived all the plotting and planning Joan did. I knew she did not want Charlotte from the beginning, but she played it sweet to keep Pete on side. Charlotte would not pander to or behave as Joan requested.

Starting with the wedding arrangements, Charlotte knew what she wanted and would not let Joan have any say. Joan pushed and pushed in a way that only Joan can. She would smile, saying, "Are you sure that is a good idea, Charlotte?" But you see, Charlotte was confident in herself then and didn't even notice Joan's put-downs. They seemed to go over her head. I felt she really thought Joan was fond of her.

I knew Joan was only biding her time. She wanted Pete to marry a nice quiet girl, that Joan could boss about. Joan is a very patient lady but Charlotte getting pregnant might have unsettled Joan at first, but then became the opportune time. Her confidence really depleted the further along her pregnancy progressed. And Joan took complete advantage of this. I would hear her put-downs, so cleverly done and I would cringe, but sadly, I was too beaten by this stage, and sure, who would listen to me?

Joan is very devious and plays a good game. I know I made my choice by marrying her, but as hard as it is to imagine, she was such a sweet girl when I met her. We met at a family wedding. I will be honest, at that time, I thought she was the most beautiful and intelligent woman I had ever met. We just clicked.

It was a whirlwind romance, and we were married within a year. Her mother was over the moon with the match. Her father said to me on the day of the wedding rehearsal, "God lad, I hope you know what you are taking on. That one is like her mother. They are devious women. Sure, what do you think turned me to the drink? Her mother chose you for a suitor and the plan was hatched to catch you."

I just ignored him, putting it down to the drink, after having had a few myself at that stage. I should have listened to the man. He was warning me as best he could, but I was truly wearing blinkers then and for a long time to come.

Things didn't change immediately. Joan was quite loving and within a few months she was pregnant and along came Pete, two years later we had a lovely little girl we named Pauline. It was after Pauline's birth that things started to change, Joan became distant and when I tried to touch her, she would pull away.

Then one day she informed me that we would need separate bedrooms. She had done her wifely duties and given me two children. From that day to this, we were never intimate or close. I am sure you wonder why I stayed, but you see, the children needed me, and we were still a family. To the outside world, Joan was the perfect wife and mother, always smiling and polite, but at home, we may as well have been strangers.

I could tolerate it as long as the kids were happy, but when she started interfering in Pete and Charlotte's marriage, I confronted her. I was told in no uncertain terms that I was imagining things as normal and to stop being such a fool.

There were times after the kids had grown up that I contemplated leaving, but I knew Joan would be seen as the victim and would take me to the cleaners. I suppose I came up with thousands of excuses, but the truth is, I just hadn't the courage.

If it wasn't for my shed and bridge twice, or sometimes three nights a week, I don't know what I would have done. It is a lovely group and strong friendships have formed over the years. Some days it is unbearable living with Joan, and I do seriously think of leaving. But after Charlotte left, it became clear that I couldn't leave Pete and Angela. You see, I know Joan would do everything to poison them against me. She would stop at nothing.

It is because of Joan's interference that we never see Pauline anymore. Her mother interfered once too often. Pauline is now living in Donegal with her partner. Living in sin, as Joan would put it. I go to see Pauline a few times a year, saying that I am away with the bridge club. It is always good to see her, especially as she is so happy. Our conversation usually comes back to me leaving her mother. She tells me she just wants to see me happy.

Hopefully, it will happen one day. Sure, nobody knows what the future holds.

I have spoken to Pauline about her mother's interference with Charlotte and she believes I could be right, but until Pete and Charlotte see it, there is no point in getting involved.

After Charlotte disappeared, Pauline phoned me asking did I think Joan had anything to do with her leaving. I told her I had no proof, but everything in my body says yes, yet how would I prove it?

"You can't, Dad. She will have hidden her tracks very well. No proof."

I know one day the truth will come out. If I could only find Charlotte to get her side of things.

Anne

That day is forever in my mind. I know I could have done more, helped more but I left my bitterness rule me. Nobody helped me. I got no support.

Charlotte was always going to be a better mother, despite me. The only thing I know I did right was to report her as a missing person to the Gardaí. They didn't have much success obviously, but at least I tried. Pete agreed with me, but Joan did not seem think it a good idea. This did seem strange to me at the time. She said how Charlotte knew what she was doing and just couldn't cope with Angela and her diagnosis.

She was not in her right mind and that is something I know for definite. Leaving was the only option she could see.

We should have got her help. She was obviously depressed and needed us to help, but we all pushed her. We all ignored the obvious. I was also worried about her physical health. She had a hard time on Angela and was only getting over the birth. She hadn't even had her six-week check-up, to see that all was healing well. Maybe if she had been to the doctor, they would have seen what we didn't – a woman on the brink and in need of help. I have lived with a lot of maybes and what ifs since then.

I was such a selfish mother putting my feelings before my own children. I just wish I had been different. If I had even a clue where she went, I would find her and tell her how beautiful Angela is and how sweet, just like she was as a child. I know she would have been a fantastic mother. There are so many things I should have told her, but the most important one was she was not like me or her father. I always felt she got the best of both of us.

All I can do is make it up to Angela, give her what I could not give my own daughter, especially when she needed it the most.

I am lucky Pete has let me be so involved. We have had our differences along the way. He does blame me at times. I know this, but I cannot deny what I did or didn't do to help my daughter. One day, I hope I will find the courage to tell him all of this but today is not that day.

Angela shows me unconditional love, something I have never known. I hope she can see how much she means to me. I try so hard to let her know. I would spend every penny I have if it would help her in any way. All I can do is make sure she still sees her consultant regularly and he is keeping up to date on any developments in medicine. At least I have the money. That's the only good thing my husband did for us. He left us very wealthy from his obsession with insurance policies.

I know I was damaged when I met Mike, so I was a prime target for someone like him. I was a very good-looking woman with no idea of what I had to offer. I fell for the first man to flatter me and make me feel special. I was only nineteen and knew nothing of the world. Before I knew it, I was pregnant and up the aisle before my bump became noticeable to anybody.

Emotions are not my strong point. I read somewhere that people in abusive relationships can just shut down emotionally and I guess that is what I have done all my life.

My father was not a kind man. He could be cruel to us all, including my mother. He hit me for the last time when I turned sixteen. I told him that day, he would never lay another hand on me, or he would never see me again. I knew this would have an impact on him as he really cared what the neighbours thought. A real-life street angel and house devil.

I always thought my mother to be a weak person, who should have stood up more for herself and others. That said, as I have aged and hopefully learned more, I have come to realise she was too beaten down and sure that her own childhood led her to my father. I digress – this is not about me. This is Charlotte, Pete and Angela's story.

Charlotte never came to me for advice or help, but I knew that Joan was not the mother incarnate she liked to portray herself as. To be honest, she was always a sneaky woman, but I could never say anything as I would be seen as the baddy, especially in the early days.

Deep down, I know she was more involved with Charlotte's choice to leave, but I can't prove it yet. I have decided to do more to search for my daughter. As I can afford it, I am going to hire somebody to search for her, this is my Christmas gift to myself and Angela.

I know Pete will not be happy, but I want my daughter to see her daughter before she gets too old and before Joan can poison her against her own mother. This, I just couldn't bear. So, it is time for me to act now.

In the new year, I will make a plan and see where I go from there. It's time to heal old wounds. I will tell Pete what I intend to do. I know he will be angry, but I need to be upfront about things for once.

Pete

What a wonderful Christmas it was. Angela really seemed happy with all her gifts and so delighted with her doll and pram. Watching her baby that doll, brought tears to my eyes. She never had her mother to do any of those things for her. I always did my best and I can only hope it will be enough. It must be the season and stuff, but God how I wish it had been so different.

I hate this anger that burns so strong still. I know it is because I really truly loved Charlotte and wanted all these memories to be ours, not just mine. I do wonder where she is and if she is ok, then I get mad for actually caring. She left us to cope on our own. She can't have loved or cared for us. Not even one letter to say she is alive and well, or how is Angela, or me. This I find so hard. How could she just have cut us off as if we didn't mean anything to her?

Why? That has always been the question for me.

Never a gift or a card for Angela's birthday or Christmas. I even wonder if she is dead. Sometimes I think that would be easier for us, at least then we could grieve and get on with our lives but this nothing…

My mother says she must have been such a cold person from the beginning and that I should move on with my life. I know she means well but that is easier said than done.

Even though I know my mother has always wanted the best for us, the one thing that has to stop is her eternal search for a nice lady for me. These women are nice, but I have no interest. To be honest, and I know this sounds a mad thing, I compare them all to Charlotte. I know it is crazy, isn't it? But I just can't help it. She was so beautiful and really, she was a kind person. I know her acting could not have been that good. Nobody could pretend to that extent. I would have known, wouldn't I?

Charlotte

Not a day passes that I don't think of Pete and Angela, contemplate going home just to see their faces. I love Pete so much. My heart aches for my family, but instead, I work hard and keep busy. I have made many friends, mainly work colleagues. Maybe friends is the wrong word, as you share everything with your friends and these people only know what I want them to and that is nothing of my past. There has been plenty of male interest, but nobody gets close to me. I am always friendly and kind, but that's it. My boss would love to know more about me and my past, but I am tight-lipped and never show my sadness in work. That would be dangerous and sure, if nobody knows anything, then I need never discuss things and work is my safe haven.

Where would you even start to be honest? How do you explain leaving your family as I did, running when the going got tough? I always make sure I am working for the Christmas holidays and this year is no exception. Where else would I want to be, and it keeps me distracted from my own thoughts.

I tried to get images in my head of how Angela would look. She was beautiful and I know she just grew to be more so. I always send a card and gift for Christmas and birthdays, and I write a little note, but I always send them to Joan's. I know she will pass them on. At least Angela will know I think of her all the time and Pete will know

I still care, even if I never get a response. I do wonder if Pete passes them on to Angela. Well, maybe she is too young yet but maybe one day when she is a bit older. It is so hard, but I truly do understand, even though it breaks my heart, I don't deserve anything better.

Isn't it funny but I would never think of sending them to my mother. For some reason, I still trust Joan more. I felt I had more of a connection with her than my own mother. I do think of my family, especially my mother. I wonder if they miss me or even care where I am. They probably saw it coming and expected nothing else from me.

Now Is the Time

Anne

T he time has come. On January seventh, I decide to tell Pete of my plans to get somebody to search for Charlotte. I have let the dust settle from Christmas, as it is emotional a time.

Today is the day, and I have organised to call to see Pete. Angela has her friend Emma over for a visit and they are playing quietly in the front room.

I have always loved this house, so bright and cheerful, with that big bay window facing the mountains and river. They are so lucky as nobody will ever build in front of them to block this lovely scenery. They have done such a lovely job on the house. It was nicely decorated but dated when they brought it. I remember their excitement at the time. They had saved so hard and had it exactly the way they wanted it when Charlotte became pregnant.

The garden was average in size but easy to maintain. It is in a nice quiet, mature terraced cul-de-sac, with older neighbours. I notice today more than any other day that Pete has not changed the decor. He has maintained it but never changed a thing. Isn't it strange that this is the first time I have noticed?

Well here goes. I have my speech prepared, but when I start talking, I stammer and stutter. Pete becomes impatient and asks what in God's name am I trying to say to him.

So, I take a few deep breaths and start again.

"Pete, I am sorry for letting you all down. Not a day goes by that I don't blame myself for Charlotte leaving. I should have talked to her, tried to understand. If only I had been closer to her, made some kind of a bond with her. Every day I ask all these questions and to be honest, they have eaten me up inside. I see what an amazing father you are and God, Pete, you were an amazing husband to my daughter, but you could never have understood how her past was the cause of her running away. I have decided it is time I find my daughter and bring her home. I know you probably don't care but I feel this need to see her and try to explain myself as the mother I was. Hopefully, I'll get the chance to build some kind of a relationship with her. Please don't cut me away from Angela if I do this. I beg you. I love her so much. She has taught me how to feel joy again." I pause to take a breath.

Pete goes to speak when I try to silence him for fear of his response, but Pete puts up his hand and what comes next blows me away. The response I get and the one I am excepting are completely different from my expectations.

Pete looks me in the eyes and says, "Anne, I think you are right. It is time. We have left it too long. Angela needs to know her mother and I need answers. Let's do it. Have you any idea how we go about this? Where, how do we start?"

To say I am stunned is an understatement. I just stare at him with my mouth open, looking like a right ape. The only word I can find is, "Really?"

"Yes, Anne. I have been doing a lot of thinking, especially over the Christmas holidays, and Angela needs to know her mother. If I never try to unite them, what does that make me? Will Angela thank me for doing this? So now it is time."

At last, I take a deep breath and throw my arms around Pete – I don't know who is more surprised, me or him. I have never been a demonstrative person, well, only with Angela and that would be thanks to her beautiful nature. Pete laughs nervously, understandably.

"Well, let's get things on the road so. It will probably cost a pretty penny, but it will be worth it. I will make inquiries and come back to you, but no matter how much it costs, I will be paying for everything. It is the least I can do. I have the money and sure, it's no good to me when I am dead, is it? I have only one big favour to ask and that is, we keep it to ourselves. I think it best until we know everything, don't you?"

Pete looks at me strangely but agrees to keep it that way if that's what I want.

I add, "It's best not to get anyone's hopes up. If Angela knows and then we fail, God knows how she would feel."

"Yes, you are right, Anne. I never thought of that and the less people who know, the less chance of her discovering anything."

I cannot tell Pete, that my main concern is Joan. My gut tells me the less she knows, the better.

We leave it at that, and I go say hello to Angela and Emma. I give them the little treat I have brought for them. They are playing with their dolls and chatting away. It is only fantastic that Emma's father enrolled her in sign language classes. It really is lovely to see them chatting away in sign.

I almost feel I am interrupting their conversation, even though it is only play chat. We chat for a while and then it is time for me to say my goodbyes. If I didn't know better, I would swear they were relieved to see me go. I get hugs and goodbyes and then I am out the door, with my plan in hand.

Angela

"Nana Anne is gone!" I sign to Emma. "I thought she caught us listening in on their conversation. Tell me everything they said again, please."

"I feel guilty, Angela. Daddy says it's bold to listen in, and not nice. But wow! They are going to try to look for your mammy."

Emma tells me everything. I know I should feel bad and that maybe Nana Anne is right, but I would love just to see my mammy. We promise to keep it our secret. I tell Emma that nobody will know she listened in for me. I will never tell them if it comes out. We pinkie promise like we always do.

Emma is such a good friend to listen in. I wasn't able to as I couldn't see their lips without being seen.

She promised to tell me everything again when we got back into the room, she was so scared of being seen signing it to me.

But I had to hide the excitement when Nana Anne came in to see us. We pretend we were just playing with our dolls and tried not to look so guilty. Granny Joan always says she knows when I am up to mischief!

Daddy is the one I am so surprised at. I thought he would say no as he always gets so angry when my mammy is mentioned, but he wants to find her too.

"Do you think they will find her one day, Emma? Will she want to see me do you think?"

"I don't know, but I hope so. Will you be cross at your mammy, Angela? You know, for her leaving you as a baby?"

"I would love to ask her questions, I think. I don't know if I would be cross. All I know is I miss having a mammy, you know?"

"I do, Angela. I just don't want you to be sad, that's all."

We decide not to talk anymore about it and go back playing with our dolls.

Pete

I am in awe. I cannot believe what just happened. Firstly, Anne apologising. I have never heard her talk like that as long as I've known her. She has bottled up so much all these years. I never imagined she felt anything or questioned her missing Charlotte at all. How wrong was I? Maybe we will truly get to know her now that she has opened up. Seamus was not a good husband. He provided for them financially, but that was it. Maybe that is why she shut down all her emotions, towards life and her family. She wants to look for Charlotte and I want her to. Never did I imagine we would both be making that decision. Now that we have, I really want to find her. I want answers and I want Angela to know her mother. No matter what my own mother says, I really believe this is the right thing.

What happens if we don't find her? I can't even imagine… Or what if we do?

I really have to put these thoughts aside and deal with whichever when the time comes.

Anne is right about keeping it to ourselves. Nobody can know as it will only make things harder.

Am I mad?

Where will we start?

Anne seems to know what she is doing. I will let her investigate and keep me posted.

Why didn't I do this sooner? How could I have waited so long? I should have searched for her immediately!

"Stop," I tell myself. I have to stop torturing myself like this. I was in bits and left holding our new baby. I wouldn't even have been able to think rationally. And then for years, the only emotions I could feel were anger and resentment.

I know now that Charlotte needed help. I suppose to say all this now is easy, but at the time I wasn't in my right mind either. I only pray that nothing bad has happened her, that she didn't do anything bad. I have to stop these thoughts. I have to stay positive and hope.

This probably sounds crazy, but the thought of finding her just makes me feel alive again. I have missed her so much.

Angela must not know anything. I have to protect her at all costs. She has suffered enough, yet she is such an amazing child. I want Charlotte to know this too.

I will not tell my parents either. I don't feel my mother would be happy. She always claims to miss Charlotte, but if I do speak of her, she says things that make me think differently. I can't put my finger on it and I never could, but I always had this bad feeling, and I am not sure why.

Finding the Right Person for The Job

✿

Anne

F inding the right person for the job.

About eight years ago I decided to do a computer class thanks to Charlotte. She talked me into it, and I have done a few refresher courses to keep my skills up-to-date, thankfully. I put private detectives into my search. It's amazing how many show up. You'd swear we lived in the States with the amount. There can't be that much need for so many in Ireland, surely, but then again, how many people are like me, trying to find somebody and God knows, the Gardaí can only do so much.

I read down through all the names of agencies and then decide I will start at the beginning, read their sites and reviews.

I must have been sitting at the computer for hours and hours. I even forgot to eat something, until I became light-headed and this reminded me. I'd reached the P's at this stage, so decided it is time for a break. The last name I see is Pearse and Patterson Detective Agency. This is a name that draws my attention. It sounds good and professional. Well, how else do you choose a PI, I ask you?

After I got something to eat, I click on their site. It's not what I expected. It is two women. I know, you can call me old-fashioned, but I thought of every PI on the telly and they were always men. When I read the reviews, I decide that these are the people for me. I lose no time in phoning them and making an appointment. This is truly the only way I will know if they are the ones for me.

Fingers crossed!

My appointment is for Tuesday January fourteenth at two o'clock. The receptionist only wanted my name and number and a quick idea of what I might be needing. Then he told me I could fill in the rest of the details when I attended my appointment. Well, I have done it. I have got the ball rolling. I am shaking as I end the call, but I know this is the right thing to do.

Audrey

Audrey Pearse and Patrica Patterson first met each other back at school, had been friends for years but as can happen to the best of us, life had taken them in different directions. Audrey married a renowned barrister at the age of twenty-one. He wooed her, swept her off her feet. He was the youngest student in his year to make it to barrister and could charm the birds out of the trees. She fell hook, line and sinker for his chat-up lines. Before she knew it, they were married and on honeymoon in Barbados within a few months. But she never minded. She was crazy about him and believed he felt the same about her. Six months into the marriage and he informed her there would be no children as it would interfere with their work and social life.

Audrey thought this would be short term and never said yes or no to this, feeling as time passed and his career was established, he would eventually want children, as was the norm. But this never happened, and the more time that passed, the more she discovered how controlling James was. He even chose her outfits, especially when it was a work occasion. Every weekend was spent entertaining or being entertained. The years passed and Audrey had given up her job to focus on keeping all in order at home and publicly for James' career. She had lost all the fight of her youth and resigned herself to being a Stepford wife (her own personal choice of name, as this was how she felt). James could be quite aggressive if she didn't go along with his plans. He had been physically aggressive towards her on a few occasions in the early days. He was always remorseful afterwards and would tell her it wouldn't happen again. He told her she needed to learn not to push his buttons in the wrong way and to just go along with his plans and not upset him.

In the later years, he never had to lay a hand on her again. She knew the look and how to behave. Looking back now, she wonders how she lasted so long. It is amazing what you will put up with when your confidence is on the ground and you are constantly being put down.

It was her suspicions about James' sexuality that got her into the private detective career. Over time, she realised that James was not as interested in her as she had first presumed. To be honest, sex was non-existent most of the time. It always felt like a chore to him, or it could happen in one of his rages – this was the worst type. She started to put two and two together when he got a new personal legal secretary. He was a lovely guy, but it was obvious to all that his preference was for the male variety. That was fine. They got on very well, they even went shopping a good few times together. Then one day, she noticed a difference in his behaviour.

Audrey invited him to lunch, he hesitantly went and was quiet throughout. Eventually, she cracked and asked him what had she done to upset him. He looked her in the eye, and she could see the pain in his eyes. He asked had she ever questioned James about his extra workload of late. Of course, Audrey said she would never question James. He works hard and keeps her well provided for. Alex just looked at her and sadly said he understands, but maybe she should not be so trusting. They parted company that day and didn't get to meet again until years later, as he had left his job within the next fortnight.

This left Audrey very suspicious. She decided to become a bit more observant of James. She started to turn up at work more often on random days, just to see his reaction. Then she started to notice, his personal secretaries were always male, and obviously homosexual. They never lasted very long in the job. It was a bit of a joke at any of the social functions. James always implied that she didn't want him having any young sexy women as his personal assistant, which was nonsense of course – as if she would have had any say!

One day, I was browsing the internet for courses and came across one to train as a private investigator. I don't know what possessed me. I wanted to do something for me, so on impulse, I signed up. The course took part at a perfect time of the day and didn't interfere with James' or my day.

This would prove to be the best decision I would ever make. It changed my life. I gained a new confidence. I decided it was time to change everything for once and for all.

One thing I knew was I would have to play it clever with James. He had not become the youngest barrister in his field for no reason. This all started the year of my thirty-ninth birthday, and I wanted to be gone from James by my fortieth. This would be the best gift I could and would ever give myself.

It turned out that I was really quite good at this PI work, probably from all the years of dealing with James and his moods. Well, he now became my first case as we needed one to complete our certificate. It took me months and a lot of deviousness to get all the information I required and a lot of undercover work but eventually, I had all the information and photos I needed. I was a woman on a mission. There are no other words for my behaviour at the time. The only way I could cope with the things I heard and saw of James and his, let's say 'relations', was to pretend it was a case I was working on for another person.

The day of confrontation came. I had it all set up. I insisted that James meet me for lunch in one of his favourite places. I told him I had a surprise for him. When he arrived, he was his usual charming self. Everybody loved him in public and I knew I would need a lot of evidence to make this work. I was meticulous. James would have been proud of me – if he hadn't been the focus.

I got up and gave him the customary peck on the cheek. We sat. I let him order – yes, order both of our meals, as always. Allowing him this last moment of control, we ate our starters and main courses. As the coffee arrived, James asked what the surprise was. This is when the fun began.

Oh, how I wished I had taken a photo or recorded the following moments.

"Well darling, I have some great news, but it is only for me. You see, I know about your relations with not only your personal secretaries but also your late-night visits to a certain – shall I say, unsavoury area in the city." I could see him start to boil.

"Audrey, what nonsense are you talking? Do you want me to get angry? You know you are not a fan of my anger."

He had that evil look in his eye, but I was not scared of him anymore. He had lost all power over me for once and for all.

"Now dear, remember we are in a public place and you know how you don't like a scene."

This shook him. He had never seen me like this before and he really didn't know how to handle it. His guard was down. His next words did make me smile.

"You have no proof of any of this nonsense, Audrey. God knows, you are not the cleverest person on the planet. Don't you know who you are dealing with? I will destroy you."

"Now, James, did you think I would say any of this to you without being well prepared? I might not be the smartest woman, but I have watched your devious methods long enough to have learned how to do things correctly."

Slowly, I took the photos out – one by one, I let him see them. "Just so you know I have left several copies with two solicitors. They will be posted to the Bar and your partners if anything happens to me."

"Who are these solicitors, Audrey?"

I laughed at this. "Do you really think I would tell you, James? And trust me, you will not find out either."

Looking at the photos, I saw his persona dropped.

"How long have you known?"

"I have always suspected, but it was after Alex left that my suspicions grew."

"Who took the photos and made the recording?"

"I did. Don't worry, I feel nothing for you anymore, James. I did once. You knocked that out of me a long time ago – literally. It is obvious you don't care about me and probably never have. I was just a trophy, a good distraction from who you really are, so let's not do the small talk, ok?" I smiled tightly. "This is what I want. Firstly, the house is mine and is to be signed over completely to me. Secondly and more obviously, I want a divorce and a one-time payment of five hundred thousand Euros. I know this is only pocket money to you, but it will be enough to get my own business started. The car is mine and of course, the final thing is that you never come near me again. Never. I don't care if I never see your face in this lifetime again."

James had never been this quiet as long as I've known him. He just stared at me in shock. Eventually he spoke, "What makes you think I will agree to all this, Audrey?"

"Your pride and your status are more important to you than anything, James. Know that I can and will destroy both of those things in a blink."

He looked at me and his words were ones I thought he would never utter. "Where did you find this new strength? I have never seen you like this, so cold and calculating. When did this happen?"

"When I discovered what a horrible man I had married, and I saw how you treated those poor boys. Now have we an agreement? Oh, and by the way, this is only the tip of the iceberg James, remember that," I said, waving the envelop. I knew he had no choice only to agree. He was cornered.

"I will have my personal secretary have the document drawn up today."

"No need James, one of my solicitors has drawn up all the needed documents. I wanted to be sure there were no hidden catches. I know how good you are at legalities and I needed to be sure. I have had them sent to your office already. Also, all your belongings are already in your city apartment. I am sure you won't mind, as we both know that has always been your favourite place."

As I stood to leave, I looked at him one more time. He is stumped, stuck for words – for the first time I can ever remember.

My last words to this man I had spent eighteen years of my life with are, "I will let you pay the bill, James. By the way, I really feel you need to seek professional help. You have some serious problems. I would be careful as one day one of those boys will be brave enough to make you pay for your abusive behaviour. Goodbye."

A few years later, Alex was one of those guys, and James got his dues, with a bit of help from Pearse and Patterson.

That was nine years ago, and the best decision I ever made. I spent the following years building my private detective firm up. It was five years ago when I met Patrica again. Our paths crossed four years after my divorce. How she came to be my partner is another story, only she can tell, I still feel she has not told me all of it.

Patrica

I was seventeen when I met Margaret, we became friends and went on to college to study journalism. I loved the whole idea of investigative journalism. As time passed and we were spending so much time together, between being in the same classes most of the week and sharing an apartment, myself and Margaret started to realise we were becoming more than close friends. Our love was different.

One night after a party, where we both had way too much drink, we went back to our apartment. That night something happened between us that would change our relationship forever.

We had a few more drinks, like we hadn't had enough already! We sat listening to some music. It was so calm. We were so easy with each other. As we were both snuggled up on the sofa, we turned to each other and started to kiss. Looking back, I don't think things would have occurred if it hadn't been for the drink. We both said we would have been too scared, but who knows.

But from that night onwards for the next fifteen years, we were a couple. I never felt love like I did with Margaret and I know she felt the same.

We graduated college and both went down different roads in journalism. Margaret went into her dream job of radio news reporter and was content, never looking for anything more. I on the other hand, was always chasing the latest stories, looking for the edge on the most up-to-date crimes.

We were so happy together. I know Margaret worried about me and the lengths I would go to find information. I had my regular sources and I know looking back now, I did put myself in a lot of dangerous positions to be first to get the story, blind to the danger.

Never ever did I imagine that Margaret was also being put in any danger but obviously she was. Especially when I decided to investigate a local politician, and his association with a criminal gang.

I knew I was getting close and even though I had been warned by one of my sources to step back, I choose to keep going. I couldn't let it go, even when all the signs were telling me to step away.

One night as I was on my way home, these guys approached me, not your run of the mill thugs but decent looking guys. One guy was a lot older than the other and seemed to be guiding the younger lad. They stood one at either side of me and walked along with me. They crushed me between them and said nothing for a bit then the older guy on my left spoke in such a menacing way that for the first time, I was truly scared. His words are ones that I truly regret not heeding to this day. If only I could turn back time and do what I should have done.

That threat was real. He was not calling my bluff.

"Step away from this case, or you will regret it, Ms Patterson. Somebody will be badly hurt if you don't."

The younger guy did not look comfortable but was doing what was expected of him.

I spoke to Margaret about it, but I didn't tell her the full story about the threat. She told me I was definitely getting too close and not to give up yet. Keep pushing and get my story, these guys had to be caught and put away.

I don't think this would be the advice she would have given me if she knew the truth and the names of those I was getting close to. So, I kept pushing. I was getting so close and the names involved should have been another sign to step back, to just let it go. But no, I had to keep pushing and pushing. I was like a dog with a bone.

Then one night about a month after my meeting with the two guys, my phone rang, the voice just said, "You should have listened, Patrica. We warned you, now you have gone too far." and then they hung up. I didn't think too much of it and I just kept working, more idle threats.

God, I was so wrong. How could I have been so arrogant...

I got home at the usual time, Margaret would always be home before me with a bit of dinner ready. She was always good like that.

But there was no sign of her and no evidence that she had been home. I checked my phone for messages and was just going to phone her when the doorbell rang.

I opened it to find two men standing there. These were not the same men I had met previously. I was met with a punch in the face... and to be honest I have no recollection of anything after that, only waking up in the hospital with my mother and father sitting beside me.

Later, I was to find out about Margaret and what had happened. To say my heart broke is an understatement, but the guilt had to be the worst part. Knowing I had brought this on us, that my beautiful Margaret was gone because of me.

They said it was a hit and run. She didn't stand a chance. The car ran the traffic lights at speed, and she was blown up into the air. These were the details that I only heard afterwards.

I never got to see her again. I wasn't able to leave the hospital for her funeral as my injuries were too bad. They weren't sure if I would ever walk again. At that stage, I didn't care, if I am honest.

I felt I had nothing to live for at that time and for a long time afterwards.

Obviously, my journalism days were behind me. Even if I wanted to continue in my job, I couldn't. I had lost all heart and my recovery took months. A lot of which were spent in a rehabilitation centre.

I refused to return to our apartment and got my father to sell it for me. He cleared it out and put everything in storage. Just until I was able to look at things and sort them myself. This did not happen for a long time. I couldn't bear to.

There were, of course, no witnesses and I didn't push things. They had done their job and I had learned my lesson. Of course, the Gardaí investigated my attackers and the hit and run, but it was well cleaned up and nobody was found. Telling me the case was left open and if they had any further developments, I would be kept informed.

I did eventually make a full physical recovery but only because of my parents and family's support. Emotionally, I could never imagine recovering, not without my Margaret. My rock, my soul mate. Life would never be the same without her.

As time passed, I decided to go back to my parents and would make plans when I was ready. It was here I met Audrey. She was home for her father's funeral, which my mother and I attended.

A few days after the funeral, we met again on the street and got chatting. She asked me to join her for a cup of coffee and I did. We had been such good friends in school, and it was lovely to catch up.

Then Audrey started telling me about her business and I was amazed, as the last I had heard she was married to a barrister in Dublin. A million miles away from the person I knew at school. But this was the old Audrey, full of life and ambition.

The more we spoke, the more interested I became. This was the first time I had shown any interest in anything in a long, long time.

We parted and Audrey gave me her contact details, and said if I was interested in a job, there was always one there for me. My journalism skills would be a great asset to her and the team she was building.

Thanking her, I walked away saying I would think about it but with no notion of joining her. Those days were behind me, weren't they?

Think about it, I did. My head was in turmoil. Did I deserve another chance after everything that had happened?

It was weeks later that my dad, whom I had told about the job offer, came to my room. He had a cardboard box in his hands.

"Thought it was time you had a look through this. I know you are ready. And it might even help with your decision, Patrica. I know it has been very hard for you, but I really feel Margaret would want you to be living life and doing what you love."

I sat on the bed for a long time, just looking at the box. I knew my father was right, but that still didn't stop me wanting to postpone this day. To lose one's love is hard enough but to know it was your fault, well, that is another thing.

Slowly, I went to the box and opened it. Inside were some really personal belongings. First, it was the photo of myself and Margaret graduating. We were so happy then.

There was a bundle of birthday cards and notes we wrote to each other. As I read them, it really hit me that Margaret loved the side of me that wanted adventure.

On one card she wrote, how I was her adventure queen, who brought fun and so much joy to her life. "We only have a short time on earth, Patrica, and I love how you live it. Never change, no matter what happens."

As the evening passed, I read everything and looked at all our photos and memories. I realised it was time for me to do something with my life. It was time to start living again.

The following morning, I phoned Audrey. I accepted her job offer. I had to do the PI course and some other training to get my licence. That is how we eventually became the PI team of Pearse and Patterson Detective Agency. Our business has thrived ever since.

We have handled a lot of cases, from missing persons to adulterers, and a lot in between – you name it.

But on Tuesday January fourteenth, when Anne walked into our office at five minutes past two, we were to take on a case that would eventually become very important to us, and change things for me in many ways.

First Meeting with Pearse And Patterson

Anne

Well, today is the day. To say I am a nervous wreck is an understatement. I must have changed my clothes ten times trying for the right look. Not really sure what that is. I eventually found it though.

When the receptionist told me to go in, I swear it was like I was stuck to the seat. He was such a lovely chap, telling me to take my time. Eventually, I moved and walked as confidently as I could to the office door.

There were two ladies sitting in the office. They were both in their late forties and attractive. You could have mistaken them for sisters. Both very dark in colouring, only one had the bluest eyes and the other's eyes were a dark brown.

The lady nearest me stood and shook my hand. She said, "Good afternoon Anne. My name is Audrey Pearse, and this is Patrica Patterson."

Patrica rose and shook my hand. "How can we help you today?"

They had a natural way of putting me at ease. Before I knew it, I was talking about Charlotte, Pete and Angela. I spoke of Charlotte's past and her childhood, then of her pregnancy and the birth, and all that occurred after it. I told them of my inadequacies as a mother, how I had let Charlotte down in so many ways, how I wanted to make things right.

They let me speak for about twenty minutes. I spoke of things I didn't even realise I had felt. What was it about these ladies that made me open up to them? Audrey made eye contact with me but Patrica took notes. When I ran out of words, Audrey asked if it was ok for Patrica to ask some questions. I agreed of course.

Well, I know it was her job, but she made it all seem so easy. She was asking personal questions without judgement or criticism.

"How was Charlotte as a child, was she a worrier?"

"Yes," I replied. "She was always worrying about school, friends and how she affected people. If she had a falling out in school, she would always blame herself. Back in the day when she would confide in me, she would tell me these things and I was awful – I never told her any different! What kind of mother would want to hurt her daughter like that? My job was to build her up, not knock her down, wasn't it?"

Patrica then asked, "How was Charlotte as an adult before she met Pete? What had she studied in college? Had she a good social life? What were her hobbies?"

I didn't understand the need for these questions and said so, but Audrey said it was to build a profile of Charlotte, so they would have a base to work from.

So, I continued, "Charlotte had many friends. She was always well liked. She didn't attend college but got a job straight out of school, working in a creche. They sent her on the relevant courses, saying she was a natural with children and they would be lost without her. She was fully qualified by twenty and just loved her job. She definitely did not get that skill from me, that is for sure. Charlotte met Pete when she was only twenty-two, and she had never spoken of anyone before him. They went out with each other for years before Pete eventually talked her into marrying him and it was a lot longer before he could talk her into having a baby. Pete spoke to me once about her terror of being a bad parent, in response I just shrugged my shoulders and said I didn't know. When I knew damned well why – she was terrified of being like me. I am so sorry for this! I have never spoken like this before. I am not sure what has come over me."

"It's ok. We do understand. It's only natural that everything just comes pouring out. Returning to Charlotte's childhood…"

"Was there any particular place you went to on holidays, anywhere Charlotte particularly liked?"

"We didn't go on many holidays around Ireland over the years, no particular favourite place. Holidays could be quite stressful with our family. There was one year, after my mother died. She left me some money, we went to Tenerife for a fortnight. It was a lovely holiday and Charlotte loved it there. She swore one day she would return or maybe even live there. She was eleven at the time. We were never a very happy family home, as I have said, but this was probably the only time we all got on as a family. I don't think we were ever as happy as we were that fortnight, either before or after. Even their father was a different man. It didn't last long but it is the only good memory we had."

At one point, I looked at the clock and it was nearly three thirty. I apologised for taking up so much of their time, but both ladies just smiled.

Audrey spoke in such a calm understanding voice, "Anne, this is the most important part of our investigation. We need to know Charlotte's frame of mind so we can begin the trace and get an understanding of her as a person. Is there anyone you feel would help us understand more?"

"Well, there is Pete, of course, and then there's Joan. She is Pete's mother. Joan and Charlotte seemed quite close, but you know, I never took to the woman. I never felt she was genuine. Something tells me she is someway involved in Charlotte's disappearance."

"What makes you say that?"

"I don't know, just something in my gut... It sounds crazy, I know."

Audrey looked at me and said, "Anne, we are given our gut reaction for a reason. Sadly, we don't listen to it enough. Do you feel Joan could help us in any way?"

My response is immediate, "No, definitely not. I have told Pete not to tell anyone, especially his mother."

The interview was coming to an end and the ladies asked if I wanted to proceed with the investigation. "There is no obligation, Anne. It is important that you are happy with our approach to things. We need to click, Anne. That is really important."

"I am more than happy. I feel you are both the right people. What do I need to do next?" I said confidently.

"We need some photos of Charlotte, her birth certificate, her PPS number and of course, we need a list of names and addresses of all those related to her. We will approach them, but they will have no idea who we are. We need to get our own impression of these people. Do you feel Pete would talk to us, just so we can get a clearer profile of Charlotte?"

"I will phone him and see what he says. I don't want to push him into anything. I was surprised he even agreed to me doing this, to be honest. He has understandably been very angry, but I know deep down he loves her and wants to know if she is alive and ok."

"That is great. We will get moving so. Our initial fee will be €600 and may increase when we start our investigation but be assured that we will never proceed until we have informed you. We are not here to rip people off but to help. We try to investigate on a budget, and we keep our personal fee to a minimum."

"Thank you. Let's get started so. I will ring Pete after I leave here and give him the option of phoning you."

They shook hands.

Anne left the office, and for the first time that she could remember, she felt light in her heart and head.

Why she had left things so long, she will never know, but today is not the day to think like that. Today is the day she has done something and is making a difference. She knew deep down that these ladies were the people to find her daughter. She knew it would take time, but it would happen.

On arriving home, Anne decided to make a cup of coffee and have that nice bun she had bought on the way home. It was a day to celebrate and she was going to enjoy this moment before she rang Pete – just in case!

Hard Truths

Pete

When Pete answered the phone, I told him a small clip of what had happened and how the duo, Pearse and Patterson, would like to contact him. His response surprised me.

"Anne, would you come with me? We could meet for some lunch first and then go meet the private investigators together?"

"Ok Pete, if that is what you want. Do you want me to make the appointment?"

"Yes please. When would suit you, Anne?"

Anne

I rang Pearse and Patterson's secretary immediately and organised an appointment with them, explaining that it was Pete and myself who would be attending.

The appointment was made for the following Thursday, at a quarter to three. I text Pete the arrangements. We decided to meet for lunch in the small bistro down the road from their office.

I have never seen Pete so nervous. He chats non-stop. Well, I suppose he is anxious. We head into our appointment. Audrey and Patrica make Pete feel as at ease as I had felt with them the previous week.

The first thing Pete asks is, "Do you really feel you can find Charlotte?"

It was Patrica who responded. "We can't promise anything, Pete, but we will do all in our power to do so."

The interview commenced. They wanted Pete to start at the very beginning, back when he first met Charlotte and his first impression.

I knew this was going to be hard as at no point would myself or the family look good in this conversation.

Pete was honest and frank, being more generous to us as a family, more than I had expected.

"I met Charlotte at a Christmas work night out. You know the ones, the party nights in the local hotel, lots of food, drink and dancing. She was out with her workmates from the creche. She caught my eye as I was going to the bar. I know it's a cliché, but I do believe it was love at first sight for me. It was her amazing blue eyes. Angela has them also, doesn't she, Anne?"

I nodded.

"Well, a few drinks later and I got the courage to ask her out for a dance. We danced and talked all night. I asked if I could take her home and she agreed. We shared a taxi. As we neared her home, I got the courage to ask her to go for dinner the following week. After that we were hardly apart.

After the first few months, I was mad to get married, but Charlotte would have none of it, 'Why not stay as we are, sure, it is perfect as it is,' she said. But over time, I was getting restless and wanted to spend more time together. Charlotte said we could move in together. I was over the moon and immediately went about finding a nice place for us to live. I was on good money and Charlotte's wages weren't too bad. We rented a bedsit for a while and one day we did the maths and decided we could manage a mortgage. We started to search for a home of our own. At the time, this was as much commitment I could have hoped for from her, but it was a step in the right direction."

He took a breath and with a half-smile at me, he continued, "You see, Charlotte was convinced that marriage changed people. They stopped caring as much and just hurt each other. I know it was because of her family life. Her own father was not a nice man and he was not nice to Anne or the children. She was terrified of becoming cold and trapped like her mother – that would be her worst nightmare. I told her I would never do anything to hurt her and she was too nice and good a person to become like her mother – sorry Anne, but I have to tell it as it was."

I could feel tears welling up in my eyes, it was so sad to imagine that that was the legacy I had given to my daughter. The wish to be as unlike me as possible. "It's ok, Pete. It is sadly the truth."

Pete nodded. "The years passed and eventually I suppose, you could say I wore her down. One night I proposed ring in hand and nearly fell over when Charlotte said she would become my wife. I was over the moon and for the first time believed that Charlotte felt the same. Don't get me wrong, she was always a very affectionate person and told me she loved me on a regular basis, but this time I knew she really wanted to spend the rest of her life with me. It was a small affair, just family and a few close friends. It was a truly lovely day…"

I could see he was remembering, thinking back to that day. I smiled too.

"When Charlotte got pregnant, we were over the moon! But I know Charlotte was also very scared she wouldn't make a good mother. I kept reassuring her over the nine months and my mother was a great comfort to her, in her own way. Well, when Angela was born, as I am sure Anne has told you, there were difficulties. I had not really understood how it had affected Charlotte, not to the degree it had, and I kept hoping things would get better with time. Now I understand they never could have. She needed help, counselling, and a lot of support. I have spent so much time being cross and bitter at her, but what I should have been doing was searching for her. I just hope it's not too late."

He took a deep breath and continued, "I have brought the note she left that day and some photos of both Charlotte and Angela. So, you can show her the beauty our daughter is, just like her mother."

Again, Audrey and Patrica let Pete speak until they felt he was finished telling his story. Then their questions began.

It was Audrey who asked the questions this time, mostly about the time during the last stages of the pregnancy to the day Charlotte left. He answered all as best he could, but he was very emotional. It must have been so hard for him to relive all that again. I never truly understood how broken he was after she left. He was always so rational and such an amazing father to Angela.

As we neared the end of the meeting, Audrey made a request we had not expected, "We will need to meet Angela at some stage."

We both answered in unison, "Why?"

"It really helps to have met someone to allow us speak about them to another. It doesn't need to be today or tomorrow, but if we get closer to finding her, it would be beneficial to us making our case. Just think about it. There is no rush."

Angela

Something is going on. Daddy has organised Granny Joan to mind me today. He said he has a work thing to do, but he's being really weird. When Granny Joan asks him if he is ok, he says yes, but we both know there is something odd.

He was speaking to Nana Anne this morning. I could read his lips, something about lunch and then a meeting. But he never said anything to me about it.

I didn't say anything to Granny Joan, cos I'm not sure yet what is happening. When Daddy collected me, he seemed much happier. He gave me the biggest hug and nearly squeezed me to death!

Granny Joan tried everything to get him to talk, but he just said, "Thank you, but we must go home now."

On the way he decides to treat us to a burger and chips, so we go to the local take away and order. This is really unusual, especially in the middle of the week.

The next day Daddy is on the phone and he looks very serious. Then he smiles and starts laughing. All I can get is, "Oh my God! That is fantastic!" and "What kind of costs are there?"

He seems to be on the phone for hours but eventually finishes all his calls. Then he sits me down and tells me he has some news for me.

The Great News

Pete

"Mr McSharry phoned this morning. He has been in contact with Mr O'Dwyer, a colleague and friend of his who has been working in a hospital in America. This hospital has been working with children born with the same hearing issues as you have, and they have been having amazing success with a specific surgery. This doctor has returned to Ireland and has opened a private clinic. The procedure is called Cochlear Implant. We will have to meet with one of Mr O'Dwyer's colleagues first. Then if that goes ok, we will organise for you to have to have a CT and MRI scan. These will confirm if you are a suitable candidate for the procedure." Pete realises this is too much information for Angela, she is staring at him like he is spouting gibberish.

Angela nods slowly and signs, "And if I am, does that mean I will be able to hear?"

The end goal – that is all a seven-year-old will think of. "I am not sure yet what it means, but we will know more when we go to the meeting with Mr O'Dwyer. Let's not get our hopes up. But it will mean an operation for you if you are a suitable candidate."

Pete did ask how much it would cost. It is expensive, but thankfully, the family are all going to pull together, that is why he was on the phone for so long. He was talking to all the family and they are all supporting them in whatever way possible.

"When will we know, Daddy?" Angela asks.

"We have an appointment with Ms Caulfield next Tuesday at ten-thirty in the morning. The CT scan is booked for that morning at eleven and the MRI is for the following Monday morning at nine o'clock. The Monday after that we have an appointment with Mr McSharry and his colleague, Mr O'Dwyer. We will know more then, pet." Pete tries to explain it as simply as possible, without scaring her too much.

Pete decides they should do something nice to distract them. They decide to go swimming, something they both love to do. He phones Andrew to see if they would like to join them. They agree to meet in the leisure centre in a half hour.

Angela tells Emma everything and she is so excited. "It is just the best news ever, Angela."

Tuesday arrives and they don't know which of them is more nervous, Angela or Pete. Ms Caulfield is nice, but she asks a lot of funny questions. First Pete is with Angela and then it is just Angela with Ms Caulfield and one of her assistants. Thankfully, she can sign. This makes it easier. When they are finished, Pete joins them again, looking so nervous. Ms Caulfield tells them that she will send her report to Mr O'Dwyer. Her assistant Francis will bring them to the scan room, where Angela will have a CT Scan.

Angela is glad when everything is finished. Pete says they can only wait and see. Angela is just hoping she answered the questions right because she couldn't tell from Ms Caulfield.

When Granny Joan asked to go with them, Pete was very clear. "It can only be the two of us, Mother. Nobody else."

Joan was not too happy with him, not liking to be left out of things.

Afterwards they go for some lunch together, before they meet up with everyone in Granny Joan's house. Pete fills them all in on how things went, but really there wasn't much to say.

The following Monday is the MRI scan, and it feels like the longest week ever until the appointment with Mr O'Dwyer.

At last, Monday is here. They arrive in the waiting room at a quarter to ten and wait to be called in. When the door opens, Angela sees Mr McSharry. She jumps up and runs over to give him a hug.

"Come on in, Pete and Angela. Meet Robert O'Dwyer, my friend and colleague. He will be your Ear, Nose and Throat specialist. I am only here in a support role, more for me than you," smiles Mr McSharry.

They shake hands. Robert signs he is delighted to meet Angela at last, that he has heard so much about her from Richard.

They all sit down and Mr O'Dwyer can speak sign really well. He tells them that they have decided Angela is a candidate for the procedure, but they need to explain everything before anything can be agreed. The fact that hearing aids never worked for Angela, is now turning out to be a plus. He goes on to tell them the name of the procedure and what exactly a cochlear implant is.

It is a small electronic device that helps people hear. It can be used for people who are deaf or very hard of hearing but is not the same thing as a hearing aid. It is implanted using surgery and works in a different way.

The cochlear implant is made up of two parts. One part of the device is surgically implanted into the bone surrounding the ear (temporal bone). It is made up of a receiver-stimulator, which accepts, decodes and then sends an electrical signal to the brain. The second part of the cochlear implant is an outside device. This is made up of a microphone/receiver, a speech processor, and an antenna. This part of the implant receives the sound, converts the sound into an electrical signal, and sends it to the inside part of the cochlear implant.

"Angela will have to have a general anaesthetic so she will be asleep and pain free," says Mr O'Dwyer.

Mr McSharry speaks next, "I know it sounds very technical, but it has a great success rate, Pete."

Mr O'Dwyer then proceeds to tell them what lies ahead. "I am not telling you this to scare you, but you need to both know what is ahead of Angela. I want your decision to be based on knowing all the pros and cons. When Angela is asleep, we will make a surgical cut behind the ear. Sometimes we might have to shave some hair behind the ear. The bone behind the ear (mastoid bone) will have to be drilled to allow the inside part of the implant to be inserted. The receiver is then placed into a pocket created behind the ear. The pocket helps keep it in place and makes sure it is close enough to the skin to allow electrical information to be sent from the device. After surgery, there will be stitches behind the ear, you may be able to feel a bump behind the ear. Then the outside of the device will be put in place one to four weeks after the surgery."

They listen and when there is something they don't want Angela to know, they stop signing. They don't know she can read lips, but it doesn't take long for Mr O'Dwyer to notice. He just laughs and says, "No secrets will be kept from you, Angela!"

Angela can't help but smile, her secret is out, but it does all sound a bit scary to her. Pete looks at her and asks how long she can lip read. "Since as long as I can remember," she signs with a smile on her face. They all just laugh and continue sharing the information.

The success rate of the procedure is amazing with great results. It will just take Angela some time to adjust to things. She will need to attend an audiologist, speech therapist and Mr O'Dwyer's clinic.

"Now you have all the information, are you still prepared to go ahead with things?" questions Mr O'Dwyer.

Angela answers before her father draws a breath, "Yes, I am ready!"

Pete looks at her and smiles. "There is your answer. When are you thinking we can get going with things?"

There is some discussion and Pete says, "We are ready, whenever you are."

Siobhan Clancy

"There will of course have to be pre-ops done, but Mr McSharry has kept Angela's medical records up to date," says Mr O'Dwyer.

A date is arranged for Tuesday three weeks from now for the pre-ops and then Thursday of that week for the procedure. Angela will have to remain in hospital, for a few days and the surgery itself can take from two to three hours.

They leave the appointment with a spring in their step and head to Granny Joan's to meet everyone and tell them the good news.

When they are in the car, Pete asks Angela how she feels about all of it.

"It sounds a bit scary, Daddy, but I will be fine."

"My brave little girl! I am so proud of you," he says and hugs her.

Angela

There is great excitement when we tell everyone that I have been accepted for the surgery. Both of my grannies cried. Grandad just hugged me. Emma and her father are over the moon for us.

Daddy said it's best not to tell anyone what is involved yet, deciding to just enjoy the celebration.

We get a Chinese takeaway. The adults have wine, me and Emma are allowed coke.

When myself and Emma get some time on our own, she reminds me of the wishes I made that day in the woods when we found the fairy ring – how I wished for my hearing and to see my mammy. Wow, and now it looks like both of my wishes might just come true. I tell Emma what Mr O'Dwyer told us. Well, some of it because a lot of it made no sense.

"Are you scared, Angela?" Emma asks me.

"A bit Emma, but imagine, I will hear what you hear!"

When Daddy and I get home, we are really tired. We decide to watch a movie and then head to bed.

Let's Get Cracking
on This Case
❀

Audrey and Patrica

We have been discussing the case and the best way to go about things. One thing that we both picked up on from talking to Pete and Anne is that Joan is not all she seems.

"I would like to meet this lady, Audrey. Something just doesn't add up with her."

"I totally agree, Patrica. We need to get things started. Let the search commence!"

Patrica says, "You are going to start with all missing persons' reports and the bodies found around the dates that Charlotte went missing. Somebody must have reported something, even a neighbour who noticed something strange. We have the estimated time Charlotte left the house, thankfully Anne did report her daughter missing, so that means the Gardaí will have a file on the case."

"So at least there is some record of her. We will find out how much investigation happened at the time. I am not that hopeful to be honest, but we will see, thankfully you have a good source in the Gardaí who will get you access to the information," says Audrey.

"We will wait until we have some information before we get in touch with Anne. We don't want to raise her hopes or frighten her. It is just a waiting game until we get more information," Patrica says, nodding.

In the end, it takes two weeks. Jack, the Garda friend of Patrica's, was actually involved in the case and even though there was an investigation, the results were inconclusive. The case remained unsolved but open. They suspected no foul play, just a mother who couldn't cope with the new world of motherhood.

Jack tells Patrica, "It is a sad story, but it happens more often than you would imagine. We agreed that there was no malice of any kind and that even though Charlotte was obviously not of sound mind, she did leave of her own choice and had left a self-explanatory note."

Jack gave Patrica a copy of the file. The contents of which were of some interest and at least gave us a building block to start with.

Anne Fitzgerald, mother of Charlotte, reported Charlotte as a missing person. Pete the husband, his mother Joan and his father Frank had all been interviewed. Pete showed us the note and it was clear. You could tell he was in a bad way and only barely functioning with the support of his family. The baby Angela was being well cared for. We had no worries for her safety at any point. Everyone told the same story of the trauma of the birth and the news that followed. We spoke to the paediatrician, Mr McSharry, and he confirmed that Charlotte had been terribly upset with the news. He feels that the hospital should have picked up on things and provided the help that was needed but sadly this family's needs had slipped through the system, as so many have over the years.

The investigation also states that Charlotte was seen leaving by a neighbour, a Mrs Hewitt. She met Charlotte at the bus stop down the street from the family home.

Mrs Hewitt statement said, 'Charlotte had not looked herself. She seemed in a bad way. Charlotte always kept herself lovely, but her hair was damp and not even brushed. She was wearing an old pair of jeans and shabby runners. She had a bag with her. I said hello and asked her if she was ok, at the time I thought her a bit rude until I took in her appearance. Then I realised that the poor girl had not even heard me. If I had known the true state she was in, I would have stopped her, distracted her maybe, I don't know... She must have really been in a bad way to leave her lovely husband and beautiful daughter. They were always such a happy couple. I did approach Pete's mother later in the week after I heard the news of her disappearance to tell her of my seeing Charlotte on that day. She asked me not to talk to Pete about what I had seen as he was in such a bad state at the minute and they were trying to protect him but that she would pass on the information to the Gardaí.'

Weeks had passed and Mrs Hewitt became concerned when the Gardaí had not made any contact with her. She decided to go down to the station herself. 'Maybe Joan was just too upset that day and my visit had gone out of her head. But you would have presumed that any information would have been vital in finding Charlotte wouldn't you, Sergeant O'Tuama?' she had asked. Jack stated that he too was surprised that this vital piece of information had not been passed on to them, but also presumed it was to do with the fact the family were in shock and dealing with a newborn and all the other issues. Jack had taken Mrs Hewitt's statement and told her it would be of great help. He had thanked her, and she left.

The local bus driver was questioned but he had said, he had noticed nothing unusual on the day. He did not recognise the lady, but to be honest so many people got on and off the bus, you stop seeing faces. Of course, he always remembered the ones who caused trouble. His bus did a round trip from the station, along his route and back to the station. He had given the information about the route.

The airport was the next place of inquiry, to be honest, they were grasping at straws. They had no idea where Charlotte could have gone. They made a few enquiries with the regular staff. One lady with Aer Lingus, who was working at the boarding gate that day, recalled seeing a woman fitting Charlotte's description, boarding a plane for Tenerife.

The reason she remembered the lady fitting that description was due to her looking so bedraggled and broken. She said, 'I asked if she needed to check in any bags, but she only had the one piece of hand luggage. I have seen a lot of people as you can imagine in my job, but not many remain in my memory.' When she heard there were enquiries been made about a missing person and the information fit the description of that lady, she had to make sure she got to speak to us. Of course, where she went after Tenerife she did not know, but she really hoped we would find her. After this we hit a dead end. Nobody else remembered her or knew any more information.

We did inform Joan, Pete's mother of this information and said that we would phone Anne with what little we knew at that point. We apologised for not being of much more help but that the case would remain open. If anybody heard anything, they were to inform us. Joan thanked me for all our help but requested, firstly that we would not contact Pete with this information as he was in such a bad state and only barely coping. She also told me she would talk to Anne and they would discuss the information we required and see where they go from there. No matter what, Pete and Angela were to be protected at all times. I did find this strange but understood her need to protect her child and grandchild."

After reading through the whole statement, the two ladies looked at each other. Patrica spoke. "Joan seems to be mentioned a lot, did you notice? And not in a good way. We need to keep an eye on her. At least we have a starting point. We will have to contact Anne and have a meeting with her."

Anne

Audrey rings Anne, saying how they have gotten some information and would like to talk with her on her own. An appointment is made for the following Monday morning at ten forty-five. They recommend not speaking to Pete until they have the meeting. Anne agreed to this but did wonder why. She knew Audrey would explain on Monday. Hopefully, it is good news and not what her biggest fear has been.

Thoughts were flying around her head that night and the one to follow. She is trying so hard to stay positive, but by the Friday evening, she just knows she can't go through a weekend of not knowing.

She decides to phone now before they close for the weekend.

Audrey answers the phone, "Hello, Pearse and Patterson."

"Hello Audrey, it is Anne here. May I have a moment of your time?"

"Hi Anne, you just caught me going out the door. Ask away, how can I help you?"

"I need to know... Is it bad news, Audrey? It's just when you don't want Pete to know, are you trying to protect him? I know I must sound crazy, but my thoughts are all over the place!"

"Anne, I should have made it clear. I am so sorry. The news is good and at last, we have a starting point. We just need to discuss a few things with you alone first, to see where you want to go with things."

Anne breathes a sigh of relief audibly.

"That's fine, Audrey. I should have asked this question when we spoke the other day. I will see you both on Monday."

"Sorry Anne, we should have made that clear. We should not have let you worry like that. See you Monday. Have a good weekend."

Anne is so relieved. At least they are moving forward with things

Regrets

Charlotte

Having a really bad day today, I know it will be Angela's birthday next week. March nineteenth. She will be eight. I have bought a card and gift for her, as always. I stopped writing to Pete a while ago.

Thanks to Joan, Angela will receive these on the day. It doesn't get any easier. If anything, it gets harder. I try to picture her and imagine her face as she reads my card and opens the gift.

One day, I just might get brave enough. I have taken the nineteenth off work and I decide to just go out on one of the tourist trips to forget as much as possible.

At least I have stopped drinking on these special days. That had been my answer in the early years – to just drink myself into oblivion, into a drunken sleep coma. But the pain never goes away. I still had to deal with it the next day. So now I just deal with it as best I can, no more self-pity.

Joseph, my boss, is very good to me. I always feel he has his own past and that is why he never pushes me too hard. I remember one night we sat having a drink after work and he did ask why I am always so sad. I just said I have a lot of regrets, things I should have done differently and now I have to live with those decisions and that it's not easy but it's my own doing.

"Oh Charlotte, we all have our secrets and regrets. I was not a nice person in my former life, and I have done terrible things. I try to make amends now, but the memories – they never leave me. Sometimes we act a certain way out of necessity at certain times in our lives. We have no other choice. That is not an excuse. But we cannot undo the past, just make the present the best we can. I don't imagine you could have done anything bad. You are too good a person. I see the way you take such good care of the younger staff. You are like their agony aunt. Getting them over the initial few weeks away from home."

"You have no idea what I have done. I am a coward, let's just leave it at that."

Years have passed since that conversation and we have never spoken about things since then.

I have been thinking a lot lately, thinking of going home just for a quick visit, just to see them. I need not let them see me. I don't think anyone would recognise me, as I have changed a lot over the years. My long hair is now cropped. I keep it short. I was always all there, as they would say, a good seventy-six kilo, but I am only fifty-six kilo now. I feel my face has changed. People have commented on my sad eyes. Before, I was described as always having a smile for everyone, having a smile that lit up my eyes.

But as much as I try, I find it hard to find a reason to smile anymore, not my real smile. Don't get me wrong it is not that I am rude or unkind. I am still always pleasant and nice to people, but that natural smile is gone, you know the one that reaches your eyes.

Maybe one day it will return. I know what would make it happen – just to lay eyes on my husband and beautiful daughter.

Keeping Secrets

Anne

Monday has arrived. I was up bright and early. It was so hard not to say anything to Pete over the weekend. I don't like keeping this meeting a secret. Especially now that he is opening up to me, but I know that Audrey would not ask me to do so, unless they had a good reason.

The lovely friendly receptionist greets me. He introduces himself to me as Alex, saying, "We will probably be seeing a lot of each other and it is always nice to know names, don't you think?"

He is a guy that just puts you at ease immediately you meet him. He asks if I would like tea or coffee.

"A black coffee would be lovely, Alex. Thank you," I say smiling.

He tells me to go in, that Audrey and Patrica are waiting for me.

The ladies greet me with a smile and I sit down.

Patrica gets straight to business, "Sorry for all the secrecy but we requested a copy of Charlotte's file from the Gardaí. We would like you to read its contents, and maybe you will have a clearer picture after reading it, Anne."

Alex arrives with my coffee and some for the others. We all sip away as I read through the file.

To say I am stunned by what I read is an understatement.

Audrey and Patrica wait for me to finish reading. They know by my face that I cannot believe what I have just read.

"Well, what do you think?" they both ask together.

"I never knew any of this. Why would she keep this information to herself? It just doesn't make any sense…"

"Just to have known she was alive, anything… but she kept this information from us all. Wait until I talk to her! Oh God, I want to murder her, I swear!"

"We would prefer if you kept this to yourself. We don't want Joan to get wind of anything we are doing. That is why we asked you here on your own today. Joan will need to be investigated. This proves that she has been holding back important information. So, we need to find out what else she does know."

"We knew that if you or Pete had known any of this, you would have shared it with us. Our suggestion is as follows – but it is your decision at the end of the day, Anne."

"Could yourself and Pete come here together on Thursday? We will not tell him about this meeting, or the full content of the missing person report – just in case he can't contain himself and goes to Joan. We will let him know about our plans to go to Tenerife to see what we can find."

"Anne, just know that we don't want to raise anyone's hopes here. This is very shaky information, but it gives us a place to start. What we will find, if anything, is inconclusive but know we will keep you posted at all times," Audrey says.

"How does that sound to you? Are you happy to go ahead?" Patrica asks.

"I agree completely and trust you both. Yes, you are right, Joan needs to know as little as possible until the time is right. I will do my best to protect Pete. He has enough on his plate with Angela's surgery coming up in a few weeks. A date has been set thankfully," I tell them. "No matter what, Joan is his mother at the end of the day, and she has always been such a support to him and Angela. I will tell you one thing from my dealings with her over the years, we need to tread carefully. She is a clever woman and as for poor Frank, well, he just does what he is told. I do believe if he knew any of this, though, he would have told us. It is all a bit fishy, isn't it?"

The decision is made. I say goodbye and head for home.

When I get home, I phone Pete about the upcoming appointment and ask would Thursday at twelve suit him. I presumed it would be fine – I knew Pete wouldn't need a babysitter, as Angela is on a school trip that day. I give him enough information so as not to worry him or raise his hopes too much. We say our goodbyes and I tell him I will see him at their office on Thursday.

At the Thursday meeting, we tell Pete the plan. He is delighted and agrees we need to go ahead. Obviously, we have to give a certain amount of information from the Garda file. He does question why we had not been informed.

Audrey is prepared with the answers to his questions. "As the case was inconclusive, the Gardaí may have felt it would have been of no benefit to give false hope to you or the family. The case was kept open, but no other witnesses came forward."

"We are delighted to hear about Angela's good news. It will be a rough road until it is over and done with but all going well, you will have a positive outcome."

You can see from Pete's face that there is a mix of apprehension and excitement at what lies ahead for Angela, but he thanks the ladies and asks them to send positive thoughts their way.

"The first place in Tenerife Patrica will visit, will be the place we went on holiday when Charlotte was young. It's as good a place as any," explains Anne.

"Well, it's all systems go now, Anne and Pete. We will keep you updated as much as possible. If we find Charlotte, we will have to be very discreet until we know how the land lies. We will have to tread carefully to see if she is ready to be approached. We can promise you we will do all in our power not to scare her off," explains Patrica.

"Please keep us posted on Angela's progress, Pete. We will be thinking of you all," says Audrey standing up to walk us to the door.

With that we leave.

Pete asks me to join him for a coffee after our meeting, so we head to the cafe across the street.

"You do think we are still doing the right thing, Anne?"

"Yes Pete, we are. I know I let Charlotte down. I need to see her and know she is ok and hopefully one day she will be able to forgive me."

"I know Anne. It's just I hope we don't get disappointed and find that she is happy in a new life. You know living with someone else… I don't think I could handle that."

"Pete, whatever has happened, one thing I know for definite is that she could never love someone as she did you. I don't believe she would have ever left if she had been in her right mind."

"I hope you are right, Anne. We can only hope."

Angela's Birthday

Angela

It's my birthday! Daddy says it's a double celebration with the surgery so close. Emma and some more of my friends arrive at two o'clock. All my family are here. Nana Anne is a bit quiet and not talking much to anyone.

I ask her if she is ok. She smiles and says, "Of course, Angela. I just can't believe you are eight today. Where have the years gone! Do you know something, you look like your mother. You have her beautiful blue eyes that were always smiling."

Just then Granny Joan comes over and catches Nana Anne by the arm, "We don't speak of her, Anne. Pete forbids it."

Granny Joan still doesn't know I can lip read, so she never turns away from me.

Nana Anne gives her a look I have never seen before, but just says, "Joan, she is my daughter and Angela is so like her. Don't you agree?"

I'm not sure why, but they both smile at me and stop talking. Granny Joan just walked away then.

I tell Emma later what happened between the two of them. Emma says maybe it's because they are not really friends. Then the party takes over and we forget everything else.

What a day it is!

Grandad is the best fun ever at the party. He arrived dressed up as a clown and was so funny. All my friends think he is brilliant. Granny Joan looked so cross when she was talking to him. I read her lips. She said he was making a show of himself. He just laughed and told her that he didn't care, that making me happy was more important to him. Well, I can tell you Granny Joan was not one bit happy with him. But I was so happy, I told him the truth – he's the best Grandad ever!

It is one of the best birthdays I've ever had. People don't go home until seven o'clock. When the parents come to collect my friends at six o'clock, they end up staying for ages.

Eventually when everyone goes, Daddy and I just collapse on the couch.

"Well," he asks, "did you enjoy your day?"

"Oh Daddy! It was the best day ever! Thank you so much!"

We just sit for a while and then I turn and ask, "Daddy, what is wrong with Granny Joan? She seems really cross with everyone."

"I don't know, Angela, maybe she is just worried about your surgery and doesn't want to say anything. You know how she can be."

"Yes Daddy, I know." I didn't tell him that she scares me sometimes.

Emma's father is leaving her off school tomorrow so we can spend the day together, as she won't see me for little bit.

The next morning, she comes to our house after breakfast. Daddy decides we will go for a walk. We go down our usual path at the back of our house. He lets us run ahead a bit. We find our fairy ring and put the flowers we have picked on the way in the middle of the fairy ring. We look around and Daddy is way back, so we talk about our wishes.

"Emma, if my operation works, and I get to hear, that will be my first wish to come true."

"I know, Angela, I hope my wish comes true. I know my mammy can never come back, but it would be nice if Daddy met a nice lady and I could have a mammy again. Does that sound stupid, Angela?"

"Tell me what you think she will look like."

"She would have the nicest, kindest eyes and will always be smiling and laughing. She'll want a little girl like me and will love to play games. But most of all, she will love my daddy and make him happy again."

We both stand up holding hands and make our wishes together. We say it three times. "We both hope our wishes come true."

When Daddy catches up with us, he asks what we are up to. "Just making wishes in the fairy ring, Daddy," I tell him.

He smiles and says, "Well, I hope they come true. Myself and your mother made a wish here once a long time ago and it came true for us."

"What was the wish, Daddy?"

He looks so sad. "It was that one day we would be lucky to have a beautiful child... and well we all know that wish came true, don't we?"

That's the first time Daddy has ever spoken of my mammy to me, and it makes me believe that wishes made here do come true.

Emma thinks this is a good thing. We are so excited! My first wish looks like it is coming true already.

Tuesday's Appointment

Pete

Tuesday has arrived. We are heading to the hospital for the pre-ops. I can't believe this is truly happening. It will be an intense day for Angela, but she is a strong and determined eight-year-old.

Angela is a trooper. She goes through all the tests without complaining once. She just smiles at me and tells me not to worry. Mr O'Dwyer is so impressed with her and tells her how proud she should be of herself. Angela just nods and tells him that it will be worth it all if she will hear my voice one day. As you can imagine, I am overwhelmed and my eyes just well up. I am so proud of my beautiful daughter.

We meet with Mr O'Dwyer and Mr McSharry after all the tests have been carried out to discuss the date. "Everything has gone to plan with the tests. Angela is ready to go ahead with the surgery on Thursday if you are both ready?"

We nod.

Thursday is here. I don't think either myself or Angela slept much last night.

I kept tossing and turning. I really hope everything goes ok. When this is behind us, I can focus on finding

Charlotte, but my main focus has to be on Angela at this moment. She is amazing, the way she is coping with everything is just fantastic.

No breakfast is eaten. Angela is fasting, and I just couldn't eat. Coffee is all I could manage. We leave the house at seven thirty, arriving at the hospital in plenty of time.

Angela is prepared for surgery, as all the pre-ops were done, so now we just have to wait to be called.

I stay with her until she is fully sedated. Leaving her there is one of the hardest things I have ever had to do. She looks so small, but Mr O'Dwyer reassures me that everything would be fine, and he will send a nurse to get me when the procedure is finished.

I walk to the waiting area and have a coffee. I just can't settle. When I go to get another coffee, I notice the little church. I am not a religious man but I decide to light a candle.

I enter and can't believe how peaceful it is in here. It's hard to believe this sanctuary is in the middle of a busy hospital. I sit down on the nearest seat and just enjoy the peaceful feeling. I find myself going over the past eight years of my life and all that has happened. I have to admit I miss Charlotte. I miss her every day.

Even though I have gotten on with things and have always done my best, Angela makes being without Charlotte bearable.

I have not spoken to God, not since my school days. But I do today. Firstly, I ask that everything goes well for Angela. Secondly, that one day Charlotte will be part of our lives again.

I didn't realise how long I was in the little church until a nurse arrived in beside me saying, "It is such a peaceful place, isn't it? I usually find people here when a loved one is in surgery."

"I am not even religious, but I can understand why that is. There is something magical about this place, a place that keeps your thoughts positive."

"Yes, I agree completely. Now, when you are ready, Angela is after her surgery and back in recovery."

She didn't have to say another word. I was on my feet immediately. I thank her, and she led me to the recovery room.

Angela is sound asleep and looks peaceful. She has monitors attached. A nurse is by her side. "Mr O'Dwyer will be with you shortly," she tells me.

I sit beside her and hold her little hand.

Mr O'Dwyer arrives and pulls up a chair. "All went well, Pete. We will just have to wait and see how things go. This is just the first stage of things, but it will be a few weeks before we will be able to tell how successful the procedure has been. Recovery is a very individual thing. It can range from one to four weeks. Only when the microphone is fitted will we know the true success. All I can tell you for now is that step one was a great success. It will be a strange time for Angela, so we will have to give her time to adjust to everything and be patient."

Around three hours pass before Angela opens her eyes. She just smiles at me, then drops in and out of sleep for another few hours. Eventually, she is awake fully and signing she is hungry. I asked the nurse if she could have some food. "Just a bit of toast and some tea, if she is up to it."

When I return my attention to Angela, her eyes are full of tears. "What is it, pet?"

Angela signed, "I can't hear you, Daddy."

"Mr O'Dwyer said it would take a few weeks, Angela. Do you remember? This is only stage one. The microphone has to be fitted yet, pet."

"I know, Daddy but I thought maybe I would be different," she signs and then she starts sobbing.

"Oh pet!" I scoop her into my arms.

It was a few moments before we settle. I speak slowly to Angela, telling her how much I love her and how lucky I am to have such an amazing daughter. When the lady arrives with the tea and toast, she brought enough for us both.

"I am sure you have not eaten. I hope you don't mind but I brought you some also."

I thank her. I am actually hungry.

Mr O'Dwyer was right. It would take time for Angela to adjust. Like her, I think I hoped she would hear immediately, but that was just silly wishful thinking.

Mr O'Dwyer arrives later and speaks to Angela. He says he would let her be for the rest of the day but would be around tomorrow to check on her progress. He wants her to remain in the hospital for four days at least, to prevent any infection.

The following morning, Mr O'Dwyer returns with his team. "The nurse tells me you had a good night. How are you feeling now?"

"Kind of sore, but it is getting better."

"The nurse gave her more painkillers. Seems they are kicking in."

Later in the day, Daniel the audiologist arrives. He explains his role in Angela's recovery. Daniel will monitor Angela during the adjustment period when her microphone is fitted. Angela and Daniel get on immediately. You can tell that he is used to working with children.

We won't be working with him for a few weeks, but it's good to meet him.

Daniel is not long gone when Ralph arrives. He is going to be Angela's speech and language therapist.

I had already told the family that Mr O'Dwyer feels it best nobody visits while we are in hospital. They all agree but I know they are finding it hard not being able to see Angela.

The morning of day five, Mr O'Dwyer and Mr McSharry arrive together.

"Today is the day, Angela, you can go home. Pete, Angela will have to continue with the antibiotics and pain killers for another four days. I will have a prescription ready for you when you are leaving. Pete, please do not hesitate to phone if you are worried at any stage."

"Thank you. Hopefully, I won't need to, but it is reassuring to know I can."

"Also, I recommend that there are as few visitors as possible. I know everyone will be excited to see Angela, but she needs this time to rest and heal."

Once I'm sure that Angela is ok, I go outside and phone the family. Everyone understands completely and agrees to stay away until I feel it's a good time for Angela.

Well, almost everyone, my mother is not too happy.

"Surely you mean everyone else, Pete? I am her grandmother and I need to be with her," she said.

I explain what Mr O'Dwyer said and that it wouldn't be fair to only exclude some people.

"Why are you excluding me from everything? I feel so pushed aside," she sniffs.

"I am sorry Mother, but it is just the nature of things. Besides, it is only for a few more days. It is quite an overwhelming and emotional time for Angela."

I couldn't believe what she said next.

"Don't tell me she is becoming like her mother."

Before I could say anything, I could hear Dad in the background saying, "Joan, you have gone too far."

When my mother spoke again, she sounded calmer, "I am sorry son, that was not very nice of me. I have just been so worried. You do understand, don't you? I do understand about the visitors. I just feel I could be some help to you both. Please let me know when I can see Angela."

I tell her I understand her concern and as soon as it was ok, she would be first to visit and I would phone to keep her posted.

Ralph arrives as I packed up Angela's things.

Ralph speaks about what lies ahead and how much work it will be for Angela. I was to sit in on the appointments as I needed to change the way I communicated with Angela. It will take time, but for the minute, just go home, rest and recover.

We arrive home after lunch and I get Angela settled into bed. I tidy away the things in her hospital bag and put on a wash.

When I return to Angela's room, she is fast sleep. I lay down beside her. The last few days catch up with me and before I know it, I fall asleep too.

We both sleep through the night. It's Angela who wakes me the next morning. I get up but insist she stays in bed a little longer. I bring her breakfast up to her.

Afterwards, I go for a shower leaving Angela to rest. The nurse had said she should only have a bath or a wash down – no hair washing for a while.

By mid-morning, Angela is a lot brighter and is enjoying reading her book.

Three days after we arrived home, we are ready for visitors. My mother and father are first on the scene. Angela is so happy to see them. We have some job getting my mother to leave.

"Angela is tired, Mother. Anne also wants to see her."

"I want to stay another while. Why can't Anne wait until tomorrow?"

"Like you, Anne is looking forward to seeing Angela. Just give it time, Mother."

"Oh ok! I suppose so… I will phone you later to see how things are." Mother says her goodbyes as Dad guides her out the door.

It's only later I realised how my Dad looks different. It's hard to pinpoint, but I would find out what and why later on.

Anne arrives and only stays for a bit. She gives us both a big hug and says how she is looking forward to when she could spend more time with Angela.

As Anne was leaving, she told me that Patrica was going to Tenerife. She would let me know if she heard anything.

"Do keep me posted if you hear anything, Anne. Sorry, I am not much help at the moment."

"Pete, you have enough on your plate. Just concentrate on Angela."

The First Visit to Tenerife

I text Audrey as soon as we land.

<Thankfully a good flight, no delays. Landed safe & sound. On way to Charles house in a taxi. will ring u when settled>

We decided that I should stay with an old friend of hers on the island. He has also agreed to help as much as he possibly can.

When I approached the gate to Charles' house, I am blown away. This is no ordinary holiday home. It's a bloody mansion! It's obvious that Charles is expecting me. As soon as I press the buzzer at the gate, it immediately opens. I am truly blown away, not only by the house, but by the grounds.

Charles walks down to meet me. "Hello Patrica, how are you? Well, aren't you just as pretty as Audrey said! Welcome to my humble abode."

I just smiled and told him there is nothing humble about this abode!

I was shown to my room by Charles' housekeeper and then joined him for a coffee on the back veranda. I can see already that Charles is a real man for the women. If I was inclined that way, I could see how he would have no problem charming you. He is quite attractive, dark hair, greying at the sides, dark brown eyes and a charming smile. We chat about my flight and how Audrey is keeping and then we get on to business.

"I have been doing a bit of investigating since Audrey got in touch, Patrica. One thing is for sure, if this lady is here, it will be easy enough to find her. Also, I have a few friends in the police and I have made an appointment to meet one of them, Miguel, tomorrow morning at ten o'clock in Los Cristiano's police station."

"I will be ready. I suppose there is not much else I can do until tomorrow, so if you don't mind, I might take a rest and make a call to Audrey."

"No worries. The pool is there for your use. Make yourself at home. The kitchen is always open, so help yourself. The only thing I must insist on is that you join me for dinner this evening. It will be nice to have some company for a change, say seven?"

"Sounds good. Seven sharp it is then, thank you Charles."

When I retire to my room, I phone Audrey to fill her in. Then she asks what I think of Charles. I can hear the grin on her face.

"I want to hate him, Audrey, but he is a lovable rogue. I think he feels he will convert me back to men!"

We both laugh at this.

"God loves a trier, Patrica, and trust me, if anyone has any chance it would be Charles. All joking aside, behind all the bravado he is a good man and has suffered his own hardships, not that you would know. But don't at any stage doubt his intelligence and ability to get information from you. Be on your guard. He is a cunning fox."

"Don't worry, Audrey. He will not get anything out of me."

Smiling, we both say goodbye.

I decide a swim is in order. Thankfully, I have brought my bikini. I put on the robe that is hanging on the bathroom door and make my way out to the pool. Deciding to take in some sunshine while I am at it. It would be a shame to waste the opportunity. Especially now while I can, as the next few days will be busy with work. I never thought I would wear a bikini again, not with the scars on my body, especially in those early days. One day a few years back, I looked at the scars and decided at least I was still alive. No longer would I hide my scars from the world but wear them with pride, not embarrassment.

Charles arrived down to the poolside just as I was getting out of the pool. I walked from the water with my head held high. I could see him trying to discreetly look at them but pretend not to notice.

"Nice swim, Patrica?"

"Yes, thank you, Charles. You have an amazing property here. Have you lived here long?"

"We moved here fifteen years ago, fell in love with the place and decided to call it home."

I noticed how he said we, but I didn't enquire further. There is a story here but if Charles wants to talk, he would. I lay on the lounger soaking up the rays. Charles asks if I would like a drink. I decide that even though I would love a beer, it would be wiser to have a coke. Within five minutes, my coke was by my side.

Charles jumps in for a swim and I just enjoy lying there listening to the water as it laps over the sides of the pool. By five o'clock I decide it was time for a shower.

"See you later at dinner," I say as I head back to my room to shower and get my paperwork in order for the morning.

Charles

As Patrica walks away, Charles thinks to himself, 'She is a very good-looking woman, with a story for definite. But Audrey did ask me not to pry and I had promised not to. I really hope she didn't notice me looking at her scars, especially the one down her back. Definitely not scars from a car accident but more scars from a bad beating,' he thinks, hoping he is wrong. 'Saying that, the scars do not take from her in anyway – she is still a beautiful woman. You have to admire how she wears them with pride and confidence. There is nothing more attractive than a confident woman, who is proud of herself, one who couldn't care less what you think of her. It is such a pity she has no interest in men, what a waste.'

Patrica

Seven has arrived and I head down to dinner. Even though the house looks so large from the outside it is well laid out. Most of the ground floor is open plan, except for the kitchen. It is easy to find where dinner is being served. Where else but on the veranda! It's twenty-six degrees today and the temperature is not set to drop much lower tonight.

Charles is already there when I arrive. He tells the housekeeper to please serve. I did like it when he asks if she needs any help.

"No thank you, Charles. I will manage fine," she replies.

He nods and he notices me looking at him. He says, "I don't think I will ever get used to being waited on. Was not reared to it and it still feels strange. I always kind of feel guilty."

Catharina arrives back just as he was speaking, "I keep telling him to stop feeling that way. I have a good job and my pay is more than excellent. I feel lucky to have such a good employer."

"I am the lucky one, Catharina. I could search far and wide and not find somebody who would treat my home and myself as you do. So, I suppose we are both winners."

Dinner is only delicious – two light fish courses and a nice wine. Conversation is easy. I fill Charles in on the case. When I finish, I can see a sadness in his eyes,

"That is so sad. I don't know who to feel sorrier for, to be honest. The mother who must have been in a bad way to leave, the husband left behind or for the little girl. Isn't life hard on people sometimes? I know some people draw a lot on themselves. But others can just get drawn into situations which are beyond their control. Would you agree, Patrica?"

When he looks at me, I feel he could read my mind, am I being paranoid? I decide to change the subject. "Yes, I suppose so, but I have to say a lot of the cases I work on have shown me that in general, people can be very selfish and cruel. Then others are so good and selfless. I like to imagine that the majority are the good and selfless, but it is not always easy to see this in my job. I had one case, a happy couple, four children, lovely home, both worked hard and had little time for each other at the end of the day. The woman decided she was bored with her life and wanted a bit of excitement. Never thought to take the time with her husband to bring some excitement back into their marriage. No, she decided to have an affair with a work colleague. A horrible sleazy man, who had no respect for her or women in general. Her husband on the other hand truly loved her and was a gentleman in every sense of the word. Over time he started to become suspicious and hired us, hoping we would tell him his suspicions were uncalled for. Sadly, he was to discover that he was correct. His wife worked in a pharmaceutical company. Would you believe, she was actually meeting this guy in his car during their breaks. No discretion or thought for her family, she didn't even care who saw her, as long as she had her excitement. When we returned with pictures to her husband, as you can imagine, he was devastated.

I asked him what he intended to do, and I was blown away at his words, 'Nothing. How can I leave my children, especially knowing that she cares so little for them that she would be so public! I want my children to have both parents in their lives. I never had that privilege and know if it came down to it, she would take my children, make my life hell and blacken me to our children.'

I really couldn't believe my ears, but his next words really struck home.

'I know you might think me a weak man and maybe I am. But sometimes we have to think of others and put our own needs on the back boiler. My kids are my world and I need to be here for them for as long as they need me. Then one day I can think of myself, I hope that makes sense to you.'

I was blown away, told him I did not think him weak, but really admired him. He was a man who did nothing wrong, but had married a very selfish woman."

We chat a while longer and thankfully Charles does not ask any personal questions. It's time to head to bed, we say our goodnights. Just as I'm leaving, he says, "Patrica, you are an interesting woman with an interesting story. Maybe someday you will share it with me."

I just smile and say, "Goodnight Charles."

After a nice early morning swim and a tasty breakfast, we drive to the police station in Los Cristianos to meet the inspector. Miguel has very good English and is interested in the story. I give him several copies of Charlotte's photo. It is the most recent one Pete had. Taken in the hospital, not long after giving birth to Angela.

Miguel looks at me, "Patrica, if this lady was trying to forget her past, she will probably have altered her appearance. But obviously, things like the colour of our eyes give us away and she has very distinguishable eyes. We will do our best to help you. I will share your photo with all the other police stations on the island. Tell them she is not to be approached at any stage, as we don't want to frighten her. I will be notified if there are any sightings."

I speak of how Charlotte had a special connection with the old town of Los Cristianos as she had visited as a kid.

"I will have my officers on lookout. There is not much more I can do at this stage. As you say, you are not even definite that she is on the island."

"I understand and totally agree, but we have to start somewhere."

"Why is it only now that the family has started to search for this lady? It seems strange to have waited eight years?"

"Emotions were running high, the family were angry at first. The baby was born with hearing problems and the father couldn't believe the mother's reaction to this news. Spent a long time very angry and now that the child is getting older, he realises it is time she met her mother and had her in her life."

"I see. I am a true believer that it is never too late to make amends. I really hope we can help. I will be in contact if I hear anything."

At this, I know we are being dismissed. "Thank you for your time, Miguel. I really do appreciate all your help. Goodbye for the moment."

"You are welcome. I will be in touch."

Charles and I leave his office.

"I really hope this works and that Charlotte is on the island, Patrica. It would be lovely to find her. And hopefully, she will want to be found and reunited with her family."

Charles decides I should see a bit of the island and we go for a nice lunch in one of the older villages. I am not flying back until tonight, so I decide what the hell, I may as well take advantage of the day. We have a lovely day and eat lunch in a small house up on the hill. It was really lovely. The family feed people lunch outside in the garden, all local produce and home recipes. It was gorgeous and Charles paid more than the amount requested. Later, he told me how this was a way for the family to make extra money and he has more than enough for one person. There is more to this man than I first imagined. I think his flirty rich boy persona is just a cover. He is a good kind man.

On my return flight, I think about the last twenty-four hours. For the time being, there is not a lot we can do. At least with the help of the police, a lot of time and money will be saved. I could have walked into every bar and restaurant on the island and not have found a trace of Charlotte. At least this way, if she is there, she will be spotted.

The following morning, myself and Audrey go over all the information and make a few decisions. We need to have a little chat with Joan but need a plan before we approach her. It is decided that Audrey is the best person to befriend her. By the sounds of things, she will be more Joan's kind of person – well-spoken and a bit posh. I jokingly tell her this often.

We are in agreement that this lady knows more about the situation. Too many things just don't add up.

Unwanted Attention

Charlotte

I am not sure if I am being paranoid, but I have had two different police officers in the restaurant this week and I swear they are looking at me strangely. This has never happened to me before. Maybe I am imaging things, but it just feels strange.

I know I have not done anything illegal so it can't be that. The way they look at me is as if I remind them of somebody or am familiar.

When I speak to Joseph about it, he just laughs and says, "Charlotte, maybe they just think you are cute. It's not the first time I have noticed men admiring you."

"It is not like that, Joseph. It's hard to explain, but this is different."

The following Monday we are doing breakfast as usual and one of the police officers comes in for his coffee, and there it is again. I ask Joseph to watch and he agrees with me. This is different.

"Are you sure you have not broken the law, Charlotte? It is really odd how he is staring at you."

I decide to go to his table and take his order. "Good morning, how can I help you?"

"Coffee please. What is your name – if you don't mind me asking?"

"Charlotte. I will return with your coffee in a moment."

I try to ignore his stares but then another officer joins him and they both stare for a moment. Then I notice they both look at their phones and nod their heads.

After they leave, I tell Joseph what I saw. "It's maybe just a coincidence, but we will keep an eye on things. Can't be anything serious, Charlotte or they would have approached you. Trust me, the police do not waste time here."

"I hope you are right, Joseph. It just seems strange."

Nothing else strange happened after that, so I left it go.

Audrey Meets Joan

They had to come up with a plan to get to know Joan. They knew she swam in the hotel swimming pool at nine sharp every weekday morning. Audrey decided this was the best place to meet her in a casual manner. At first Audrey just smiled and kept to herself. Joan was always polite and as Anne had said, she liked to know everything about everyone. Never liking to imagine she was not always in the know. Audrey was a new member, so of course Joan would need to know everything. She would want to be the person to tell the other nine o'clock ladies.

One morning Audrey was in the steam room when Joan joined her. She didn't hesitate and introduced herself immediately.

"Good morning. My name is Joan. I see you have started to come here regularly. It is always nice to see new members. I hope you don't think me rude if I enquire into your name."

"Not at all. My name is Alice. Nice to meet you, Joan."

"You are not from around here, are you Alice?"

"No. We just moved here. My husband is a barrister. We decided to get another house outside of the city. It is so much smaller – only a five-bedroom detached, but it is so quaint."

As predicted, Joan's face lit up. The snob in her was taken in – hook, line and sinker.

"Oh, how lovely and is your house in Dublin a large one?"

"It is a private residence in Donnybrook, but you know, city life is so hectic. We decided to have a little getaway. I am sure you understand."

"Oh of course, and it is such a beautiful little town. We have such a variety of beautiful places, from the sea to the woods. We are very lucky to live here. Have you been down by the harbour yet?"

"Oh yes! It is such a sweet little place."

Each morning for the next fortnight Joan would get chatting to Alice.

Audrey was having great fun adding to her story and Joan was enjoying every minute. Audrey didn't feel bad, this lady was a complete snob for definite.

Little by little Audrey started slipping in questions and finding out snippets of Joan's family. One morning Audrey invited Joan to join her for morning coffee. As you can imagine, Joan jumped at the chance.

Over coffee, Audrey asked more about Joan's granddaughter. Then smoothly slipped in, "You never seem to speak of her mother, Joan. I hope she hasn't passed away or anything so dreadful…"

"Oh her? Now there is a story if you are interested in hearing it."

"Well, of course but only if you want to tell me."

"Of course. Besides, it's not as if you know anybody around here. I feel you are not a person to gossip. To be honest, it would be nice to confide in somebody. It has been so hard since she left. Since that day, I have always been there for my son and granddaughter."

Joan proceeded to the tell Audrey how Charlotte had left her poor son Pete to cope on his own with Angela. Everything she told me was exactly as Anne and Pete had said, maybe we were wrong, maybe she was just as upset as the others were at the time. At the end of her story, I asked her was it a surprise to her that Charlotte had left. Here is where things got interesting.

"To be honest, Alice. I never liked the girl from the beginning. My Pete was way too good for her and her dysfunctional family."

"Really Joan, so you didn't trust her from the start?" I thought it was good to let her feel I was on her side from the outset.

"Alice, I see you understand completely. I was always nice to her and I did try to guide her in the right direction, but she was a strong willed, opinionated young lady. I blame her mother, no discipline. You know the kind? When Pete announced he was to marry her, well, you can only imagine my dismay but there was nothing I could do. So, I went along with things, you know, as you do. My son was my confidante, and she was taking him away from me, but I smiled and even assisted in the wedding plans, not that Charlotte let me get too involved. She would always be polite but tell me herself and Pete had it all organised and I should just relax and enjoy the day. As if, Alice! I had to ensure it would be done correctly."

I responded with, "Really? I do understand, it was your son getting married, Joan."

"I know but what could I do? Pete was besotted and I couldn't lose him no matter what happened."

"And did your relationship improve after the wedding Joan or how did things progress?"

"It went ok. Pete and Charlotte lived their own lives. My son just didn't seem to need me anymore," I noticed her eyes well up at this point and if I am truly honest, I started to feel a bit sorry for her at that moment. Then her expression changed, and that pity disappeared with her next words.

"Well, as you can imagine, I had to play that lady at her own game, and trust me, I played it well, Alice. Very well indeed."

"Really, well I can see you are a very clever lady. I am intrigued, do tell me more." I had a look of complete interest in every word Joan was saying and she was loving the attention.

"I have so much to tell you it can't be done in one sitting. Are you doing anything Friday after our swim? If not, perhaps we could meet for a coffee then?"

Even if I was booked solid, I was making that appointment. "That sounds like a great idea. Oh, it is lovely to have met such a like-minded person, Joan. I feel we could be great friends." I hated lying, but I felt in comparison to the lies Joan had told, this was only a white one in comparison.

"That is lovely to hear and I feel the same myself. Sorry I have to run off, but Angela has a half-day from school, and I told Pete I would collect her and bring her to the speech and language therapist. I will see you at the pool in the morning. I look forward to coffee on Friday. See you then, Alice."

When I returned to the office, I filled Patrica in on my progress with Joan, my new best friend.

Patrica laughed and said, "You are such a charmer, Audrey."

"It is from all those years of living with James and putting up with all our false so-called friends and of course, charming the important clients."

"I nearly forget the life you lived before. I am sure you have met a lot of Joan's in your day and are just a pro at playing them."

"Patrica, I have learned a lot about Joan in these past weeks. She is so good at manipulating others. Even sucks me in sometimes, then her true colours show. It's in her eyes. God, they are so cold most of the time, like she has no feelings whatsoever. I do find this quite sad. I wonder what in life made her that way. I know we always talk about the nature-nurture theory and even if her nature is not the nicest, what happened or influenced her personality to be so cold. I know I am overthinking again. I can't help it, Patrica."

We both laughed as Patrica always thinks I am both too understanding and analytical. I feel with Patrica there is never any grey matter. I suppose that is why we work so well as a team. We balance each other.

"I could be wrong, but I feel Joan is one of those people who could never keep friends. You know the type? They like everything to be about themselves and as long as they have an audience and you are in agreement, they are happy. But the very minute you start to disagree, you will be blown out. Her way or the highway. I will have to play her carefully until the time is right. I want to get as much information from her as possible. I feel now more than ever that she knows more than she is letting on. I would bet my house on that."

"Hopefully, this Friday will tell more."

"I got a phone call from Anne asking how we were getting on, so I have arranged to meet her in town on Friday. She will have Angela with her and has cleared it with Pete. He is ok with me meeting her. She's had the receiver fitted – that was a fast four weeks since her surgery. He feels it will help our case if we can talk about Angela in a personal manner if – when we find Charlotte. What do you think?"

"It can only help and sure, it can't do any harm. How are you going to play it?"

"We are going to pretend we met on one of Anne's computer courses and that we are just having a catch up."

"Sounds good, keep it simple and casual."

"It will be nice to meet the little lady."

"We have a busy Friday ahead of us."

There is a knock at the office door and Alex puts his head in, "Patrica, it's for you. A Miguel from the police in Tenerife. I thought you might want to take it."

"For definite! Put it through and we will put it on speaker."

"Hello Patrica, we have had some progress. Two of my officers feel they have found the lady, Charlotte. One of my officers casually asked her name, and guess what? It is Charlotte. She matches the photos. She is a lot slimmer and her hair is short, but her eyes and cheekbones give her away. We obviously cannot approach her but can just keep an eye on her, ensure she doesn't move on."

"It would be great if you could keep an eye on her if that is not too much bother. It will be Monday of next week before we can do anything. We need to discuss things with our clients, as you can imagine."

"No problem, my men love the coffee where she works, so they will not complain. Let me know your plans as soon as you can."

"Thank you, I will do. Chat soon."

"That is great news. Where do we go from here, Audrey?"

"I know you are meeting Anne on Friday, but I think we should check things out first. Before we say anything. No reason to raise their hopes. We need to know it is definitely her. What do you think? Also, you can use the fact that Angela was there as an excuse as to why you could not talk openly with her."

"I agree, Audrey. I will fly over Sunday night and visit the police and go to the restaurant and check things out. I will fly back Tuesday. We can decide from there. I am curious as to what information you will get from Joan on Friday. It should be interesting."

New Friends

Joan

Joan skipped along to the school to collect Angela.

Oh, to meet such a lady. Of course, she is the kind of person I am most suited to, not like that Pat woman from the pool. I imagine she is green with envy now that I have made friends with Alice. I am so looking forward to our coffee on Friday. She seems so interested in me and my life, my family.

It is nice to have someone to tell how I really feel about Charlotte. I just know this is a woman I can trust. We are so like-minded, and her husband is a big barrister in Dublin. Just wait until I tell Frank. I think I will treat Angela to a visit to the park and an ice cream after her speech and language therapy. She is coming on so well. I can't believe how quickly she has recovered from the procedure and how much she has progressed.

Angela

My appointment with Ralph is good but a lot of hard work. I started to make out sounds about two weeks after the operation. When I returned to Mr O'Dwyer, he was really happy with me and I had the receiver fitted. It has been quite strange, but I can make out more and more sounds. My speech is improving every day. Daddy says I am really good, especially with my exercises.

Granny Joan is in great humour. After my appointment she tells me we are going to the park. She even buys me an ice cream before dinner.

"You seem happy, Granny."

"Oh, I am, Angela. I have made a lovely new friend at swimming. She is just my kind of person."

"That's lovely, Granny. I hope she is as nice a friend to you as Emma is to me."

"Oh, she will be, Angela."

That is the first time I have heard Granny Joan talk about friends. I suppose adults need friends too. I never thought of that.

We arrive at Granny's house and I run inside to see Grandad. Secretly, he is one of my favourite grown-ups, after Daddy, of course.

"Granny brought me to the park, and I had ice cream, Grandad. Before dinner and all!"

"Well, that is a first, Angela! Is that a smile I see on Granny's face?"

We both laugh at this because usually Granny Joan is not happy when we do this. But today is different. She doesn't seem to mind.

"What's making you so happy?" Grandad asks Granny.

"Oh, I had a lovely morning! I went for coffee with a lady from the swimming pool. I think we could be friends. We are so like-minded. Would you believe it, her husband is a barrister in Dublin? Our kind of people, dear, well-educated and well-mannered."

Frank

"Oh, that sounds lovely. It's always nice to meet new people."

Even though I say these words to Joan, in my head, I am wondering how long this friend lasts. It has always been the same. She meets a new person, and they are the bee's knees. Then one day, they either question or contradict Joan and that's that. They are gone. Never has a friend lasted more than a few months, mainly because Joan only likes people she thinks are very grand or posh. And now here we go again. It has always been the same in all the years I have known her. It is quite sad. Once I would question her on the choice of friends, but now I just smile and tell her I am happy for her. Another sign that I have stopped caring for her, I suppose.

I am so very thankful for my bridge club and my friends there. They are so different from Joan. These friends keep me sane, especially Mary. She seems to have had the same friends for years, some even going back to her childhood. I feel honoured to be a friend of hers.

I am preparing things to leave soon. Now that Angela has had her surgery and it has been so successful, I have no excuse not to. Even Pete is standing up a bit more to her. It still worries me that she will be able to turn him against me. Though I am not sure how his sister will react. I am allowed to be happy at some stage of my life.

We celebrated forty years marriage last year. Well, celebrated is a bit of an overstatement. Joan organised a dinner for all our family and neighbours. She hired a private company to cater it. She flounced around like the lady of the manner, giving me drink orders, not that I complained. I am used to it.

It just felt so false when everyone was congratulating us on our successful marriage and how we are still so happy after forty years. I just smiled and nodded, leaving Joan to do all the talking.

As I said, I have been organising things in the background, getting my finances in order. I will take good care of Joan and make sure she is comfortable. She can keep the house. I will sign it over to her, with a weekly allowance.

I intend to buy my own house when the right one turns up and turn up, it will. I know it.

Pete

It has been such a strange few months. Angela has recovered so quickly from the surgery. Into the second week, she told me that it felt strange. She was actually getting sensations in the cochlear implant. At the four-week check-up, Mr O'Dwyer was really happy with her progress. He fitted the receiver and told us it would take some time for Angela to adjust. But she has been amazing. Her progress has blown us all away. She has speech and language therapy three times a week with Ralph and he works with the therapist in Angela's school. Between everyone, Angela has had such great help and support. Angela never complains or gives out about all the exercises. She just works really hard all the time. She is so determined, telling me how she just wants to be able to hear.

I know it must be really hard for her, but you would never know it.

We have a meeting with the team tomorrow – Mr O'Dwyer, Ralph the speech and language therapist and Daniel the audiologist. We need to see where we go from here, to see how Angela is progressing.

After school we go straight to the appointment. We all sit around the table. Daniel tells us how he is happy with the adjustments he has made. Ralph speaks of the hard work Angela is doing, how she is doing her exercises every day, and this is showing in her progress.

Mr O'Dwyer is really happy with how the procedure went.

Angela is given most of the credit, understandably.

Ralph will be seeing Angela once a week from now on and Daniel is only a phone call away if we have any issues.

Mr O'Dwyer ends the meeting saying, "Angela, you should be so proud of the hard work you are doing. Onwards and upwards, keep up the good work!" Then he turns to Pete, "We will call Angela for an appointment in two months and then every six months after that. If at any time you have any worries or questions, please do not hesitate to phone my secretary."

The adults shake hands, and we say our goodbyes. Angela is now making clearer sounds and even though it is strange for her, it is also great.

Leaving the clinic, I asked Angela, "How does it feel to hear everyone's voices, Angela?"

Angela

"It is quite strange, Daddy. Some people sound like I imagined but then others sound completely different."

"Who sounds the most different to you?"

"Granny Joan. She sounds really different."

"How?"

"I always thought she would have a soft gentle voice but it's a bit cross. I thought Nana Anne would sound that way, but she has the softest, gentle voice."

"That is strange. I never really thought about it. I suppose because I am so used to hearing them speak that it never entered my head. I must start to take notice of that, food for thought. Do I sound different from how you imagined?"

"Nope, you sound exactly like I imagined. You do swear a lot though. I think we need a swear jar."

We both laugh and Daddy promises to try to stop swearing so much.

Friday Meetings

Audrey

Both myself and Patrica text each other the best of luck today. We have a busy one ahead of us. I am in the pool bright and early. I have to admit, I am enjoying these early morning swims. It will be hard to give it up when this case is over.

Of course, Joan is here sending a big smile and wave my way. "See you for coffee," she says loud enough for everyone to hear.

I give her the thumbs up and start my swim. I am pleasantly surprised how fast I have progressed. I am up to twenty lengths now, not too bad.

Joan is waiting for me at the reception when I come out.

"How would you fancy some breakfast, Alice? If you are not in a rush. I know a lovely place up the town."

"Sounds great, Joan. I am in no hurry today. A leisurely breakfast it is."

We stroll to the coffee shop and just chat in general. Joan speaks of a lady. Pat, I think her name is. She is the lady I thought was her friend on that first day.

"Oh, Pat is raging that we have become friends. She is a bit of a snob you know. She would love to have made friends with you. But luckily, I met you first, Alice. She wouldn't appreciate your friendship like I do."

How sad that these people have no real idea of friendship. I smile and nod along with Joan.

We settle ourselves in a window seat, of course. Joan is afraid she will miss anything. Seems to always be making comments about people – how they dress, their family business. I really couldn't care less, and I hate gossip, but I have to tolerate this as it is a means to an end. I leave enough time before I bring up the subject of Charlotte.

"Joan, you have me so intrigued about your daughter-in-law."

"Oh yes, you have no idea what I have had to endure because of her. All I hope is that she will never return. I am doing my best to make sure she never does, for all the right reasons, of course. My priority is to protect Pete and Angela."

"I understand. They are so lucky to have you, Joan. Have you had contact with Charlotte since she left?"

"What makes you ask that, Alice?"

"Just curious, that's all," Audrey says, inwardly cringing. She will have to be more careful.

"As I told you the other morning, I never took to the girl. She was so single-minded and confident. She never appreciated my advice. Well, not until she fell pregnant, then it was questions all the time. Is this normal, Joan? Is that how I should be feeling, Joan? I don't think she ever confided in her own mother. As the pregnancy progressed, she became more reliant on me. I tried to be as supportive as I possibly could. She was terrified of being a bad mother. I don't think even Pete knew how scared she was, to be honest. I never told her she would be a bad mother, but I never said she would be a good one. One mustn't tell lies and I honestly didn't feel she would be a good mother, judging by her own mother's skills.

My Pete could have had so many lovely girls. Have I told you how handsome he is? Girls were always mad about him, but he never seemed to have any interest in anyone until Charlotte came along. True love, he called it. I personally don't believe in such nonsense. You meet someone suitable and marry them. Get on with things, that is what I was told by my mother and that is what I did."

I sit here and try so hard not to show my true feelings to Joan. I am not sure whether to hate her or pity her, to tell the truth. I nod at all the appropriate times. She doesn't notice my silence. She is on a roll now.

"Frank told me I wasn't been supportive enough to Charlotte but sure what would he know, I ask you. When Angela was born, the way Charlotte reacted to the news just proved to me that I was correct. I couldn't abide the weakness she showed. So, one day I went in to see her when I knew she would be on her own, to give her a little advice. Well, somebody had to, Alice."

"Of course, Joan. Somebody had to take the situation in hand."

"I knew you would understand! Well, I suggested to her that Pete and Angela might be better off without her. How she had shown she was not up to things. And that day she left – now Pete obviously knows none of this, he wouldn't understand, you know. Well, that day she left, I phoned the house to see how things were going and

Charlotte answered. She told me her fears. Well, this was an opportunity I couldn't resist. I told her she was doing the right thing for everyone. I felt a bit bad. She really was in a bad state, quite hysterical. I think the hardest part about that day was knowing Angela would be left alone until Pete got back, but it had to be done, all for the best you see."

I really cannot believe this woman. She doesn't seem to have an empathetic bone in her body and truly believes she did the right thing.

"It was hard to watch Pete suffer, but I knew one day he would see it as the best thing to happen for us all. I have tried to find a nice lady for him, but he has no interest, saying the only lady in his life is Angela. I think he still hopes that Charlotte will return. I simply don't understand this. After what she has done to him and Angela? I will make sure this never happens."

"How is that, Joan?"

"Now here is the bit you really must never speak of. I know where she is. I have kept in contact with her. I tell her how she can never return, how angry Pete still is with her. How he has moved on with his life. That it is for the best, of course. She is better off where she is, and they are better off without her."

"So, you know where she is then, Joan?"

"Oh yes. The silly girl even sends cards and gifts to me for Angela every birthday and Christmas. She believes I pass them on to Angela. I keep her sweet and let her feel I am on her side. I will go to any lengths to keep her away."

"I understand, Joan. I do hope it is for the best."

"Of course, it is. I am sure my secret is safe with you, Alice. It is good to have someone to share this with. I have had to keep it to myself all these years."

"Your secret is safe with me, Joan. Would you like another cup of coffee?"

"That would be lovely."

We finish our coffee, and it is time to leave. I tell her I will see her Monday at swimming, and we part company.

As I walk along the street, my mind is racing. One thing is for sure, I will not be swimming on Monday or any day after that. Thankfully, we have not exchanged full contact details – intentionally on my part. I gave her a mobile number I use for work purposes. I actually despise this woman. She has no heart. I can't imagine how she justifies her behaviour, but she seems to be ok with it. I had to put on my best acting skills to cover how I really felt. I wanted to shake some sense of feeling into her, but I think she is well past that. Thankfully, I do not think I will have to meet her again. Hopefully, I have gotten all the information I need. Thank God for modern technology. I have recorded both conversations on my phone.

Patrica

I have arranged to meet Anne in the shopping centre at half past eleven. Angela has a day off school, and she has offered to mind her. Pete knows her plan and agrees that it's ok. We think it will be good for us to know Angela on a personal level so we can speak of her to Charlotte.

Anne greets me and introduces me to Angela as a friend from her computer course. We chat for a bit and then order some food. Angela is such a sweet child and has the most beautiful blue eyes and a smile that would light up the dreariest of days.

After we have eaten, we go for a stroll around the shops. Anne tells me how well Angela is adjusting to hearing and is working so hard with her speech and language therapy. She still uses sign language, but her speech is really improving.

As we walk along, Angela holds my hand and looks up at me with her beautiful smile and her words are slow but clear. They do shake me a bit, "Why do your eyes look so sad?"

At first, I didn't know what to say, then for some reason and I don't know what, I told her the truth. "I lost a very close friend and I still miss her, Angela."

"That is sad. I think your friend would want you to be happy. I know I would want my friend to be happy even if I wasn't around anymore." There are long pauses between her words, which is probably why it impacts on me even more so.

"Yes. Angela, you are right. My friend would be actually very cross with me for being like this."

As the morning progresses with Anne and Angela, I really start to feel better about things. Angela just has that way about her. Also, I thought if this little girl can be so happy and kind after all she has been through, then I should learn from her.

When we were saying our goodbyes, Angela gave me a big hug and we promised to meet again, maybe someday in the park.

I realised I actually wanted to really meet her again and get to know her more. I told Anne I would phone her Wednesday and hopefully would have some news for her.

"Chat then, Patrica."

We went our separate ways.

When I returned to the office, I found Audrey in a right state. She wasn't herself at all. It was like we had swapped personalities. Usually she is the one all calm and relaxed and I am the one who needs calming.

"Oh Patrica, you have no idea what a morning I have had! That woman is evil. Pure evil, I swear."

Friday Afternoon Meeting

We sit down and Alex brings us in some coffee and buns. "I thought you could do something sweet, Audrey."

"Thank you, Alex," she nods.

Audrey asks him to join us. We all listen to the recordings as we sip our coffees.

Our faces are frozen in a look of horror when the recording finishes. Nobody spoke for a few minutes.

It's Alex who breaks the silence. "Oh my God, I have heard of horrible mothers-in-law, but I have to say she wins hands down! She is horrific. Evil is too kind a word for her, Audrey."

"I know and the scary part is, she really believes she is doing the right thing by everyone. I suppose that is how she justifies it. We need a serious plan of action. This news will be hard to pass on. What should we do and who should we tell?"

"One thing I do know is we have to play this correctly. Joan is a dangerous woman and if she gets any idea about what is going on or what we know, I am sure she will do all in her power to stop us. What do you think, Patrica?"

"Well, telling Anne or Pete is definitely off the cards. There is no love lost between Anne and Joan and I don't think Anne could contain herself if she had this knowledge. She would understandably lose the plot with Joan. As for Pete, he would just be devastated at this information. To imagine his mother caused so much heartache in his life, being instrumental in him losing his wife and Angela her mother. Especially when she had the opportunity to help Charlotte. So personally Audrey, I feel we should keep this information to ourselves and see how things go. It will all come out eventually. All at the right time."

We all agree to keep this between us for the time being.

I have decided to go with Patrica to Tenerife on Sunday. We feel both of us should be there when we go see Charlotte.

The weekend is spent in preparation. We need to get this right. A meeting with Miguel at the police station is first on the agenda. We need to speak to the two police officers first and then proceed to the restaurant where Charlotte works. We have decided to play the recording to her if we get no joy. It will be our final card to try to bring her home.

Pete

"Hi Anne, just ringing to see how Friday went. Angela told me you met a friend, Patrica. She was really taken with her."

"Angela and Patrica really hit it off. She's always so good with people. Thankfully, she had no clue about anything else and just chatted away."

"It went really well, Pete. I think Patrica was totally smitten with Angela and sure, who could blame her! I think Angela made a friend there, they got on so well."

"Funny, I felt that too. It can only help if – when, she finds Charlotte. At least when she speaks of her, it will be in a personal way."

"Pete, Patrica said she would call me during the week and hopefully she will have more news for us."

"What will we do if they find her? What if she doesn't want to see us? I'm not sure I could handle that."

"I know Pete, I have been thinking the same way. I suppose all we can do is hope and deal with things as they happen. At least we will know we have tried. We can do no more than that."

"Let me know as soon as they get in touch, won't you? Chat soon."

"I will, Pete. Chat during the week."

Pete nearly jumped out of his skin when he turned around and saw his mother standing there.

"Hi Mother," he stuttered.

"Who were you talking to there, Pete? It seemed serious."

"Just a friend. How did you get in?"

"Angela let me in. I did knock but you were obviously busy on the phone."

"Sorry. Do you want a cup of tea Mother?"

"Yes please."

Pete is wondering how much his mother has heard. The last thing he needs is for her to get wind of what they are doing. In his head he is wondering could she have picked up anything from the conversation, and decides she couldn't have, as no names were mentioned. It's the one definite thing himself and Anne totally agree upon, is that his mother should not know anything for the time being.

Joan

'I wonder does Pete know how long I was there? I know it was Anne he was talking to. I'm not sure why he didn't tell me. They are up to something, I am sure. I wonder what though? Nothing too exciting with it being Anne. She is such a boring lady,' thought Joan.

Angela

Emma is coming over today. Daddy says he is going to bring us to the park for a while. If we are good, we can get a take-away afterwards. I can't wait to tell Emma everything, about meeting Patrica and Daddy's chat with Nana Anne.

When she arrives, we head to the park and run ahead of my dad so we can talk. I tell her all my news and about Daddy and Nana Anne.

"Do you think they have found her, Emma?"

"I don't know but it looks like it, Angela."

We chat away and as we near the park, Emma says, "I have some news too, Angela. Daddy brought me out for dinner the other evening. Telling me he wanted me to meet his friend. Well it turned out to be a lovely lady named Annmarie. Oh Angela, she is so pretty and nice and I saw them holding hands under the table. Do you think my wish came true, just like yours did?"

"Sounds like it to me, Emma. I am so happy for you."

"Daddy asked me what I thought of Annmarie and I told him I thought she was lovely. He said that is great as he would like us to spend more time together, all three of us. We are going to the zoo on Saturday, all three of us. I can't wait. My Daddy looks so happy."

"That is great news. I hope we get to meet her soon."

When Emma's daddy comes to collect her, himself and Daddy have a great chat in the kitchen. When they leave, it's time for bed. As Daddy is tucking me in, I tell him Emma's news.

"It is lovely news. I haven't seen Andrew that happy in a long time. He would love us to meet Annmarie, but he wants Emma and Annmarie to get to know each other a bit better first."

"I understand, Daddy. Emma is delighted and she really likes her. Looks like her wish is coming true."

"Is that what she wished for that day up at the fairy ring?"

"Yep, that was it, Daddy. I made my wishes too."

"What did you wish for, Angela?"

"Well, I can tell you one of my wishes as it came true, but I can't tell you the second one as it might not come true if I do. The first wish was that I could hear and that has come true. I believe my second wish will come true someday."

"I hope it does, Angela. I can't wait to find out what it is."

We pinkie promise as Daddy tucks me in. It has been a busy day and so much fun.

"Sweet dreams, Angela."

Detectives Travel to Tenerife

A very early start to our Monday morning. Our flight is at six. I collect Patrica en route. Before we know it, we are landing.

"Didn't feel that flight, did you Audrey? I suppose we have been planning our day and script all the way."

"I know, Patrica. I just hope we can pull this off and everything goes to plan. The Joan card is our last resort, ok?"

"Yes, for definite Audrey. Hopefully, we won't have to use it but if needs must, we will."

Charles is waiting for us as we enter the arrivals hall.

"Good morning ladies, hope you had a good flight."

"Didn't expect to see you here, Charlie!" exclaims Audrey.

"Thought I would give you a lift to the station. Save you getting a taxi. Also, I am curious to know how the case is going."

"Well firstly, let's go to your car and we can fill you in on the way. Thank you, Charlie," beams Audrey.

"Yes, thank you, *Charlie*. Audrey always says you are quite the gentleman," says Patrica.

"Does she now? You are both more than welcome."

When we are in the car, we tell Charles the latest and our plan.

"What do you think?"

"It is worth a try, but I have a proposition to make. I could go in for a coffee and engage her in conversation and see how the land lies. You know see if she is interested in other men and has moved on with her life."

"I suppose. What do you think, Patrica?"

"Well, if anyone can charm the pants off her, it would have to be Charles!" They all laugh.

"Patrica, you take my character! I am just a nice guy. I wouldn't imagine flirting." This, they all find the funniest.

We arrive at the police station at eleven. We have to wait about fifteen minutes for Miguel to be ready to meet us.

"Good morning ladies, Charles. Please follow me."

As we enter Miguel's office, we notice two young officers sitting to the side. Miguel introduces them as Officers Pedro and Philip.

I can't help but notice Miguel himself. I truly cannot remember the last time I noticed how attractive a man is.

"Please take a seat. Firstly, my men will tell you what they know about this lady. They recognised her from the photos you have provided. They are one hundred percent sure it is the same lady. When Pedro asked her name, she responded with Charlotte. Too much of a coincidence, yes?"

Pedro speaks first, he is very professional and seems by the book. "When I entered the Cafe de Rosa on my first visit, I immediately recognised this lady. She is the same as in the photo provided. She is a lot slimmer and her hair is shorter, but she has very distinguishable characteristics. I observed her and while doing so, I messaged Officer Philip. I requested he come to Cafe de Rosa to confirm the identity of the lady in question. He arrived ten minutes after receiving my request. We both ordered coffee and waited on the arrival of the waitress, the lady in question, to bring them to our table. When she approached, Philip agreed with the identity of the lady. We ordered coffee, and I requested her name. At this question she responded, Charlotte. We did not want to arouse any suspicion, so we did not ask any more questions. We finished our coffees, thanked her and left the premises and reported to our sergeant."

"Officer Philip, have you anything else to add to this information? Anything that would help with the investigation?"

"I found the lady quite pleasant and professional, also if I may add an observation, sir?"

"Of course, Officer Philip."

"I found the lady although pleasant and friendly, she seemed quite sad. Her eyes seemed hollow and empty."

"Thank you, Officer Philip. If you have no more to add, you may both leave."

Both myself and Patrica thank the officers as they leave the office.

"I hope this information is of some help to you both. We could not do any more as this lady has done nothing illegal in our country. I cannot use up too much of my officers time on this, as I am sure you understand?"

"Of course. We both thank you for all you have done. We really appreciate it. You and your men have gone above and beyond. Hopefully, we will reunite the family. Thank you again." I say.

"You are very welcome. I would be interested to know how things go, Audrey. If you would let me know, that would be very good of you. I truly do hope you are successful with this."

"I will, of course. It has been a pleasure to meet you, Miguel. I hope we will meet again."

"The pleasure was all mine. I also hope we meet again, Audrey."

When we are back in Charlies' car, both Patrica and Charlie are staring at me with a strange expression on their faces. "What?"

They both burst out laughing. As you can imagine, I am getting quite annoyed at them.

"Oh Audrey, I have not seen you flirt like that as long as I've known you. It was like neither me nor Charles were even in the room. It was brilliant to watch," splutters Patrica.

"Hey, it wasn't only Audrey. I think our friend, Miguel was also quite flirty. I hope we meet again Audrey, hmm?"

"I don't know what you are talking about, we were both very professional. I admit he is a very handsome man and he truly has a presence about him but that is it."

"Of course, Audrey!" They say in unison and burst out laughing again. I choose to ignore their juvenile behaviour.

To be honest though, deep inside I am quite happy that they felt Miguel was acting the same way. It is a long time since I have felt so attracted to someone. It is quite scary if I am honest but nice at the same time.

As we near the Cafe de Rosa and look for a parking space, we decide to have some lunch. There is another restaurant across the road. We decide we will eat there, and Charles will enter the Cafe de Rosa and dine there.

"Well, wish me luck, ladies. I will be my most charming."

"I don't think you need luck, Charlie! We will meet in that bar up the road after lunch as we do not want you to be seen joining us. We don't want her to notice any connection between us and cause any suspicion," I explain.

"Roger that. I think I quite like this undercover stuff. I might get used to it, ladies."

"Well, not if you keep calling us ladies like that."

"Like what?"

"In that patronising male chauvinistic manner," sniffs Patrica.

"Oh, you are very sensitive, Patrica, but if it bothers you, I will stop saying it."

"That would be great, thank you."

"See you both soon then, my dears," were his last words as he walks to the other side of the street and heads into the Cafe de Rosa with a big grin on his face.

"I know you like him, and he is a nice guy, Audrey, but he really is a chauvinist, isn't he? I find it quite irritating."

"Patrica, he is only doing that as he knows it is irritating you. He is a bit flirty but that's put on, honestly. Give him a chance. You know something though, if he was interested in more work, he would come in handy.

He can charm the birds out of the trees and has women eating out of his hand. A great man to get information out of people, I can tell you this for a fact from personal experience."

"I will take your word for that and I will give him more time. I promise to try and not let him know how irritating he can be. I do agree he would be great working undercover, especially with the women. We will see how he goes today with Charlotte. See how much information he can obtain from her."

We take our seats and order the lunch of the day with a large bottle of still water. We need a clear head for us to succeed with our plan.

Pete

Meanwhile, back in Ireland Pete and Anne are both hoping they will hear some news this week. Thankfully, they know nothing about what is happening in Tenerife, otherwise they would be on tender hooks. Pete has asked Anne if she would collect Angela from school today. He has a staff meeting and can't get out at his normal time. Being a teacher is a job Pete has always loved doing. He wanted to be one since primary school.

This was another thing himself and Charlotte had in common, their love for children. Both having a way with them and a great understanding of children's needs.

The hours were ideal, especially now. As he was able to be there for Angela and only on a rare day like this, when there were parent teacher meetings or staff meetings would he need someone to collect her. He was very lucky to have both Joan and Anne on board to help. He tried never to take advantage of either of them as would be so easy to do.

He had encouraged Charlotte on numerous occasions to return to college and get her teaching degree. But she said she loved the creche, even though she was underpaid, as were most people in the childcare sector. They had discussed this on numerous occasions. Charlotte would say how the job she did was one of the most important jobs. Taking care of peoples most precious gifts, their babies, and yet being paid less than people in other sectors.

Over the years, she had heard people trying to bargain down the price on their childcare. Even though she understood the financial side, she could not imagine doing so herself. "Really Pete, the state should be helping people. Other countries can do it, why can't we?"

I had to agree with her, but still I always felt her work was undervalued and unappreciated. But she loved it and that is all that counted. I wonder if she is working with children now, or what is she doing.

I really wish I knew. It is funny, I have been shut down around Charlotte these past years. Now that I have opened up again, I can't stop thinking about her. She is always on my mind. I really hope we can sort things out. I know I will have to apologise for deserting her when she needed me the most. I can only hope she will forgive me. All I can do is hope and wait. What will be will be, I suppose.

I am sitting in this meeting, but my thoughts are elsewhere will we hear any news soon? Patrica did say to

Anne that she hopes to have some news this week. I really don't want to get my hopes up, but it is hard, this waiting game. It is just as well people can't read your mind or everyone would know that I have not got a clue what we are discussing at the minute. These staff meetings can be tedious sometimes, especially when we are discussing how many centimetres a margin should be. I find these debates quite comical, considering it is hard sometimes to get most of the kids to actually draw a margin at the best of times. When we are broken up into groups to discuss this topic, I join in. If for nothing but the distraction from my own thoughts. Some of the teachers, the ones not in the real world become quite passionate about this topic. So, I decide to put the cat among the pigeons, a kid in my class made a very valid point the other day.

He said, "Sir, why do we need to draw a margin in our copies? There is one there already?"

I really found it difficult to argue his point and had to respond with a quite unsatisfactory answer but the best I could do. "Darren, that is a very valid point, but it is school requirements."

His reply was priceless. "Well sir, I think the school may start looking at their requirements."

I seriously had to turn to the board because I could feel a grin on my face. "Let's move on kids, page two. Margaret you start, please."

After I relay this story, I comment on how I really think that Darren had a good point.

Well, if I had said I was going to murder a student, I wouldn't have got the same reaction. Honestly! Of course, from the same three teachers, who are so far detached from the real world, it is actually scary.

"We can't believe you would agree with that point. The margin is very important on the page. It teaches children order and structure."

The other teachers in our group just looked at me, threw their eyes to heaven. At the coffee break, the few rational ones in our group had a good laugh about it.

I never knew a margin could cause such passion, at least it took my mind off Charlotte for a while.

Anne

Pete asked me to collect Angela today from school. He has some meeting in school. When Angela sees me at the school gates, she runs into my arms.

"Hello Nana!"

This child has brightened my world and softened my heart like I never believed anybody ever could.

"I was thinking we might go to our usual place, Angela and have a little bun. What do you think?"

"Yippee! Sounds lovely!"

When we are sitting in the little cafe shop down the road, we order and have a little chat about our day and Angela's day in school.

"How is it now, Angela, now that you can hear things in school?"

"Oh, it is great now, but it was so strange at first and it took a while for my friends to get used to, but now it is a lot easier."

"That is so good, Angela. I am so proud of how you have dealt with things. You are doing so well."

"Thank you, Nana. I am doing my best. Did you hear Emma's news? Her daddy has a new friend. She's a girl. Emma really likes her. Her daddy is so happy. She made a wish, and it has come true, Nana, just like my one did."

"What wish was that, Angela?"

"I wished that I could hear, and it came true, so hopefully my other wish will happen too."

"Oh, that sounds lovely, Angela! I hope it does also. Are you allowed to tell me the wish?"

"No, as it may not come true if I tell anybody."

"Ok, Angela."

As we are walking to my house, Angela looks up at me. "Nana, do you ever think about my mother?"

It takes me a moment to compose myself. This is the first time Angela has ever directly asked me about her mother.

"Yes Angela, of course I do. She is my daughter. I wish I could see her and know how she is."

"Do you think she thinks of me, Nana?"

"Of course she does. She is your mother Angela. I believe she thinks of you every day."

"I hope so, Nana. I really do."

I try to hide my tears and look off into the distance. My beautiful granddaughter is never cross or shows her sadness. But this must all be so hard for her, especially now that she is getting older and noticing more. I can only hope we find Charlotte and they can be reunited. Maybe even one day be a family again.

I hope we get news soon. This waiting is so hard for us all, thankfully Joan has no idea, some part of me wants to see her face if – no, when Charlotte returns home. We will just have to wait and see.

Angela

I am so glad I spoke to Nana. I was scared to at first, but I want to know more about my mammy. What if they find her, will she want to know me? What if she doesn't like me or want me? What if she does?

Café de Rosa, Tenerife

Back in Tenerife, Charles has taken a seat and Charlotte is on her way over.

'Well Charles, now is the time to turn on that famous charm everybody jokes about.'

Charlotte places a menu on the table in front of me.

"What would you recommend, my dear?"

"Oh, you speak English! I will get you the English menu."

"No need. I live here and speak fluent Spanish, thank you. You also speak English – Ireland? What part of Ireland are you from – if you don't mind me asking?" Charles asked, eyebrow lifting. "I am from Waterford originally. What part are you from, yourself?"

"I am from the south east of Ireland originally, but it is been a while since I have been home."

"Why is that? Oh, excuse me, I am being quite nosy."

"It is a long story but thank you for your interest. May I take your drinks order, or are you ready to order your food, sir?"

"Oh, please don't call me sir! I will have a beer, please."

When Charlotte returns, I place my food order. When she returns with my lunch, I make my second move.

"I see you are quite busy. I am sorry, I never caught your name?"

"My name is Charlotte, sir, and yes as you can see, I am quite busy. Can I get you anything else?"

"No thank you, Charlotte, but maybe if you were free one day, we could meet for coffee? Maybe I could get to know more about you?"

"Thank you for the compliment but I am always very busy. I work long hours and trust me, I am not that interesting. Enjoy your lunch and please let me know if you need anything else." Charlotte walks away.

Charmer indeed, I don't think there is a man that could charm this woman. Shut down would be an understatement. Well, that's some good news for the girls.

Charlotte

As Charlotte walks away, she thinks to herself how men make her laugh. He must think he is a right Casanova. God, I have met so many like him, but to be fair, at least this one was handsome if a bit sleazy. Nobody will ever compare to Pete. He would never be so intrusive to a person. Funny though, this is the second person to ask me my name in the last couple of weeks. Maybe it is just a coincidence. I need to stop being so paranoid.

Charles

When I am finished eating, I ask for the bill, wave and say thank you to Charlotte. I walk up the road to the bar, as arranged. Audrey and Patrica join me about ten minutes later.

"Well how did it go, charmer?" asks Audrey.

"I don't think there is a man that could charm that woman. I tried my best, to no avail. She did tell me her name and that she comes from the south east of Ireland. That is as much information as I could get."

"How is your ego, Charles?" Patrica says laughing

"My ego is perfectly fine, thank you Patrica. That lady has no interest in any man. I can tell you that for a fact."

"Well, that is good to know. At least we know she is as Pete and Anne described her."

"We better move on to plan B, but I think we will wait until tomorrow, lest she become suspicious."

We all agree, and we head back to Charles' house.

"Thank you so much for letting us stay with you, Charlie."

"Hey, it makes me look good, having two beautiful ladies staying over."

"I didn't know you're called Charlie? I thought it was just Charles."

"Only two people ever call me Charlie, my beautiful Rachel, and Audrey. They were friends a long time, and they both decided it suited me best. I personally think I am more a Charles. It is much more sophisticated than Charlie, don't you agree Patrica?"

At this we all burst out laughing.

"I suppose so – Charles. Has he been this delusional for long, Audrey?"

"As long as I've known him."

"Glad you find it funny, ladies."

We decide it is time for a swim and a bit of sunbathing. "Work can be done as we sunbathe."

After a lovely relaxing evening, we get cleaned up and join Charles for dinner. We have a lovely evening, but an early night was necessary as tomorrow would be the day we visit Charlotte. Hopefully, all will go well. We will have to be very careful.

Awake bright and early, we enjoy a lovely swim to start the day. "I could definitely live like this!"

"Me too," Patrica says arriving to join me.

"We have been really busy lately, Patrica. One case rolling into another. It is time we took a break. Maybe get another staff member? Someone who will work well with both of us."

"Well, we are doing very well. But are we financially in a position to do so?"

"I think we are, but of course I will have to look at the figures and see from there. Maybe in the next six months. Let's get this case sorted first."

"Perfect. Well, a few more lengths, then a shower and breakfast."

"I wonder if Charles has risen yet. He has the life, that's for sure."

"Do I hear my name being mentioned?"

"We were wondering when you would join the rest of the world."

"I always start late but I can work into the early hours. You know that, Audrey."

"I know that, just winding you up, Charlie. I can't wait to read the next book. Any hints on what it is about?"

"Can't tell until it is all finished but hopefully it will be as successful as my last two novels."

"Patrica, did you know that Charlie's last two novels were made into tv series, and became very popular?"

"Really? I didn't know that. I must read a few of them when I get a chance. Now back to the real world. We have a busy day ahead of us. Let's get showered and get moving," Patrica says walking into the house.

"Patrica's not too impressed with me being a writer, I take it."

"Take no notice. She is very sceptical of writers. She thinks they are always looking for a story and she isn't going to be one."

"I just knew there was a story there! Do you think I could talk her into telling it?"

"Let it go, Charlie. I don't want you to upset her. Patrica has been through enough. Trust me on this one, ok?"

"Will do, Audrey. Just the writer curiosity. You know what I am like. Now you better get going."

The women meet at the top of the stairs and go down for breakfast. "I hope he isn't looking for a story, Audrey. He is a nice guy and all that, but I won't talk to him about anything, ok?"

"I have warned him off, Patrica. He won't ask you anything, I promise."

"Thanks, Audrey. I feel better now. Well, let's eat. I am starving."

Breakfast arrives and the general chat is about today's meeting with Charlotte. Nothing much else is discussed, much to Patrica's relief.

By twelve thirty they are on their way into Cafe de Rosa. They ask for two white coffees, but it is not Charlotte who is serving them. The young girl arrives back with their coffee and asks if they would like anything else. "Not at the moment, thank you."

"What if she isn't working today? We didn't think about this. Now, that was silly of us."

"Maybe she is on a later shift. We can't chance asking, we don't want her getting suspicious. What now, Audrey?"

"I think we will have our coffee and then go for a walk. We can return around two thirty and see if she is here or not. We can always have some lunch and take our time over it."

So, they finished their coffees and pay, leaving a tip. They had only gone about ten minutes when Charlotte arrived at work.

Charlotte

"Thank you for the morning off Joseph, I got everything sorted. I'll fill you in later."

"No worries, Charlotte. I must admit I am quite curious as you never look for time off. We can talk later when things quieten down."

"If it ever quietens down, Joseph! We are so busy, and it is not even our peak season yet. I suppose it's more that the weather has been really bad in most of Europe. I think people just want to get away from things. A good thing for you and your business. But I tell you, we are earning our keep early this year."

"I know I am looking at asking our seasonal workers if they would like some extra work at the moment. Take some of the pressure from you and the other staff."

"I am not complaining, Joseph, but that sounds like a good idea."

"Done. I will phone them later. Oh well, smiles on, the tables are filling up. I will take the left side as usual, you take the centre and Catrina to the right. Let the fun commence!"

Café de Rosa

Audrey and Patrica return just after two, but they are hard pushed to get a table. Thankfully, a couple are just leaving. They are shown to their table by the same nice girl, whose name they now know is Catrina.

"Can you see her, Audrey?"

"Not yet. I hope we get to see her today. The chance of having a chat are not looking great. It is way too busy."

Catrina arrives with their menus and tells them the specials for today. Just as they order, Charlotte arrives out of the kitchen. It is hard to get a good look at her but from the description she fits the bill.

"What will we do, Audrey?"

"We will eat our lunch and enjoy it, then have a coffee and see if things settle down. I really didn't expect things to be this busy at this time of year, did you?"

"No, holidays are all year round these days."

Charlotte

At around four o'clock things settled down a bit, the mad rush was gone. Charlotte and Catrina took a small break after making sure all their customers were ok. "God Catrina, it has been crazy. We need this break."

"We absolutely do, Charlotte. Have you noticed those two ladies?"

"No Catrina, why do you ask?"

"Well, it's just they seemed interested in you. I could be imagining things but it's like they recognised you or something."

"I have been too busy to be honest."

Just as they were discussing the women, Catrina noticed one of them was approaching.

"Can I help you?"

She looks directly at Charlotte as she speaks. "Hi, my name is Audrey Pearse. Would it be possible to talk in private? It is really important. I hope you will give me some time to explain."

"What is this in relation to?"

"It is hard to explain in one short sentence. We really need to talk."

"Did Joan send you, is something wrong at home?"

"No, Joan did not send us. Why would you feel she would?"

"She said she would always let me know if something was wrong at home."

"Oh, did she? I really wish you would sit and talk with us so I can explain everything to you."

"I finish work at seven tonight. I will meet you here then."

"Thank you and I promise you will be interested in what I have to tell you. See you at seven then."

"What was that about, Charlotte?" asked Catrina

"I don't know but I am curious to find out."

Patrica

When Audrey arrived back to the table, Patrica was just staring at her with disbelief. "That was not in any plan, Audrey. What was that about?"

"I am not sure, but everything told me it was the right thing to do. It just felt right. I can't explain it to you, but something told me this was the moment to approach her."

"You and your gut instincts, but I can't say anything because you are generally right about these things."

They paid the bill and left the restaurant, as they walked up the road, Audrey told Patrica what Charlotte had asked her. "Was it Joan who sent you? – Interesting one that, isn't it, Patrica?"

"For sure. Joan really has her trust."

Charlotte

When they had left, Joseph asked Charlotte what that was all about. She told him she would explain everything later.

"Do you know those women, Charlotte?"

"No, I have never seen them before. God Joseph, you look like you've seen a ghost."

"I think I have, Charlotte. I really think I have."

They worked away for the evening. It was busy but not too crazy. Charlotte couldn't understand Joseph's reaction to the ladies. He wasn't himself all evening. Just as well she didn't tell him they were coming back at seven, or they would have gotten no work out of him. At least worrying about him, took her thoughts from why these ladies wanted to talk to her. She should have been nervous, scared even. But that lady Audrey made her feel safe and she just felt everything would be ok. She hoped it was not bad news. Not now, not when she had finally gotten the courage and had everything organised. I suppose there is nothing else to do but wait until seven and see what happens next.

Audrey

"Are you ready? We better be on our way, Patrica. I don't want to be late for our meeting."

"Hope we didn't scare her off, Audrey?"

"I don't think so. She seemed genuinely interested in what we have to say. I will do the initial talking if that is ok with you, Patrica?"

"No problem, I know I can be quite blunt sometimes and you are much better at the gentle approach."

"That is why we work so well together. It is all about balance. Let's get going."

We arrive back at seven on the dot. Charlotte is waiting for us. We sit at a table together and order some coffee. Charlotte has a white wine in her hand.

"I feel I might need one of these, for some reason. Now is someone going to tell me what this is about, please."

"Well, let's start with a proper introduction. My name is Audrey Pearse, and this is Patrica Patterson. We are private detectives. We have been hired by your mother Anne Logan and your husband Pete Williams."

"Are you joking me? How? Why? Why now after all these years? I don't understand."

"Let's start at the beginning. This could take a while."

"I have as long as it takes. It's not like I have anyone to go home to."

"Anne rang our office one day requesting an appointment, which was organised. When she arrived at our office, she told us the story of your disappearance and how she had reported you as a missing person to the Gardaí on the same day."

"Really?"

"Yes, well they could not find you and were a bit hindered in their investigation. We found that out when we took on the case. Well, then as your mother said, life went on. At first, as you can imagine there was a lot of anger. Then of course the baby had to be cared for. The time just passed but not a day went past that she did not think of you. Not knowing if you were alive, and if so, where you were."

"Are we talking about my mother here? Anne Logan?"

"Yes, Charlotte. After the interview we advised your mother to talk to your husband before we moved forward. She was a bit dubious about this, as she felt he was very angry and bitter about things. Little did she know that Pete had been feeling the same way. They both felt they should have done more, Charlotte, more to help you. They both felt they should have been there for you when you needed them most. But you were always so strong and independent, they felt you would get over this and move on. We requested a meeting with both your mother and Pete. Both of them were enthusiastic to start the search for you. The investigation started straight away. To be honest, the first thing we had to do was to ensure you were not dead. We went to the Gardaí to see what had been found on the initial investigation. It was easy enough to find you. There was a lot of information there. It just had to all be put together."

"Are you ok, Charlotte? I know this is a lot to take in?"

"I am just stunned. Why did Joan not tell them? I have been in touch with her since I arrived here. She was the only one I trusted. You see, she understood how I felt and encouraged me to stay away. She has kept me up to date on Angela. There are a few other things I am finding hard to take in."

"Such as?"

"Well, everything you are telling me is the opposite of what Joan has been saying. She says Pete is doing well and even dating again. That maybe it's time I give him his freedom. So, what you're saying is not making sense, as I am sure you can understand."

"Oh, we do, Charlotte. Maybe it is easier to believe Joan. We are two total strangers, and it is hard to take in everything we are telling you. But you must know this – neither Anne nor Pete wanted Joan to know about this investigation, at least not until they knew what the full story is. Look, I feel you have had enough to process for one evening. Will you meet up with us again and we can chat more?"

"Yes, I will but I need to take in all of this. I don't start work until four o'clock tomorrow, so we could meet before that, say two o'clock? There is a coffee shop on the beach front, I will meet you there."

"Great. One more thing. Charlotte, please do not contact Joan about this. It is really important that you keep this between us. I know it is a lot to ask, but you will just have to trust me on this. I know it is a big ask."

"I won't say a word. I just don't know who to trust. You will have to give me some time."

"We do understand, truly."

After a quiet journey back, we arrive at Charles' house. When we get in, Charles is there waiting with a nice white wine chilling for us.

"Thought you might be in need of a drink after your evening."

"You couldn't be more right, Charlie. It was certainly an interesting night. We didn't expect the response we got. Charlotte seemed really open to hearing what we had to say. We didn't want to overdo things, so we didn't tell all of it yet. So, I am afraid you will have house guests for another night, if that's ok? We don't want to outstay our welcome."

"Will you stop, Audrey, after all you have done for me over the years! It is my pleasure to be able to have you both as my guests for as long as needed."

"Thank you, you are a good friend."

"Your welcome, my friend. Now sit down and taste this amazing wine."

After a few hours of sitting and chatting, Charles said it was past his bedtime.

"Well Audrey, what do you think of our chat tonight?"

"It went well, but I have one worry and that is Joan."

"I know, I feel the same. How has she gotten Charlotte to trust in her so much. What has this woman said and done to deserve this trust?"

"Remember, I did tell you she is a clever lady, Patrica. Especially when she wants something, and it looks like she wants Charlotte far away from her family. We will chat to Charlotte tomorrow and hopefully find more answers. We need to tread carefully with the Joan situation."

"I know. We are two strangers to her, and Joan has been there for her all these years – or so she believes. If only she knew the truth."

"I know, Patrica, but I think that would be way too much for her at the minute."

"I agree totally, Audrey. Tomorrow is another day. Right now, it's time for bed. Goodnight friend."

"Goodnight, Patrica. See you at the pool in the morning."

"I could definitely get used to this lifestyle."

We pass the morning catching up on some paperwork. Alex has phoned, telling us we have two other clients waiting on us. We have decided that after the meeting today, if things haven't progressed much, then Patrica will fly home and I will remain until we get somewhere.

When we arrive at the coffee shop, Charlotte is there already. Coffees are ordered and we start our chat.

"How are you feeling now, Charlotte? Have you had time to digest the information we have given you so far?"

"I have something I need to tell you both first and then, we can go from there. I have been doing a lot of thinking these past few months. I have only recently decided to go home and give Pete a divorce. Joan feels it is only fair of me to give him the chance to move on and I agree. I can only hope he will let me meet Angela, and that they will somehow find it in themselves to forgive me."

"Charlotte, Pete has already forgiven you. It is himself he is finding it hardest to forgive."

"I have booked my flights and made an appointment with a solicitor."

"By any chance, would it be a solicitor that Joan recommends?"

"Well, yes, it is."

"Ok. Here goes… Charlotte, I wish you would believe what we told you last night. I know this is difficult as you don't know us, but your mother and Pete sent us and they trust us," says Patrica.

"What would be your one wish, Charlotte?" interrupts Audrey.

"I wish I could turn back time and have never left. To have gotten the help I needed. I was depressed after the birth and then with Angela's diagnosis, well, I just couldn't cope. I know that in time I would have been ok but at that time, I just couldn't cope. It's funny how I was so hard on my mother and I turned out to be worse than her."

"I have no idea what your mother was like back then, but she has told us a lot about your home life. She really does want to talk to you. Please give them a chance. One of us can sit in on the meeting, if that would make things easier?"

"Look, what have you to lose? Is it not worth a try?" added Patrica.

"I suppose so. I will have to speak to Pete once things are in place. Joan thinks I should leave it to her to sort things but the least I owe him is an explanation, don't you think?"

"Yes, I feel you do. What dates are you booked to travel home?"

"I fly on a Wednesday in a week's time. It is the soonest I can get off work. Joseph my boss is very understanding and has given me two weeks' break. Even though he has no idea what I am doing, and the restaurant is really busy at the minute. He just knows it is important if I am looking for time off."

"When do you meet the solicitor?"

"We meet on the Thursday afternoon. I have a two thirty appointment. Joan is going to meet me there."

"Well, could we arrange to meet up in our office that morning? Say ten?"

"And please don't tell Joan just yet. You just need to trust us a little longer. You will understand when we meet up. I really cannot say more than that at the moment, only that it is vital you come. It will greatly influence you getting to meet Angela. I promise not to do anything underhand but just give us the chance to explain it all. Then you can decide what you want to do, ok?"

"Ok. I will meet you on the Thursday morning, but I am not making any promises. Joan has always had my best interest at heart, so I will trust her to continue with this. But I do promise not to mention any of this to her for the moment. Do you really think you can help me get to see Angela?"

"Yes, Charlotte. I have met Angela."

"Really? What is she like?"

"She is a beautiful kind young lady. She has your eyes."

"Not a day passes that I don't think of her. How do I contact you and where is your office?"

"Here is our card and if you have any problem finding us, please just phone. We can arrange for you to be collected if needed."

"We will see you on Thursday. Thank you for giving us this opportunity and your trust."

As we are about to leave, Charlotte turns to Audrey, "Do you really think I will get to meet my daughter? I don't want to raise my hopes and then have them shattered, you understand?"

"I promise you, I would not do that to you. All I can say is everything we tell you is fact. We will talk in Ireland, Charlotte."

Charlotte leaves with a new spring in her step. "I really hope you can keep that promise, Audrey?"

"I had to say that or else we would have lost all chance. Angela is our carrot to get her to our office. Getting her there is our priority. It will be easier in Ireland than here. Meeting Pete and her mother will help her see there are options. Sorry for changing the original plans, but I wouldn't have done so if I thought they would work."

"I know, Audrey, and you were right. If we had gone with the original plan, I feel Charlotte would have run off and we would never had found her. At least now there is hope of the family being reunited. Imagine if we hadn't found her? The first thing Pete would have heard from her was when he received the divorce papers. Is it terrible that I can't wait to see Joan if and when this meeting happens, and she finds out? I know people will get hurt, but that lady needs taking down a peg or two."

"I agree totally, Patrica. We have really started to make this case personal, haven't we? And it's all thanks to Joan, what a woman."

We return to Charles and phone Alex on route. He organises our flight for that evening.

Charles insists on driving us to the airport. We say our goodbyes. Charles makes us promise to return on a holiday the next time.

"Charles, what is a holiday? We haven't had one of those in years. You know, Audrey is such a slave driver," scoffs Patrica.

"Oh, don't I know it, Patrica!"

"You're both very funny."

When the laughter settles, I give Charlie a hug and to my surprise, so does Patrica.

"Thank you, Charles I have enjoyed both my stays and thank you for not prying. You never know, one day I might get the courage to tell you my story but I wouldn't hold my breath, if I was you!" says Patrica.

I don't know who is more shocked, Charlie or me but it is a massive breakthrough for Patrica.

We don't speak again until we land in Dublin. Walking through the airport, Audrey turns to Patrica saying,

"You must really have taken to Charlie. I am so glad. He is one of the good guys. Trust me."

"I am not going straight or anything, Audrey, but I agree, he is one of the good ones."

"Now let's get home. I am wrecked and so in need of my own bed."

We collect my car and I drop Patrica to her home on the way home.

"See you in the morning, bright and early! We have a lot of decisions and plans to make."

"Night Audrey, see you tomorrow."

News Update

Anne

The phone rings at ten o'clock. It is Patrica.

"Morning Anne, hope all is good with you?"

"Yes fine, what's the news?"

"Anne, could you organise for yourself and Pete to come to the office? We need to talk to you both in person."

"Off course, I will. I'll phone Pete. It will probably be this evening after school, is that ok?"

"Perfect. Come when you are ready. We are here all evening doing paperwork. Talk to you later."

"It's not bad news, is it?"

"No, it is not. I promise. Chat in a while."

As soon as I am off the phone, I send Pete a text message. <Phone me as soon as you can please. It is very important.>

The phone had only left my hand when Pete phoned.

"What's wrong? Is everything ok with Angela?"

"Yes, yes! Sorry for worrying you but it is important. Patrica phoned me and they need us in their office today. They have news and no, it is not bad – I checked. What time can you make it, Pete?"

"Let me think. I have to organise Angela first. Give me a few minutes. Thankfully, the kids are doing their hurling training, so I have time to organise things. I will phone you back in a few minutes."

True to his word, ten minutes haven't passed, and he is back to me. "My mother is going to collect her. I had to lie. I told her I had a meeting with a parent. I really don't like lying to her, but I know it is the right thing to do at the moment. She won't be too happy with our plans. I don't think she has ever really forgiven Charlotte for leaving. Well look, I must go. I will meet you at the office at four, ok? Fingers crossed it's good news."

"See you then, Pete."

I always have to change the subject or ignore it when Pete speaks of Joan. I am afraid I will say some of how I feel about her out loud, and she is his mother after all.

Well, that's the spare room cleaned out. I am doing everything I can to keep busy. My head is all over the place. I keep crossing my fingers and if I could, I would be crossing my toes. I hope they have found Charlotte and that she wants to see us. I am terrified to get my hopes up, but I can't help it. Just to get the chance to see her and say I am sorry.

Pete

I am not sure how I am feeling about things. What if she is happy with someone else and doesn't want to meet up. What if she doesn't forgive us? Thankfully, hurling training is over, and I will be kept busy enough until later. I am on yard duty today, that will keep me distracted. One of the great things about my job is the kids keep you busy, no time for brooding at work. I hope Anne is doing ok. She has nothing to keep her distracted. She has really changed. I would never have imagined that we would become close. But we really have in the last few months. It is great to have her support with this. I'm not sure I would ever have had the courage to go ahead with looking for Charlotte if Anne hadn't initiated it. Let's hope things turn out ok.

At last it is home time. When the last of my children are collected, I return to the classroom. Tidy up the room, collect the English copies that need correcting. Finally, it is time for me to go.

I park up with a few minutes to spare. I stroll down to the office building. It's just as well people can't see what you are thinking – I would be locked up for definite. My head is genuinely all over the place.

I am truly grateful that Audrey and Patrica did not give us more notice for the meeting. I would be a definite basket case if I had to wait any longer.

Next Step

Audrey and Patrica

"Well, have we decided what we are going to tell them? Do we mention Joan and her input?"

"I think we will not plan anything this time, Patrica. What needs to be said, will be said. Of course, we will tell them we found Charlotte but after that, I am not really sure how much we should tell them. We can only wait until they arrive and go from there."

Pete

It is four o'clock and we are sitting in the waiting room. I don't know which of us is the most nervous. We have hardly said a word to each other. Honestly, I think we are both lost in our own thoughts. Alex tried at first to make small talk but soon realised he was only wasting his time.

Alex is looking at us both strangely. Then I realise he is telling us we are to go into the office. I have to nudge Anne. She is truly lost in her thoughts.

"Good evening to you both," Audrey says as she rises to shake hands with us. Then Patrica gets up and does the same.

"I can only imagine how you both are feeling. We will make this as painless as possible, we promise. As you know, we had gotten a few leads on Charlotte. You will be glad to know we found her."

"Where? How is she?"

Both Anne and Pete speak together, asking questions, understandably.

"If you can give us a moment, we will tell you all we know. You will have to be patient. I know this is not easy."

Audrey picks up the phone. "Alex, could you please come in?"

When he opens the door, she asks him to get some drinks. "Tea or coffee?"

Pete responds with, "A good stiff whiskey would go down well at this minute, to be honest."

"I can only offer you tea or coffee, sorry about that," Audrey says with a smile.

We get our orders in and just sit and chill for a few moments, giving us time to digest things and calm a bit.

"Patrica will start as she was the person who initially found Charlotte."

"After following up on the information I received from both yourselves and the Garda report, Tenerife seemed the best place to start the ball rolling. Luckily, Audrey has a good friend with contacts in the police force over in Tenerife. He organised for me to meet one of them, who very kindly passed Charlotte's photo to his officers and others on the island. They were informed not to approach Charlotte as we did not want to spook her, not yet knowing her frame of mind. Officer Pedro and Officer Philip were the ones to come across her first. She is working in a local bar not too far from the station.

Pedro recognised her from the photo, even though she is wearing her hair shorter and is a lot slimmer than in the photo. He got chatting casually and asked her name, and obviously she said Charlotte. We took this as a good sign, as anyone who doesn't want to be found, would use a different name. Miguel got in contact with us and filled us in on the information. We decided it would be good for us both to go over. We needed to confirm for ourselves that this was definitely Charlotte. We visited the police station and had a meeting with the officers in question and they informed us of their experience and confirming her identity."

"Oh, thank you Alex."

Audrey & Patrica

Both Anne and Pete took their cups and just sat quietly, eyes wide. They did thank Alex for their coffee, but I am sure they did not remember this later.

"Well, this is where Audrey comes into things."

"After this meeting, we decided to come up with a plan of action. The last thing we needed to do was to tip Charlotte off or scare her away. So, my friend Charles, played his part and went to her restaurant for some lunch. To be honest, Charles is a very charming man and we wanted to see if Charlotte had moved on, or where her head was at. She was not impressed by Charles much to his disappointment. I hasten to add, as he is always successful with the ladies, well maybe he tries to imagine he is at any rate! He informed us that Charlotte was a very friendly lady but seemed to him to only have interest in her work, not much else by the sounds of things. Well, the next step of our plan was for us to go meet her but not approach her, just get our own idea of her as a person," explains Audrey.

"Now here is where Audrey, changed the plan, much to my surprise," says Patrica.

"I know. I do, and did, apologise. Anyway, back to the story. I became aware that Charlotte and her co-worker were discussing us and were becoming suspicious. I suppose there was just too much interest in her in such a short space of time. She is a clever lady and was becoming quite curious as to why all of a sudden, she was gaining such interest. So, I decided to approach her and asked to speak to her. She was startled at first but agreed to meet up when she finished work at seven. To cut a long story short, we filled Charlotte in on some details and left her to digest the information. We met her the next day for lunch and we had a good chat. Charlotte informed us that she herself had at last gotten the courage to travel back to Ireland. Her trip is next week. With a lot of persuading, we convinced her to meet us in this office on Thursday week at ten o'clock."

There was silence for a few minutes. Uncomfortable would be an understatement.

Pete spoke first. "After all this time, I am just finding it so hard to take in… She is alive and well. How, why has she never made contact with us?"

"Pete, remember we let her down and she probably never felt she could approach us. To her, we turned our back on her."

"No, that is not how she feels, Anne and Pete. Charlotte has been riddled with guilt and believed it was best to stay away. She always felt you would be so angry at her and would never forgive her. Look, just give her a chance to explain. I had to tell Charlotte that I would not tell you both, so she would agree to a meeting. But again, I have a little plan and I am not sure if it will work but it is worth a try. I really feel if you were sitting together in the same room, things could be worked out."

"It is a tricky one, but I feel Audrey's plan could work. It is worth at least a listen. But first things first, how are you both with this? Has it scared you both off? Tell us your thoughts on all of this. It is a lot to take in and we do understand that."

"Anne?" prompted Audrey.

"I am just so relieved that my daughter is alive and well. I am angry at myself for not even trying to find her and not thinking of traveling to Tenerife. Oh, I know I can't keep wondering what ifs but it's not easy. I am her mother, and it doesn't say a lot for me that I let my daughter get into this situation. I should have been there for her when she needed her mother most."

"Anne, that is not achieving much. You know, as you keep telling me, the past is the past and we cannot undo it. We can only move forward and change the next chapter."

"I know, Pete. I am not great to practice what I preach, am I?"

"Pete, what about you? What do you think of all this?"

"You have both been so professional in all of this and I really appreciate this. I hope you realise this."

"Yes, thank you. Pete, how do you feel about meeting Charlotte again?"

"To be honest, bloody terrified – for all of us, not just me. I have to think of Angela and how this will affect her. There is just so much at stake and I am trying to take it all into consideration. My mother will not be too impressed, that is one thing I do know. She has always only had myself and Angela's wellbeing at heart, so I know this will be hard for her to digest. But Audrey and Patrica, deep down, I personally want to see her again. If nothing else comes from it but closure for us all. Now, what is this plan? It can't do any harm to hear it anyhow, can it?"

"Pete, I understand your concerns truly, but I am going to ask you to not say anything to anyone at this early stage, not even to your mother."

"Why not, Audrey?"

"Can you please just trust me on this? It is important to keep things as quiet as possible. We don't want Charlotte to get wind of anything just yet."

"Ok, but I am not sure how telling my mother would change that?"

"From our personal experience, we have found that the least number of people in on a plan, the better. Less chance of news traveling, and you would be surprised at how easy that can happen."

"Are we all in agreement to keep this to ourselves for now?"

"Yes," they both said in unison. "Of course, you both know best."

"Let's tell you both the plan."

The plan was put into place and all were in agreement on things.

Anne is to arrive just after nine o'clock and wait for the go ahead from the ladies. She will sit in another office and will only enter when called. "We don't want to spook Charlotte. We need to give her time to settle and then we will give her the option. Pete, you will stay in the coffee shop across the road and we will text you, if all goes well with Anne. We can only hope all goes well, but if at any time I feel that Charlotte is just not ready, we will cancel it all. Best to give her the time she needs. I hope you both see the sense of this?"

"I do but it will be very hard to know she is here, and I can't see her. I know it is the right thing to do but it will be hard."

"I know, Anne. And it will be hard on you also, Pete. But it is for the best. This has to be when Charlotte is ready, or it might all go wrong, and we might lose her if she panics."

They say their goodbyes and Anne and Pete leave.

Outside, they give each other a hug. "See you Thursday morning, Pete. Fingers crossed all will go as planned."

"See you then, Anne. We've a tough few days ahead of us." and at this, they part company.

Suspicions

Joan

When Pete arrives home, his mother and Angela are in the sitting room. They are both reading their books. He says his hello's and Angela runs into his arms for her usual hug.

"Hi Daddy, how was your meeting? Did it go well?"

"Yes pet, it went very well. How was your day?"

"I have cooked a bit of dinner for us, Pete. I know you won't mind me joining you. Your father is on one of his outings with the bridge club."

"No worries, that would be lovely. What's on the menu?"

Even though Pete is smiling, he really would prefer if his mother left as he hates lying to her and if she starts to ask questions, it will make it even harder.

"We are having your favourite, son, homemade steak and kidney pie. We made it together and there is a surprise for afters. Isn't there, Angela?"

"Yes, me and Granny Joan made that together too."

"Wow! You both have been busy. I will just go have a shower and get changed for dinner."

"No worries, son. Take your time. We will get things ready."

When Pete is upstairs, just about to get into the shower, he remembers he left his phone downstairs. 'I am sure it'll be fine. Neither Angela nor my mother would ever look at my phone.'

Meanwhile downstairs, Joan tells Angela to sit down and read for another while. She will call her when she needs her. Angela does what she is told and reads her book.

"Call me when you need me, Granny."

When Joan is sure that Angela is settled, she listens to make sure that the shower is running. Then takes Pete's phone into the kitchen. She just knows there is something going on and she will find out one way or another. Between spur of the moment meetings and the amount of contact Anne and Pete are having, she just knows something is going on.

She knows Pete's password as she has always kept a check on his phone. Just in case Charlotte ever got brave enough to contact him.

"As she scrolls down through the calls, she notices that there seems to be a lot of calls from a landline number. As quickly as she can she writes the number down. Then checks the text messages and just as she suspected, there are a lot of messages from Anne. But the last two take her interest immediately. One is from just twenty minutes ago.

<That meeting went well, Pete. Sorry for texting, but my head is bursting since we left the office. Imagine it is only a few more days. I just hope we're ready to meet. Not sure what will happen then but at least we will have met and hopefully get the chance to talk about how we feel. See you on Thursday morning. Let's keep fingers and toes crossed it all goes to plan.>

The other message was from earlier today, <See you at the office this evening. Remember, don't tell anyone anything yet, not until we know more. See you later. Anne>

Joan hears movement upstairs and she swiftly runs out to the hall to return the phone to the windowsill, where Pete left it. Just as she is about to put it down it beeps with a message, when she turns around Angela is staring at her.

"Why are you at Daddy's phone, Granny?"

"Oh! I thought I heard it ringing and I was checking it wasn't work or anything. No need to say anything to Daddy as I would hate him to think I was at his phone, dear."

"Ok Granny, I won't."

"Now let's get this dinner ready and set the table."

By the time Pete arrives down, the table is set, and the dinner smells delicious. They chat away about this and that and then Angela helps Joan get the dessert. A lovely homemade apple crumble, another of Pete's favourites.

"Wow, ladies! You have me spoilt. What did I do to deserve all this?"

"Because you're the bestest Daddy in the world."

"And son, of course," Joan says this with one of her false smiles. But this is not what she is thinking. Deep down she is raging, the fact that they are going behind her back, do they really think she is that stupid?

When they have finished and the cleaning up is done. Joan says she is going home, smiling she gives a hug to both Pete and Angela.

As she drives away, she is relieved to let her anger really show. Pete, Anne and that nuisance in Tenerife! She should ring her and ask her what she is playing at. But knows this is not the way to handle things. Instead she goes to her local greenway and walks it out for over an hour, pounding the footpath. By the time she has returned to her car, she is calmer and thinking straight.

First things first, I will ring this number in the morning and see what and where it is.

There is not a lot I can do until then.

Thankfully, I have the house to myself tonight. Frank and his bridge! Well, it suits him, he is such a boring man. He wouldn't know excitement if it jumped up and bit him. I can watch that lovely movie in peace with a nice glass of wine. That will keep me distracted until I can plan what to do next.

Frank

Little did Joan know that the last place Frank was, was playing bridge at that moment. He was actually viewing a house outside town. Bridge was not until eight tonight. Joan never had any interest in where he was but if she knew about him viewing houses, now that would be another story. He is sure she would not be happy.

Joan

At nine o'clock the next morning, Joan phones the landline she took from Pete's phone. It rings for a few seconds and then a male voice answers, "Pearse and Patterson Detective Agency, how can I help you?"

"Oh, I am sorry! I must have dialled the wrong number. Please forgive me."

"No problem, madam. Have a nice day."

So that's what they are up to. Right. Well, what is Joan to do?

She makes herself a nice cup of tea and sits down.

'I need to do this correctly,' she thinks. 'I know Charlotte will believe whatever I tell her, so I better come up with a good story.'

After about an hour, Joan has her head straight and a story in place. She picks up her phone and dials.

Charlotte

"Hi Charlotte, how are you keeping?"

"Joan, how are you? Is everything ok at home?"

"Are you in work or at home, Charlotte?"

"At home, I am on this evening, so not starting until four o'clock."

"Well I have something to tell you, dear. This is not going to be easy for you, the last thing I want to do is to hurt or upset you. This is so hard for me, but I know it is for the best. Are you sitting down, dear? If not, it would be best if you did. I was talking to Pete last night. We were having a lovely meal together, just the three of us. I had collected Angela as he had a meeting with Anne and some detective agency. When Angela was settled in bed, Pete filled me in on everything. You are meant to have meeting with these private detective ladies on Thursday morning. Yes?"

"Oh Joan, I should have told you, but they asked me not to tell anyone. You know, in case things went wrong. I was going to tell you when we met."

"That is ok, dear. I understand. Well, let me get on with things. I believe they promised you would get to see Angela and some other things."

This I am only guessing but Charlotte doesn't know that.

"Charlotte, it is a trick. They want you to sign away any rights to Angela. Make you promise never to see her, even when she is an adult."

There is silence at the other end of the phone.

"Are you ok, dear? I hate having to tell you these things, you know that."

"Yes Joan, I do. You have always been there for me."

"I know it has been so hard for you. If you come to Ireland and file for divorce, this will be forced on you."

"What will I do, Joan?"

"I think the best thing to do is to stay where you are and not come here at all. Another thing they have organised is for Pete and your mother to come to the interview. Oh Charlotte, I feel so bad! Firstly, for betraying my son. Secondly, having to be the one to tell you. It just breaks my heart." I let my voice become emotional, just enough. This is one skill I am blessed with.

"Joan, this must be terrible for you and I really appreciate all you do for me. Honestly."

"It is ok, dear. I am all you really have and can trust at this time."

"Joan, there is another problem. These investigators know where I am. I can't believe I was taken in by those ladies. They just seemed so genuine."

"They had this well planned out, I can tell you that much. You will have to stop all contact with them. Do they have your phone number?"

"No, I didn't give them my home address either. They only know where I work."

"Can you change jobs?"

"Joseph has another business. I am sure if I asked him, he would let me work there. What about the solicitor and the divorce?"

"We will have to put all that on hold, Charlotte. We don't want you signing away your rights to Angela, do we? They seemed to have everything well organised. They obviously know about your plans to divorce Pete."

Another guess but I bet I am right.

"Yes, I told them why I was going and what I intended to do."

"Do they know about me helping you?"

"I did mention it. I told them how good you are to me. Is that a problem?"

"No dear, I will send you some money to help with the move. Let me know how things are going. Best not to mention my help though, Charlotte. It puts me in a very awkward position."

"I know, it just came out, Joan. Don't worry, I won't be fooled like that again. You are the only one I will trust."

"Very good, Charlotte. Talk soon."

After the call, I sit wondering why that girl is so silly, why couldn't she keep her mouth shut. Though why didn't Pete ever mention anything to me? He didn't seem to know anything. He wouldn't have been able to keep that quiet, that's for sure. Seems strange, maybe it is Anne keeping it from him. I best just keep my distance and see what happens. This is all very curious indeed but at least I have Charlotte back on track. It is a pity about the divorce but can't be helped. Keeping her away from Pete and Anne is my priority. Hopefully, she will get things sorted with work and move as soon as possible."

The Move

Charlotte

Sitting on the couch, going over the conversation with Joan, Charlotte berates herself. What was I thinking trusting those women? Joan is right. I have to move. I can't sign away my rights to Angela. One day I want us to at least meet, even just so I can explain. How stupid could I have been to imagine that Pete would forgive me and want me back in his life? I feel like such a fool for being so gullible, my need to see them has made me blind. Well, that won't happen again for sure. They will be rightly let down when I don't turn up on Thursday, their plan will be ruined.

When I look at the clock, I realise it is time for work. I will talk to Joseph tonight and see what we can come up with. I hope he will help me out.

It is a busy evening and I only get to talk to Joseph when we have closed and cleared up. I ask him if we could chat. He opens a bottle of Muscadet wine and we sit down.

"Is everything ok, Charlotte? You haven't been yourself all evening. Is it the visit to Ireland on Wednesday?"

"Firstly, that has been cancelled. I won't be going."

"Ok, do you want to talk about things?"

"Yes. Joseph, I am going to tell you a story and I hope you will not judge me. That you will understand and be able to help, but I will understand if you don't."

"I will do what I can, Charlotte. That is all I can promise you."

Charlotte tells him everything, from her leaving home to the last call she had with Joan. She tried not to leave out anything. She is watching Joseph's expression at all times. Not once did he look disappointed or disgusted with her. The only thing she saw was sadness, this she didn't expect but to be honest, it was a relief.

"Well? You're very quiet."

"Charlotte, that is the saddest story I think I have heard in a long time. How have you been coping and now this?"

"It is ok, Joseph. It is all of my own making."

"No, it is not. They were your family. They should have been there for you. One thing is puzzling me. Joan. Is she really to be trusted?"

"Oh yes, she has been there for me since the beginning. It was she who told me about the plan."

"I know and that has me curious. If she was as close to her son as you say, why is she helping you?"

"I think she just felt sorry for me, Joseph, that's all."

"If you say so. I am just not that convinced, that's all. Now what's this favour?"

"As you know, the private detectives know where I work, and it won't take them long to find where I live. Well, I was wondering, how would you feel about me working in your premises in Maspalomas? I know it is a big ask but I feel it would be better to move."

"If that's what you feel is the right thing, of course. You will be missed here, but I would rather have you move than to lose you altogether, Charlotte. I don't just think of you as an employee but as a friend also. Have you thought about accommodation? If you want, there is a small apartment attached to the restaurant, you are more than welcome to stay there?"

"Oh Joseph, that would be brilliant. You are the best! Between you and Joan I might just get through this. When will be a good time for you?"

"Charlotte, whenever suits you. To be honest, I could do with someone keeping an eye on the Cafe Maria. How would you fancy a management job? I haven't been able to find anybody reliable since Magdalena left to return to Poland."

"That makes moving a lot easier. Thank you, Joseph. I will try to be moved by the end of the week and if anyone comes looking for me, you know nothing. Only that I never returned to work when I got back from Ireland."

"Are you sure you want to do this, Charlotte? Maybe it's time to face everyone and get things sorted, once and for all."

"But what if they make me sign something and I never get to see Angela. She will always believe I never wanted to see her. I couldn't bear that. I am not saying I won't go back. I just need time to clear my head and see where to go from here."

"If you are sure. I will travel with you to Maspalomas and settle you in. Show you the ropes and introduce you to the staff. Now go home and get some rest, we can talk again tomorrow. And one more thing, Charlotte. Think about what I said about Joan and her motives. It still isn't making sense to me."

"Night Joseph. I will think about Joan. I have a lot of things to sort out and the change will give me a chance to do so without the fear of being tracked down. I just need time and space, until I figure out where I am going next. Chat tomorrow."

Angela

Today, we have an appointment with Mr McSharry and Mr O'Dwyer. It has been two months since I had my last appointment. We arrive at ten o'clock and both doctors are there to meet us. Smiling, I tell them there is no secret keeping now, as I can hear everything.

I have the usual different tests and they seem to be happy so far. By one o'clock, the tests are done and we get some lunch in the hospital and then return to the office. Both doctors are sitting across from us.

"Well Angela, how do you feel things are going?"

"I am very happy. I feel things are getting better and easier every day."

"That's good. We have had time to look at all the results and we are very happy with your progress. Everything is going to plan, and you are doing great work."

"Where do we go from here then?" asks Daddy.

"Well, Pete, as I said at the last appointment, Angela will have an appointment every six months. Unless you have any worries in the future. Truthfully, Angela has progressed beyond even our expectations. This, of course, is down to her pure determination. Now it is just onwards and upwards for you all."

"Will Angela be able to go into mainstream school now?"

"Yes, of course. That is, if it is what she wants. Well Angela, what do you think?"

"I love my school, Daddy and I am not sure I want to leave."

"Ok pet, we might wait until the end of the year," says Daddy. "We can wait until this year ends and see where you go from there."

"Are you happy with everything, Angela? You have done such good work, you should be very proud of yourself."

"Oh, I am very happy, Mr McSharry, except for one thing. I won't have an excuse to visit you anymore. We always have such good fun."

"Sure, we are friends, Angela. We will organise other ways to meet. I will talk to your father and organise something."

"That would be great! Thanks doctors!"

"Your very welcome, Angela. It has been an honour."

When we leave, Daddy says we need to celebrate when we get home. When we get there, Nana Anne, Granny Joan and Grandad Frank are there. It's all hugs and how proud of me they are. It's lovely but I haven't told anyone what I believe. That it was the wish I made and that my second one is in the making.

We have a lovely time, but my nans are being funny with each other. They are being polite but hardly talking.

They think I don't notice but it is very obvious. The doorbell rings and when I answer, it is Emma – she has come for a sleepover. Granny Joan tells Daddy she has organised for him to go out for a few drinks with Emma's dad and that she is babysitting.

When everything settles down and Daddy has gone out, myself and Emma are playing in my room and we start talking about our wishes. She tells me her daddy is so happy with Annmarie.

"She is lovely, Angela. We have great fun together, all three of us. And your first wish has come true! What about your second wish, have you any news about that?"

"I know that Daddy and Nana Anne are still working on things. But I don't know a lot more than that. I can only keep hoping they find my mammy. I would really love us all to be together. It would be lovely to just know my mammy and what she looks like. Do you think she'd like me, Emma?"

"Of course, she would. We need to get to the fairy ring again and make the wish, just in case. Do you think your Daddy will bring us tomorrow if we ask?"

"We can ask him when we get up."

Granny Joan comes into the room a few minutes later and she looks funny. Her eyes are all red and puffy.

"Are you ok, Granny?"

"Yes of course, dear. I am just a bit tired, all the excitement, you know. I have popcorn made and a movie ready to watch. Pj's on and let's go downstairs."

When we are ready – pj's and fluffy socks on, we go down to Granny.

After the movie and popcorn, it is time for bed. Granny Joan tucks us in and reads us a story, my favourite story. When she says goodnight and I give her the biggest hug ever. "You're the best Granny ever! I love you loads."

"Love you too, pet. Night night."

Joan

Best Granny ever... If only she knew, my heart nearly broke when I overheard her telling her wishes to Emma. Never have I even imagined she thought about her mother. How could I have been so stupid? Of course she would, especially as she gets older. I have to keep my resolve. She must never know of my involvement. How would I explain that I am only trying to keep her safe from her mother? I just know I am doing the right thing.

Even if I wanted to, I can't let Charlotte ever come home or she might tell of my involvement. No. I will stick to my plan. Everything will work out for the best. This is my family, and she will be kept as far from them as possible.

Pete comes home early enough.

"Son, you should have stayed out a bit later."

"I have an early start in the morning but thank you for minding Angela. You're so good to us."

"Your welcome, son. Oh, by the way, the girls are hoping to go for a walk tomorrow morning. You won't be able to bring them – do you want me to come around and bring them?"

"I forgot completely with all the excitement, that the girls are off school. My brain is in a muddle, would you be able to come and mind them until I come back? I am not sure how long I will be. It depends on how things go. You never know, I might even have some good news to bring back with me."

"Really son? Tell me more."

"I can't, not until tomorrow is over with. Thank you again for all your help. You are the best."

"See you bright and early, son."

Then out of nowhere he gives me a big hug. I really don't know what to do. We are not a family for hugs. Angela is the only one that hugs everyone.

"Good night, Mother. I love you."

"Love you too, son."

What is happening? I never feel like this. I love my son and granddaughter. All I want to do is protect them. Or is that really my reason? I need to stop these thoughts. All this emotion has just unsettled me. I am doing the right thing. I must not lose sight of that. They would never forgive me if they found out the truth. Whatever is done, I must make sure they never discover where Charlotte is and never know my part. That is my priority.

Thursday Appointment

Audrey & Patrica

Anne arrives just after nine o'clock, as requested. Alex showed her into Patrica's office and gave her a coffee. She is well settled in and I can see she is a nervous wreck. It is so hard on them both but thankfully it will be over soon.

It is the slowest half hour we have ever put down. But ten o'clock passes and there is no sign of Charlotte.

Five past ten.

Ten past ten.

"It is not looking good, Audrey."

"I know but I really felt she would show up. What could have happened her?"

Alex knocks and says he has just received a phone call from a woman. "Said she is a friend of Charlotte's. I tried to put her through to you, but she would have none of it. Asked me to pass on the message. Charlotte will not be coming today or any day, she found out how you were all setting her up. Wanting her to sign away any chance of seeing Angela. Also, she said there is no point in trying to find her, she has moved jobs and house. Just leave her alone. She just wants some peace."

We just sit there with our mouths open, "Your joking, Alex?"

"Sadly, no."

"Do you think Joan could have had a hand in this?" asks Patrica immediately.

"But how would she know, unless someone told her."

"I don't know but she has gotten to her somehow. Now for the hard part. How are we going to tell Anne and Pete? We can't mention what we know about Joan yet. We have no proof it was her who influenced Charlotte."

"We can tell them Charlotte panicked and didn't come. We will keep up our side of the deal and keep going until we find her and get her home. Patrica, I am going to suggest we do this for free. I just don't want Joan to get away with this. What do you think?"

"Audrey, you're the boss, but I am with you one hundred percent."

"Good stuff. Alex, call in Anne. Patrica, will you go get Pete? If we message him, he will think Charlotte is here."

"Will do."

Anne

I just know something is wrong. They would have called me by now. Maybe she doesn't want to see us. Maybe she isn't ready yet. This waiting is just torture. I have gone to the door about a dozen times and have had to talk myself into sitting down again to wait.

As I was about to have another internal battle, the door opens. It is Alex. He is not looking happy at all.

"Audrey wants you to join her in the office. Patrica is gone for Pete."

As we walk into the office, it is obvious Charlotte is a no show.

"She never turned up, did she?"

"No Anne, I am afraid not. I have no idea what happened. We have a proposition to put to you both. We will wait until she arrives back with Pete to discuss it."

"Ok, Audrey." Anne is just sitting there with the tears running down her face, heartbroken and confused.

Pete

As I sit here in the coffee shop across the road, waiting for the text message to arrive. Drinking my third cappuccino, I think about Charlotte and the happy times we had together. Wishing I could turn back time, for the thousand time. Do things differently, but sure hindsight is great, isn't it? Never once have I taken my eyes away from the entrance to the office. The girl serving me must think I am a lunatic. She is giving me the strangest of looks. How could I have missed her going in, maybe it was when I was ordering my first coffee. It is amazing you watch and watch and the one minute you blink you miss what you are looking for.

Then the door opens, it is Patrica, her face tells me all.

"She never came, did she? It was too good to be true."

"Come over to the office, Pete. We need to talk to you both."

"Is there any point really?"

"Yes, there is, Pete. Please."

"Ok, I'll come over. I'm sorry. I didn't mean to be rude to you, it's just, well, I am gutted. I had my hopes set so high, I think I've hit the ground with a bang. Does that make sense?"

"Yes Pete. Look, I can only imagine how you feel, I would be pretending if I said different. Just give us a chance to put something to you both, please."

We walk the rest of the way to the office in silence. I walk straight to Anne and put my arm around her.

"Well, where do we go from here then?"

"Is there any point in going forward? She obviously decided she is not interested in meeting up with us."

"I know this is hard for you both. I really feel she just panicked. She must have been overwhelmed by everything. Patrica and I have been talking and have decided we want to go ahead with this case. You can pay us what is owed to date, but any work further work we do is at our own cost."

"Why?"

"We feel we have left you down. Both of us really thought we had Charlotte on her way home. Our intention was never meant to raise your hopes at any time, but we did. And only because we were so convinced. We need to know what happened to change her mind and we intend to find out. This case has become personal to us, Pete and Anne. We want your family back together and will do all we can to achieve this."

I look at Anne and she is as stunned as I am.

Anne says, "Thank you both. This means so much to us."

"Do you really think something happened to make her panic?" I ask.

"Yes Pete, we really do. We will do all we can to find out what, that we can promise you."

"Ok, if we can help, please let us know."

"We will."

"Just send me on the bill and if you need any more money, I have it and I don't mind paying to find my daughter and bringing her home."

"We know Anne, let it with us and we will keep in touch with our progress."

Detectives Decision

When Pete and Anne leave the office, it is nearly noon and we have a lot of planning to get on with. Alex brings in fresh coffees.

"How did things go with Pete and Anne after the no show?"

"Alex we are going to continue with the case, we are not giving up. It took a bit of persuasion, but we have convinced them both that it is a good idea, without mentioning Joan at any stage. I can't believe I haven't even a home address or phone number for Charlotte. What was I thinking? They are the first things we get usually."

"Audrey, don't beat yourself up. I never thought of it either and we were so convinced she would be here today."

"Why won't you tell them about Joan? I really don't understand that. You have the recording, surely that would convince them," asks Alex.

"Alex you haven't met this woman. We need to have a lot more than a phone recording for proof. She is a devious woman and will stop at nothing to get her own way. I know her type, she is a female version of my ex and needs to be handled right. It is no coincidence that Charlotte didn't arrive. Somehow Joan got wind of things and put a stop to it."

"So, Audrey, what's next?"

"Back to Tenerife for me next week. I will not travel until Thursday, let the dust settle. I will go to Cafe de Rosa and try see Charlotte. Hopefully, I will find out what happened."

"Not really a lot else we can do until that happens. Are you going to meet Joan again and see if you can get anything out of her?" asks Patrica.

"As much as I dislike that woman, I feel that has to be done. I think I will wait until after Tenerife. I want to speak to Charlotte first and then I will know what Joan has done to influence her."

Anne & Pete

When they come outside the office, Anne and Pete decide to go for some lunch. Not that they are hungry, but they are just not ready to face anyone else at that minute.

"What are you thinking, Anne?"

"Pete, I am devastated. I really thought we would get to see her today. I had visualised it over and over again and it didn't end like this, not even once. There is nothing we can do, Pete, only see if the ladies find out more information and go from there."

"I have decided to go to Tenerife and see if I can find her. I just can't sit around waiting for something to happen. I will phone Audrey and tell her my plan and look for the name of the place Charlotte works. I should have done it sooner and took things into my own hands."

"I will come with you, Pete."

"No, I need you here with Angela. Besides, I don't want my mother to get wind of things. She will be suspicious if we both go away. I know this might sound like a terrible thing to say but I am starting to agree with Audrey, Patrica and yourself about keeping my mother out of the loop. I don't know why, but I have a gut feeling, it doesn't make sense, yet I am going to trust it."

"I do understand and can't explain it either. When are you thinking of going, Pete?"

"The May bank holiday weekend is next week, so that would be a good time. I don't want to take time off work, as I missed a lot with Angela's treatments and appointments. I'll go online and see what flights I can get, probably be a bit pricy at this time of year but it will be worth it if I find her."

"Ok, sounds like a good plan to me, Pete. Now let's try to eat some lunch or we will be hungry later."

Pete

After lunch they go their separate ways. Pete phones Audrey and tells her his plan. He can tell she is not too happy with his decision, but she really cannot blame him. She understands his need to do something.

"Pete, I am going to travel on Thursday, but I can change it to Friday, I have nothing booked yet. Why don't we travel together? I can bring you to the Cafe de Rosa? If nothing else, I would be support for you."

"That sounds good. I will book flights and accommodation for the Friday to the Monday evening."

"Listen, let me book everything. I will get cheaper flights and you can fix up with me. As for accommodation, we can stay in my friend's house. I know he won't mind. I will contact him when I have the flights booked."

"Are you sure, Audrey? That's a big ask of your friend. Are you sure he won't mind?"

"Trust me, he won't mind. He loves to meet new people as he is a writer and is always in need of new characters."

"If you are sure, that would be great. Let me know what you arrange and how much I owe you. Thank you so much, Audrey. Sorry if I didn't seem appreciative earlier, but I was just so disappointed. You and Patrica have been amazing through all of this and we really do appreciate everything."

"No problem, Pete. It has been our pleasure and I truly wish today had turned out different. I will text you the details when I have them. Talk to you on Friday."

"Thank you, Audrey. See you then."

Pete feels lighter in himself after making this decision.

Joan

When he arrives back at his house, Joan is surprised to see him in such a good mood. This was the last thing she expected. 'He doesn't look like a man who got bad news. I wonder what happened,' she thinks to herself.

"Hello son, how did your meeting go?"

"Hi Mother, it wasn't what I expected, but it turned out ok in the end."

"Well, what is this news you were going to tell me?"

Pete had forgotten all about saying that to Joan, with all the excitement this morning.

"Oh that, well it didn't come about so no news to tell you. Sorry."

"Right, you are a funny fish. I am not sure what is going on with you these days. I was only saying to your father the other night, how you seem so distant these days. Not yourself at all. Not that he listens to me either. Is there anything you want to talk about, son? You know I am always here for you."

Pete

Even though it's tempting, something is telling me not to tell my mother anything. It's strange because I have always confided in her. I can't quite put my finger on it, but something has changed.

"No Mother, everything is fine but thanks for the offer. You're very good."

Joan

Not the answer I was expecting. I thought when Charlotte was a no-show, he would tell me everything, like he used to. But he is keeping quiet about it. This means we are not out of the woods yet. I will have to watch him carefully to see what's going on.

"You know I am always here for you, son. We have always been so close."

"I know, Mother. Now I will let you go. I am sure you have enough to be doing yourself. Thank you for minding the girls last night and again today. I will bring them off for a walk and a bit of a picnic. Chat soon," says Pete, hustling me out the door.

'Well, that's me told!' thinks Joan. 'I'm only useful to mind the children and now my use is done. Pete never made me feel like this before. But I won't show how hurt I am.' I just smile and say my goodbyes.

I am on my way home when I start to think about Alice. I haven't heard anything from her in a while. When I get home, I will phone her, and we can organise meeting up for a bit of lunch.

Audrey

The mobile phone rings. It's the one I gave Joan the number to.

"Are you going to answer that Audrey?" says Patrica.

"It's Joan phoning, Patrica. What will I do?"

"Answer and tell her you are in Dublin at the minute, or something like that."

"Hello Joan, nice to hear from you!" It's just as well she can't see the face I am pulling. Patrica smirks.

"Hi Alice, how are things with you? I haven't seen you swimming in a while. I hope all is good with you?"

"I have been very busy in Dublin. Entertaining, the usual, you know! But I am looking forward to getting back towards the end of next week. Would you like to meet for some lunch?"

"You read my mind, dear. I was just going to suggest the very same thing. What day would suit you best? We could meet in the usual place."

"It would definitely have to be the end of the week, by the time I will be free to meet. Perhaps Friday? I do hope that suits."

"That is perfect. Oh, I do look forward to seeing you. I miss our chats. See you then. Lots of news to tell you."

"Lovely! I look forward to it. See you then, Joan."

"Well that saves me a phone call, Patrica. 'Our usual place' – what is she like? I only met her twice. You would think we had been best buddies for years."

"As you said yourself, Audrey, the woman hasn't many, if any, friends. She is not letting you go."

"Ooh! Lucky me."

Then they both burst out laughing, a relief after the intensity of the morning.

Joan

Joan is a lot happier in herself when she ends the call.

It is so nice to have such a lady for a friend. She understands me and it will be great to have a good chat with her. I am sure she will totally agree with me and know that it is all for the best.

Do Wishes Come True?

Pete

P ete and the girls go for their walk once Joan has
gone. They go their usual route.

The two girls run ahead.

'It is so good to see Angela so happy,' thinks Pete.
'These little girls are such good friends, I really hope they
have each other and remain friends through the years.'

When he catches up with them, they are at the fairy
ring. "We always end up here, girls. Do you want to have
a picnic down by the stream?"

"We have something important to do first."

Both girls have made little paper flowers and put
them by the fairy tree.

"They are lovely. Girls, are you sure you want to leave
them here?"

"Oh yes we do! We want to say thank you to the fairies for making our wishes come true."

"That's lovely. Are you going to tell me those wishes? I
think the fairies will be ok with that, you know."

"Well, we can tell you two because they have come
true but I'm not sure about the third one… What do you
think, Emma?"

"I'll tell my wish. I wanted my Daddy to meet someone nice and kind and he did. Maybe one day they will
get married and I will have a mother again."

Pete tries not to show the sadness he feels at that minute and smiles saying, "Oh that is lovely, Emma. Annmarie seems like that person. And you'd never know what will happen."

Pete smiles to himself but does not say anything else to the girls. 'And Andrew was only telling me last night how serious things had become between himself and Annmarie, and how his biggest worry was Emma. I'll phone him this evening and tell him he need not worry about that. I'm sure he'd be interested to know about the wish that Emma has made. That should put his mind at ease on that part of his plan. Annmarie saying yes – that I can't help Andrew with!'

"Emma, I think you should tell your Daddy your wishes. Maybe he can wish for the same thing and make it stronger, then it might happen sooner," suggests Pete. He turns to his own daughter. "Well Angela, are you going to tell me what your wish is?"

Angela just stands there. She isn't sure what to do. 'If you tell your wish, will it come true?' she wonders.

"Daddy, my first wish was that I would be able to hear and that's come true. I am not going to tell you my second wish because it mightn't come true if I do and I really want it to. But you should make a wish and if my wish is meant to come true, then maybe your wish will be the same as mine."

"Not sure it works like that, Angela, but if you want to keep your second wish between you and the fairies, that is alright by me. I think I will make a wish. Remind me what I have to do again."

Both girls talk together, "You have to walk around the fairy ring three times. Then tell the fairies your wish and ask them politely to make your wish come true."

Pete does exactly as the girls tell him and when he stands in front of the fairy ring, he thinks, 'Sure, what have I to lose!' So, he makes his wish. 'Please let me find Charlotte and bring her home.'

"What did you wish for, Daddy?"

"No telling, remember! Now let's go have our picnic."

The rest of the day is a joy. When they return home after Pete dropped Emma home, he gets time to really think of everything that happened that day. They had gotten so close, maybe, just maybe, they will find Charlotte when they go to Tenerife and he will get the chance to explain everything. He tucks Angela into bed and tells her a story.

He says to Angela, "I really hope your wish comes true. Night pet."

"Goodnight Daddy. I hope yours comes true too."

The next morning Alex phones him, telling him the flight times and that Audrey will meet him at the airport. They will be flying at seven o'clock Friday evening, which suits him perfectly.

Anne says she will take Angela away for the weekend. It will give him a cover story for Joan. Angela is all excited about going away on holiday with her Nana Anne. It is all a big mystery, so this just adds to the excitement.

Pete has decided it is best not to tell Joan his plans. He phones her to tell her himself and Angela are going away for the weekend. They won't be back until Monday evening.

"Oh, that sounds lovely, dear! Where are you going? Maybe you would like some company. Myself and your dad could do with a little break."

"Sorry Mother, but it is just the two of us. We could do with a break away together. It has been a busy few months, and it will be nice to spend some time together, just the two of us."

"Alright, I know when I am not wanted. It was just an idea."

"Mother, don't be like that. We can organise another weekend together." I forgot how moody my mother can be, not a side of her everyone gets to see. She always did like her own way. Now that I think about it, my poor father never had any say.

"Don't worry about us, son. We will be fine, here on our own for the weekend."

"That's good, Mother. Say hello to Dad for us. Do something nice for the weekend together."

"Enjoy, son. Goodbye then."

"Bye Mother."

As soon as the call ends, Pete gives a sigh of relief and decides to give Anne a call.

"All sorted with Joan. She wasn't a happy camper. She wanted to come with us. I had some job to put her off! I am most definitely in the bad books. You know the story, just in case she phones you, I don't think she will, but it's no harm to have a story in place, just in case."

"Don't worry, Pete. I have it all rehearsed in my head. It will be fine. What have you told Angela?"

"Just that she is going away with you for a mystery weekend. That we are not going to say anything to Joan, as you just want it to be just the two of you and that you don't want to upset or hurt Granny Joan. She was ok and understood, a bit too well if you ask me but maybe I am just being a bit paranoid at the minute. I hate lying and always feel guilty, especially when it comes to my mother."

"I understand this is hard for you, but it is for the best. Now go get yourself organised and I will see you tomorrow after work."

Joan

Joan hangs up the phone, thinking to herself, 'Strange. That's not the son I reared… What has happened to Pete? I could always make him feel guilty, but he doesn't seem bothered any more. I do feel he is up to something. I am not sure what, but I will find out, that's for sure!'

Anne

Anne is not surprised when the phone rings or that it is Joan. Pete might have not thought she would, but Anne knew Joan would not rest until she knew more.

"Hello Anne, how are you today?"

"Well, this is a surprise, Joan! I didn't know you had my number."

"Yes, well, I got it from Pete a while ago, just in case I needed you to help with Angela or anything like that. But of course that need never arose, so I never had to use it until now."

"To what do I owe the honour of this phone call today, do you need my help with something?" Anne grins to herself. She knows it is killing Joan to have to phone her. She must really be desperate to know what is going on. Oh, a part of her would love to rile her. Tell her that Pete and herself are in cahoots but she won't for obvious reasons. But just for a moment she imagines the reaction she would get. Oh well, back to the phone call…

"I was wondering if you know where Pete and Angela are away to for the weekend by any chance?"

"I didn't know they were going away, Joan. I am surprised Pete hasn't said anything about it."

"He phoned there about a half an hour ago to tell me, and myself and Frank were going to surprise them by turning up. I just wondered if he had mentioned anything to you."

"That was a lovely idea, but obviously when he hasn't even said he was going, he must want a bit of quiet time with Angela. You know, just the two of them. It has been a busy few months for them between all the appointments and the operation."

"Oh yes, I know. We have all been quite busy alright, but especially Pete. He seems to have a lot of appointments with work in the last while."

"That's true. I am sure you will be glad of the break yourself. You are so good to help out." I nearly choke on those words but to be honest, they are the truth.

"Hmmm… I will let you go now, Anne. Thank you for your help, not that I am any the wiser. And by the way, I would never need a break away from my beautiful granddaughter. That is where we differ, isn't it?"

It takes everything in my power not to retaliate, but I know that is what she would love, and she could be the victim again. I never understand why people like to play the victim. The funny thing is, the people who play the victim the most, are usually the ones to leave a wake of victims behind them.

"Goodbye Joan. I hope to hear from you soon."

Joan is already gone. Her usual polite self! She didn't get what she wanted, so my use is done.

From Clare to Tenerife

F riday is the longest day I have ever put down. It's the poor kids that have to put up with me. One of my students even uses one of my quotes against me, "Sir, you are away with the fairies today!" and he's dead right. I may as well have been sitting up in a tree… At least it's test day. Fridays are always the day for revising the week's work.

When the home time bell rings at three o'clock, my class are the first to leave. "See you all Tuesday. Enjoy the long weekend!"

Our bags are in the boot and it is straight on to Angela's school. She is in the car and we are on our way in minutes.

"I am really looking forward to my holiday with Nana. I wonder where we are going?"

"I have no idea, Angela."

"Nana is very good to take me away for the weekend. It will be lovely to spend some time together."

"It will, Angela."

Sometimes I swear I forget she is only eight. I think she has more sense than the lot of us put together.

Anne is waiting at the door. She has her car packed and is ready to get on with their journey. I put Angela's bag in the boot.

"Good God, Angela! We are only going away for the weekend – it looks like you packed for a month away."

"Well, I didn't know where we were going, so I had to make sure I had everything, just in case."

Pete says his goodbyes gives her a hug and straps her in. "Enjoy yourself and I will see you on Monday."

"Don't miss me too much, Daddy."

"I will try my best not to." He closes the door and turns his back on her, remembering she can read lips. They walk back to the house as if checking all is ok inside.

"Your mother phoned me last night."

"I had a feeling she would."

"I went with our plan. That's why it is best for us to also go away for the weekend. I think she knows we are up to something."

"Me too, but we can tell her all when the time is right. Now, safe journey and text me when you arrive in Clare."

"Am I that predictable?"

"Yep."

Pete waves them off and then returns to his car. Out of the corner of his eye, he sees a car just like Joan's but surely it couldn't be hers. He really has to stop this. He is becoming quite paranoid these days. Charlotte always said he's a useless liar because he hates to lie to people and always looks guilty.

Without a backward glance, he takes off in the direction of the airport. Giving himself plenty of time but at least the Friday rush hour traffic will be coming the other way. Everyone will be on their way out of Dublin, going home for the weekend.

Joan

Joan is stunned.

The lies they have told me! And they are in this to-gether. I really can't believe this and to think that Anne lied so blatantly to me. The anger is just bubbling inside me!

How could Pete betray me like this? Anne must be laughing her head off at making a fool of me like that! They will both regret this. There is no need to follow Pete, if he is going to these lengths, he must be going to find Charlotte. I will get there first though.

When she arrives back to the house, she is in foul mood and poor Frank has the misfortune to be home and get the brunt of it.

"Have you done nothing today, Frank? You are as much use as a wart, do you know that?"

Frank

Frank wonders what has happened now. She is on a right rant. The tirade of abuse is unbelievable. He never got used to Joan's temper and her name calling. But whenever she is in one of her moods, she fires every name she can think of at him. The polite lady-like behaviour goes out the window.

Something just snaps in Frank at that minute. He wonders why he is putting up with this abuse and has done for years. He knows for a lot of years it was for the kids, as he knew deep down if he ever left Joan, he would never again see his children. Joan played the victim to perfection and she would have definitely turned the kids against him. But the kids are grown up now. He doesn't need to put up with this woman anymore. He tunes her out and gets up to go upstairs.

But Joan stands in front of him shouting her usual abuse, "You're not a man, Frank. You are just a weak excuse for one."

"Yep, that's it Joan. You know me so well. Now, I am not going to row with you, just because someone annoyed you. Shout away to yourself. I am going to go for a walk. Chat later."

Joan

After he leaves, Joan is sitting in her chair, her anger spent. Tears of frustration – not regret, run down her face. She feels she is losing her power over everyone. Well, everyone except Charlotte.

Frank doesn't seem to care anymore. He didn't even try to calm me down. Oh. he is such a weak man, but I have never seen him stand up to me like that and just walk out the door without looking back. I am just exhausted after the day, but I have one more job to do and that is to phone Charlotte.

"Good evening, Charlotte. I hope things have settled down for you. Is everything going to plan for you?"

Best to let her do most of the talking and see what she has done before I mention anything to her.

"Hi Joan! Oh, it's nice to hear a friendly voice. It's been a hard few days but I am settled in my new job and apartment. Joseph, my boss, has been fantastic to me.

It will take a bit of getting used to and of course, it's not easy starting all over again."

"I can only imagine but you are doing the right thing, Charlotte. At least you have made it possible for you to get the chance to meet Angela one day."

"That is true, and thanks to you, she will know I care and tried to keep in touch. With all the excitement I never asked, did she like the present I sent for her birthday?"

"Ahm… Oh yes, the present! Of course, she liked it." I had forgotten to peek at the present so I could mention it and Angela's reaction to it.

"She did like it, didn't she?"

"Of course, dear. I must be slipping. I forgot to mention it to you."

"Right. No worries, Joan."

Charlotte

For the first time ever, Charlotte is doubting Joan. Joan usually goes on and on about Angela's reaction to my gifts, but not a mention. Maybe Joseph is right, and I should doubt Joan a little bit and be more cautious.

"Are you there, dear? You have gone very quiet," Joan's harsh tone interrupts my thoughts.

"Yes Joan, I'm just a bit tired from the move and everything. I'm sure you understand."

"Of course, dear. Now, you never mentioned where your new apartment and job are."

"No, I didn't, that's true. How are you and Frank keeping?"

"All good here. You know, Frank being Frank. Charlotte, are you going to tell me where you are, dear?"

"Joan, I don't mean to be rude, but I am keeping my whereabouts to myself for the time being. I just need some space. I am sure you understand, after everything that has happened."

"Hmm… Right… Well dear, after all we have been through, I thought you knew you could trust me. You know I would never tell anyone until you wanted me to."

Charlotte can hear the edge in Joan's voice. She had forgotten how Joan can be when things are not going her way. But she has promised Joseph not to tell a soul, even Joan where she is for a while. "Just leave the dust settle, Charlotte, until you sort your own head out," were Josephs exact words.

"Don't worry, you will be the first to know, Joan. I just need some time. Now take good care and I will be in touch soon."

Joan

"Well, I never! Charlotte, I am a bit disappointed in you and your lack of appreciation for all I have done for you…" just as she was about to continue berating her, she realised that Charlotte had hung up on her.

This did not help her mood one bit.

'How dare she! The little upstart! How dare they all turn on me like this! The lack of appreciation after all I have done for them!' she fumed silently.

With nobody to take things out on, Joan decided it was best to try calm down. She poured herself a vodka. She had a nice little stash and well, it was for medicinal purposes. Nobody knew that Joan liked a little tipple during the day. She always did her shopping in different supermarkets, so nobody knew how much she bought. She had heard once that if you wanted a drink that others couldn't smell, vodka was it.

Her stash was in a wardrobe in the small back bedroom. She used this room for storage and Frank never went in there.

As she opened the wardrobe she looked up at the suitcase on top. It had not been used in years. If anybody knew what was in it, there would be right trouble. But nobody ever would. She wasn't sure why she had kept all the gifts and cards. Maybe one day she would have a little bonfire and dispose of them all.

Frank

Due to the terrible mood she was in, Joan forgot to stop drinking and fell asleep in the armchair. When Frank came home, he found her out cold. This was not the first time. He was the only one that knew about Joan and the vodka. Usually, he would try to wake her and get her to go to bed. That would always gain him a mouthful of abuse. Tonight, he just was not in the mood for more of Joan and her temper. Her face even though she was asleep, was twisted in bitterness and anger.

'Where is that beautiful woman I fell in love with?' he thought but he had to stop himself. 'Nothing will change now, Frank. Go to bed, man. Leave her there.' At that moment he just felt tired and sad. They could have had such a good life, especially since he retired. But nothing he did was ever enough or good enough. Today is the day he stops all that and he goes to bed with an easy conscience.

As he lay in his bed that night, he knew it would be only a few more months and everything would be in place and he could leave this unhappy life. "Goodnight Frank, sleep well," he said. This was something he had been saying to himself every night for a long time – as sure as hell, Joan never said it.

Joan

Around three in the morning, Joan wakes up, groaning, "Oh God!" She has a thumping headache. She gets up, hides the evidence and goes up to bed. It is only when she lies down that it hit her – Frank never woke her to go to bed.

'I need to sort things out. They are all running away with themselves!' she thought.

After two paracetamol, she starts to feel drowsy and her head only hits the pillow and she is asleep.

Next day, as usual, neither of them discuss the previous night and both go about their business. Joan does notice that Frank is exceptionally quiet.

"Are you going to sulk all day, Frank?"

This is typical of Joan. She always blames others and never sees that she has done anything wrong.

"Not sulking, Joan. I'm just in a quiet mood. Off for my walk now. Enjoy your swim. I hope it helps with your hangover. Oh, and by the way, I won't be back until later. A few of us from bridge club are meeting up to have a few games and some food. You work away with your dinner. I won't need anything, thank you."

Before I can answer, he is gone out the door. What has gotten into that man? I better sweeten him up. I suppose I have been a bit hard on him lately. I will cook a nice Sunday lunch for him tomorrow and get a good red wine.

Frank

Frank jumps into his car and drives off down the road with a new sense of purpose. He has a few viewings today. One is an apartment and the other three are houses. Thanks to his retirement package and always having been a great one to save for a rainy day, he is in a good position financially. Joan can have the house and her car, even if he did buy both, he could not be that vindictive to her. He has a bank account set up for her and she will manage on the money in it. She will be fine. This has to be done right and it will be, if all goes well today.

He meets Tim, the estate agent, at the first viewing. It is an apartment on the second floor, there is no lift and two flights of stairs – that is the first X against it. When they go in, the apartment is nicely decorated but very modern. Tim is showing him this mod con and saying things like, "It has the top of the range dishwasher, cooker and induction hob (whatever that is)…" Frank nods away, but deep down he knows this is a non-runner.

"Tim, this is a lovely apartment, but I don't think it is for me. It is more suitable for an up and coming youngster."

"I agree, Frank. I just want to show you all of the options, so you will know what's out there."

The first house is also a non-runner. When he said a doer-upper, I did not envision having to rebuild the thing!

"No, this is not it either, Tim."

"Well then, on to house number two. I feel this might be more like it, yes?"

And he is spot on.

It is a nice little two-bedroom, semi-detached bungalow in a quiet cul-de-sac. When we arrive, I notice there is a driveway leading up to a garage. When we go inside, on first sight, I know it is exactly what I want. Nice and homely, tastefully decorated, a big open fire – I always loved an open fire before Joan insisted that we needed one of those new fancy gas ones.

The best part comes when we go out the back. It is nicely paved with a big shed at the end of the garden.

"Tim, you couldn't have built a house more perfect for me."

We discuss the price and I tell him I will be a cash buyer.

"That's great, Frank. The owners are looking for a quick sale. They said something about moving to a country cottage. I will let you know as soon as I discuss everything with them. Now would you like to see the third house?"

"No thank you, Tim. This will do me perfect, thank you. You have my number. Chat soon, I hope."

As we are parting, who do I notice coming out of the house across the road but Mary. It is funny we have been bridge partners for years and I never knew where she lived.

"Hello there Mary, how are you today?" I forgot completely that nobody is meant to know what I am doing.

"Hi Frank, what brings you to this neck of the woods?" she says this as she looks over at the house with the for sale on it.

"Mary, would you mind if I didn't discuss this with you at the minute and if you would kindly forget you saw me here?"

"Not a bother, Frank. I wasn't prying, you know, just being a bit curious. You don't have to tell me anything, honestly."

"I want to, it's just that the timing isn't great at the moment."

"Not a bother, Frank. See you at bridge club later."

"Thank you, Mary. See you then."

I feel so rude, but I know Mary understands. I will tell her when things are sorted. That is one thing I have promised myself – Joan will be the first to know I am leaving her. It would kill her to imagine I had spoken to anyone about things. Even though she has treated me so... well, as she has, I still could never do that to her. Maybe she's right and I am a weak man, but I couldn't be any different. God knows, I have tried over the years and it has taken more out of me than the other person.

Anne and Angela's Holiday

Anne

I t was a long drive but worth it. The house, or I should say cottage, I rented is only gorgeous. We are only a five-minute walk to the beach and can see it from our bedroom windows.

After settling in, unpacking our clothes (and half of Angela's bedroom from home) and unpacking the shopping we bought on the way, we get on our coats and go down to the beach. It is a nice crisp dry day, not the usual heat in it for this time of year, but nice.

The journey was an interesting one. It was lovely to get some time on my own with Angela. Sometimes, I forget how young she is, especially with some of the things she comes out with! I think she knows more than we give her credit for. She is a very observant child and I suppose this all comes from her life. Angela has had to overcome so many challenges and not having a mother's support. We, myself and Joan (I will give Joan that), have always done our best by her and will keep doing so. But there are times when a mother is the only person to help, especially as Angela gets older.

As we were walking along, Angela looks up at me and says, "You and Granny Joan don't really get on with each other, do you?"

I take a few moments to answer and decide not to lie to her. The child has eyes, and you would want to be blind not to notice the bad feelings between us.

"We do try, Angela, but sometimes people are so different that it makes it hard for them to get on together. Do you understand that?"

"Yes, I do. I know you are very different. Did she like my Mammy?"

'Oh God! How do I answer that?' was my first thought. "I think she did. They seemed to get on well. Why do you ask?"

"She just looks so cross when you or Daddy mention her, that's all."

"I don't think she means to, but she finds it hard to talk about Charlotte."

"Nana, would you tell me about my mammy? You know, stories of when she was small? Do I look like her?"

"You know what, Angela, this weekend we will have a good chat about your mother. I was hoping you would ask. I brought some photos with me if you want to see them?"

"Really? That's great! This is going to be the bestest weekend, just you and me. We can talk about Mammy without worrying about upsetting Daddy or Granny Joan."

"Is that why you never ask about your mother? Are you afraid of upsetting everyone?"

"Yes. I don't want to see Daddy sad. And Granny Joan is kind of scary when she is cross."

I do have to hold back a grin when she says this. "Angela, this weekend we will not have to worry about any of those things."

The beach is gorgeous, typical west of Ireland, wild yet beautiful. If it's a warm sunny day, you could imagine that you're somewhere tropical. The sand on this beach is so fine and smooth. The sun is shining today and there is heat in it, until the wind blows and nearly cuts you in two!

We return to the cottage and decide on dinner. It is amazing how in the last few minutes, the light has vanished from the day. Thankfully, we had the fire lighting, and the heating was on when we arrived, so it is lovely and snug.

Lasagne and garlic bread for dinner is the overall winner. I only brought easy to cook meals, so we can spend time together, not me being stuck cooking in the kitchen.

When I arrive in the sitting-cum-dining room, Angela is busy colouring. She is such a good child. She never causes an ounce of bother, just like her mother when she was a child. I can feel my eyes welling up, because of my bad parenting, my beautiful granddaughter has been deprived of her mother. I know I can't undo the past but if I was to pray for anything – which trust me, I never normally do – it would be for Angela to have her mother around, especially when she nears her teens. I know Charlotte would be a fantastic mother. I had so many chances to tell her and I never did.

As I sit staring into the fire with my regrets at the forefront of my mind, I don't notice Angela coming over to me until she put her arms around me.

"Nana, why do you look so sad? Is it because I asked about my mother?"

"Yes and no, Angela. I love that you are speaking about her. It's just that it makes me sad that she's not here with us. I really wish she was. It would be lovely to see her. You know you are so like her, in so many ways. Did I ever tell you that? Even in your beautiful personality."

"No, Nana, you didn't. Do you really wish she was here?"

"Yes, of course, Angela."

"Can I tell you something, Nana? It's a really big secret."

"Of course, you can! You know I would never tell your secret to anyone."

"You know the fairy ring near our house?"

I nod that I do.

"Emma and I made a wish. Well, I made two."

"Really? That's lovely."

"I can tell you Emma's because it came true for her and one of mine did. Emma wished for her daddy to meet someone really nice and he met Annmarie."

I sit quietly, just listening, afraid if I say to much that I will put her off telling me.

"My first wish was that I could hear and that has come true. Now Nana, I know I am not supposed to tell you my wish because it might stop it happening. But now I know that you have the same wish, I can tell you. I wished that my mammy would come home. Promise you won't tell anyone?"

I don't know how I am holding it together. None of us even imagined that Angela thought about her mother. She has hardly spoken of her.

"I promise, Angela. What a lovely wish."

"Pinkie promise, Nana."

"Pinkie promise, Angela."

How could we have not noticed? I suppose we were all so caught up in protecting her, we lost sight of what was really important. But not anymore. Hopefully, Pete will be successful at finding Charlotte and bring her home.

Dinner is served and we decide to sit in front of the fire and eat. No rules on holidays. After our dinner, I show Angela some photos of her mother when she was only a baby and tell her what she was like. The rest of the weekend flies by with lots of photos and stories. Angela's face is alight with every story and photo. I know now that no matter what happens, this weekend has been one of the best gifts I could ever give Angela, except of course her mother in the flesh.

Monday morning arrives and we pack the car. Angela has more to add to her baggage, as I had made a copy of all the photos for her and put them into albums. Adding some handwritten stories about her mother. She is delighted.

"Nana, you are the best! I will always have a bit of my mother now, even if my wish never comes true."

"I have a feeling it will come true one day and you will be able to show your mother these albums when she returns."

The journey home seems shorter, it always does, I have noticed.

Pete has kept me posted all weekend and the news is not looking too good at the minute. It seems Charlotte can't be found anywhere. Her boss has no idea where she is gone, or so he says. Pete said he didn't trust him. He said that the man looked terribly guilty when he spoke to him, especially when he told him who he was. I will find out more when he gets back. We decided to keep contact to a minimum just in case Angela overheard anything. God, the last thing we want to do is raise her hopes. Especially after all she has told me this weekend. I feel so privileged that she trusts me enough to tell me. I asked her if she had spoken to her Granny Joan about any of this. Her answer didn't really surprise me.

"I don't think Granny Joan would like me to be wishing things like that. I don't think I will show her the photos, Nana. Do you mind?"

"No, of course not, Angela. You do what's best for you."

To say I was relieved would be an understatement. It is not that I am in competition with Joan. I was never that kind of person. I just know deep down that she has some part to play in all of this. I have no clue how or why, but it is my gut feeling.

Disappointment in Tenerife

Audrey & Pete

After meeting at the airport, Pete and Audrey go to their gate. Thankfully, everything was running on time. They hardly spoke until they were seated on the plane.

"I hope you don't mind that I got seats together. It is just we need to have some kind of plan in place before we get there," Audrey explains.

"No, not at all. It makes a lot of sense. What are you thinking?"

"Firstly, we can't just rock up and surprise her. She might see us and make a run for it. There is a cafe across the road, we can go there and wait until we see her enter work. Then when the time is right, I can approach her, explain everything to her. Then you can join us when she is prepared to see you."

Pete nods.

Audrey continues, "When we land, we will go to Charles' house and unpack. He is expecting us. There, we can have a good night's sleep, then go to the cafe in the morning. There is no point in going tonight, it will be too late when we arrive."

"Ok. Are you sure your friend doesn't mind me staying with him?"

"Not at all, Charles loves to meet new people. To be honest, I think he is enthralled with this case. Ever since he did a little bit of PI work for us."

We land on time, and as we are coming out of arrivals there is a man there with a sign, it has our names on it.

"Hi Charlie! Pete, this rogue is Charles."

"Hi Audrey and you must be Pete? It is nice to meet you," said Charles with his hand outstretched.

"You're very good to come and collect us. Thank you. What was the sign about?" Pete says laughing, shaking hands with the man.

"Not a bother. Looking forward to doing a bit more PI work, if I am needed. Just in case Audrey didn't recognise me with my new haircut."

"I think you're safe there, Charlie. About the PI work, we'll see how things go."

In the car, Charles tells them both that he has been going to the cafe across the road from the Cafe de Rosa and hasn't seen Charlotte in over a week.

"She may be off work, as she would have had the time booked off for traveling to Ireland. Maybe she still had to take the time off, or she didn't tell her boss that her plans had changed," suggests Audrey.

"Maybe, Audrey."

As usual, Charles' housekeeper had a lovely meal cooked and waiting to be served along with a nice wine. It takes Pete a bit of time to relax but after a while, thanks to Charles, they are talking like old friends.

Around eleven o'clock, they decide it is time to hit the hay.

"Pete, please make yourself at home. The pool is there and help yourself to the fridge."

"Thank you, Charles."

The next morning after a swim and breakfast, it is time to leave for the cafe. They sit there for two hours, drinking coffee but there is no sign of Charlotte. They had spoken of her work hours and decide to go away for a while and return at four o'clock when the next shift starts.

But she is still a no show.

"Do you think she has spotted us, Audrey, and is avoiding us?"

"I don't, Pete. Even if she did, she would still have to work, and we would see her from here."

"What now?"

"We go speak to her boss or the other members of staff. We could spend days waiting and watching."

They both agree to this and walk over to the restaurant. It is busy but there are a few empty tables. They take one near the counter.

"There is the girl that was working here the day we spoke to Charlotte. We will ask her."

When she arrives over, she starts to recognise Audrey and her expression changes. "You again. Have you not done enough damage? I have lost my friend over you." Then she pales under her tan as she realises she wasn't meant to say anything, but she has the words out now. She composes herself and asks, "How can I help you?"

"What do you mean you lost your friend?" Pete asks her and you can hear the worry in his voice.

"Nothing. Now, would you like to see some menus?"

It is obvious that we will not get any information from her. She has shut down completely.

"Can we speak to your boss, please? And yes, we would like menus, please."

"I will see if he is available."

She goes into the kitchen and tells Joseph that the lady who was there speaking to Charlotte a few weeks ago is outside but with a guy this time.

"She wants to speak with you, what do you want me to do?"

First Joseph has a look out and with a sigh of relief, he tells her to say he will be with them shortly. "May as well get some custom out of them first."

She returns with the menus and tells them that her boss will be with them shortly.

They chose two steaks and two beers when she returns to take their order. They could not say she's rude but she's definitely being cool with them.

Audrey says to Pete, "I suppose it is not her fault. We haven't a clue what she has been told about us and the situation."

As they are nearing the end of their meal, Joseph arrives at their table. "Good evening, I hope the meal was to your satisfaction? How can I help you?"

"I am sure you remember me from a few weeks back. We were talking to Charlotte."

"Yes, I remember. You were with another lady."

"That's right. Well, Charlotte was meant to come to our office when she returned to Ireland, but she never turned up and we are quite worried about her. I am sure you can understand our concern."

"I am sure you are very concerned, but maybe it would have been best if you had been up front with her in the first place."

"Firstly, I do not understand what you mean about being up front with Charlotte. We were very honest with her, trying our best to help her and her family."

"Oh, are you here to ambush the poor woman? Tell her how she will never see her daughter?" Joseph asks.

"So, you know the truth of Charlotte's story?"

"Yes. After she received the phone call from a close friend. Who filled her in on your plan, she came to me and told me her story. She was very upset. She told me she was handing in her resignation and was leaving the island. I pleaded with her to stay but she would not. She said she could not bear the thoughts of never seeing her daughter and needed time to sort things out."

"So where did she go?"

"And who might you be?"

"I am her husband, Pete."

Pete immediately sees the change in Joseph. Audrey notices it also.

"Oh right… I have no idea, Pete. I have not heard one word from her since that day."

"Did she give you any idea where she might be going?" asks Audrey.

"No, not an inkling."

Pete butts in, "Sorry to interrupt you both, but what are you talking about? Never seeing Angela again? You are not making any sense. I would never do that to her. I want her to come home and even if we never work out, I want our daughter to know her mother. Where did she get these ideas from?"

Joseph sits down with them when he hears this and says, "Her friend in Ireland – she never mentioned the name, just that they are the only person who has been there for her all these years. That friend told her it was a trick, this meeting. That both you and her mother were going to make her sign away any rights she had to Angela."

"I really can't believe this! Do you know who this friend is, Audrey?" Pete splutters.

"Not at the moment," she lied and both herself and Joseph knew it. They were both lying about not knowing it was Joan.

"But I will find out. Joseph, if you have any way of contacting Charlotte, will you please tell her that myself and Pete have called here and tell her this – she has been given the wrong information and maybe she should question this friend's motives. Seems a bit fishy to me. Tell her to phone me. Anytime. Here is my card. Please. It is so important that you do this. I am sure that you, like us, only want Charlotte to see her daughter and get to know the beautiful young lady she is."

"Obviously, I cannot make any promises but if I hear from her, I will pass on your message."

"Thank you. We really do appreciate this."

Joseph

They pay for their meal and as they leave, Joseph is struck by Pete's demeanour. The man looks devastated and seems genuine. He is now sure that his gut reaction to this 'friend' Joan is spot on. He is glad he never mentioned her name, but something tells him that Audrey also knows it is Joan. He is not at all sure what that was about, it seems strange.

Then again, he has the feeling that this Joan might be a force to be reckoned with. He will phone Charlotte later. Things need to get sorted. He does not want that lady back here, especially not with her partner. Patrica is part of a past he never wants to relive, a past of shame and regret.

Pete

Pete just walks along with his head hanging. Knowing he was silly to get his hopes so high and now they are back to where they started. He needs to find out who this friend is that has been there for Charlotte. He racks his brain. Who would she have been that close to?

Audrey

Audrey leaves him with his thoughts. He will talk when he is ready. Today is such a hard blow for him. She is used to this kind of thing, the disappointment more often than not. But she should have known things were coming together too easy in this case.

Eventually Pete comes out of his thoughts and looks at her.

"Audrey, we need to find out who this friend is. I have racked my brains and I can't come up with one name."

"I will get Patrica on to it first thing Monday morning."

"We may as well go home. I suppose, we are not going to get any further here."

"Oh, we have other avenues to look into Pete. I will get Charles to phone his friend Miguel in the police force to ask for a meeting tomorrow. We will also print off some more photos and hand them around. You would be surprised at the things people remember when they see a photo. Maybe Charlotte only left this locality and told Joseph she was leaving the island in case he wanted her to stay on and work for him. Don't give up yet, Pete. It is early days. Trust me. I have had cases run on for over two years. We have achieved so much so soon, this is just a lull. Honestly, Pete."

"If you say so, Audrey. It is just very hard."

"I understand. Why don't you go for a swim when we get back? It might help clear your head."

"Sounds like a good idea. Thanks for everything, Audrey."

Joseph

Joseph is in a serious quandary. He really felt sorry for Pete earlier. He seemed really genuine about his intentions but there seems to be a lot of things not adding up. Like, why didn't Audrey tell him it was Joan that is Charlotte's so-called friend. As much as he wants to help, his biggest fear is that his secret will come out. He will have to think about things and see what the best course of action to take is.

If anybody knew his past, be they friend or family, they would find it hard to forgive him the things he has done. God knows, he will never forgive himself. Why hadn't he listened to his brother when he started doing odd jobs for his old boss, he will never know. Especially the day he said, "Joe, it is bad enough that I am so far in, there is never a hope of me leaving. Don't make that mistake. Promise me?"

Oh, he'd been young and stupid. It was only a few months later that his brother's body was found down by the canal. They said it was a mugging that went terribly wrong. At least, that was what the police told his family. It was only years later, when he was so deep in the job that there was no way out, did the realisation kick in about his brother's death.

'I got out. Eventually. And not the easy way. I managed to turn my life around. But I sure as hell do not want to draw attention to myself now by becoming involved in this case,' he thought to himself.

Pete

Pete had a good swim, something he hasn't done in years. These days it was more about hovering in the shallow end with Angela. He returned to his room, showered and then sat on the bed. He sent a quick text to Anne, <Things not going to plan, will know more by Sunday. Hope you are both having a lovely time. Give Angela a hug from me x>

That was as much as he dared to text, just in case Angela picked up the phone.

The next morning everyone was up bright and early.

"Morning Pete, hope you slept well? We have a little bit of good news. Charles contacted Miguel. He will meet us today at eleven am in his office, even-though it is his day off. I have printed some more photos of Charlotte to give to him."

"That's great. Thank you, Charles. Your help is really appreciated."

"No worries, Pete."

At ten forty-five they go to their appointment. When they arrive, they are brought straight through to Miguel's office.

Audrey and Miguel shake hands, "Good morning. I did not think we would meet again so soon."

"Good morning, Miguel. Thank you so much for seeing us on your day off. We really do appreciate it. This is Pete, Charlotte's husband."

They shake hands. Pete also thanks Miguel for meeting them and for all the help he has given.

"I am sorry to hear about your situation and I was really hopeful you would come together as a family. My officers and I, we will do all we can to help you."

Audrey gives him the envelope with the prints and tells him what has occurred up to now, finishing with our visit to the restaurant last night.

"We will keep our eyes and ears open. Unfortunately, we cannot interview her boss or any staff, as no crime has been committed."

"We understand that. Of course, any help you can give us, will be great. We will go and leave you in peace. We feel terrible bringing you in on your day off."

"It is my pleasure, Audrey. Pete, would you mind if I had a moment with Audrey please?"

"Of course not. I will wait outside, Audrey."

Audrey

Audrey is intrigued as to why Miguel wants to speak to her alone, but just nods at Pete and tells him she will be with him in a moment.

When the door closes behind him, Miguel looks at Audrey. "There is only one thing I request from you for dragging me in to work on my day off, as you say."

"And that would be, Miguel?"

"I insist that you join me for dinner this evening. Please?"

"Oh! Ok, that would be lovely. What time?"

"I will collect you at eight o'clock, if that is ok?"

"Lovely. See you then."

As she walks from Miguel's office, she notices his big smile. She is not sure what it is about him. She has sworn off men but thinks that there is no harm in dinner with a friend. No harm in that, is there?

Pete is smiling when she meets him, "What are you grinning at?"

"Oh nothing, bit of a spark there between you and Miguel, I see?"

"Not at all. We are just business associates."

"If you say so. Where to now?"

"Let's grab some lunch and we can decide from there."

As they sit and chat, Audrey has a few questions she wants to ask Pete, but she doesn't want to make him suspicious of Joan.

"Pete, is there anyone among your family or friends who was against you and Charlotte? You know, not entirely happy with you as a couple."

"Why do you ask?"

"It's just this friend Joseph spoke about. Seems she is happy to keep you apart. That information they passed on, only someone who knows you well could have done that. Would anyone have access to your phone or to any of your plans?"

"Audrey, neither myself nor Anne have told a soul. I just know Anne would have said if she had told anyone. We might not have seen eye to eye over the years but there is one thing Anne is and that's as straight as a die. She couldn't lie if it was to save her life. Sure, you could see she was just as blown away as me when Charlotte didn't show."

"I agree, there is no way it's Anne, but can you think of anyone else?"

Pete is racking his brains. He knows he told nobody and no one in work would care less about him looking for Charlotte. Angela would never go near his phone that's one thing. She is not a nosey child thankfully.

"The only other people who have access to our home, are my mother and father. Mother and Charlotte always got on ok. My mother can be a bit bossy and she didn't like that Charlotte did her own thing. But I know she was devastated when Charlotte went. My Dad was always crazy about Charlotte. They got on so well. So, I can't imagine him doing anything. I really don't know, Audrey. But I can tell you one thing, I will be keeping my phone by my side until we solve this."

'Oh no! I had hoped he would come to the obvious conclusion himself, but now I will need as much proof as possible. A confession is what will be needed,' thinks Audrey.

"You do that, Pete. I am sure we will eventually find out. What did you make of Joseph?"

"I think he knows more than he is telling us, but I am sure if he is Charlotte's friend, he is only trying to protect her. What do you think?"

"I agree, there is something about the guy… I'm not sure what, but from what Charlotte told us, he was very good to her. A bit of investigation into him would not go astray. Let's see if he has another restaurant and if so, where? We will get on to Patrica this evening and get that in motion."

"What can I do?"

"You know what, Pete, maybe a few beers and chilling out with Charles would do you good. You need a night to switch off. You are strung out. I hope you don't mind me saying so?"

"I don't and you are right. I never really chill out. It hasn't always been easy, and the last few months are starting to catch up with me. I will take your advice and if Charles is up to it, we can have a few beers."

"Oh, trust me, he will be delighted. He loves company, and since his wife died, well, he doesn't socialise like before. Only the occasional book launch when he has to. Says he has done enough of that. He does have a few close friends, of which I feel privileged to be one. It is hard for him not having his wife there anymore. Life is not the same, I would imagine."

"I didn't realise he had lost his wife. We can have a few beers and I won't let on I know anything about his loss."

"Thank you, I would appreciate that. I would never have said anything except I feel you both have more in common than you know."

When they arrive back, Charles is delighted at the idea of a boys night, saying, "Haven't had one of those in years!"

Of course, Audrey had told Charles earlier about her idea of Pete and himself having a boys' night for Pete's sake, but deep down, she feels it will do them both the power of good.

"Audrey, tell me, so you have a date with Miguel? Interesting. Are you not the lady who swore off men?"

"We are meeting as friends. He has been helpful with the case. It would have seemed ungrateful to turn his invite down."

"Oh of course! If you say so... I knew there was a spark between you both. Good man, Miguel."

"You are so funny, Charles. Two adults can have a meal on a friendship basis. You know, it's not unheard of."

Charles and Pete just look at each other nodding and laughing.

"You two have your fun and think what you like. I am going to have a shower and get ready."

She leaves the two of them to their laughter and thinks to herself how nice it is to hear Pete laughing. That is something she hasn't heard him do since she has met him, even if it is at her expense.

When she comes downstairs, the two boys are sitting outside, eating pizza and drinking beer.

"Classy night ahead of you, boys."

"Boys' night! Audrey, don't you look lovely. I am sure Miguel will be a happy man tonight, having such a beauty on his arm."

"Charles, thank you for the compliment but please stop seeing things that are not there. Now enjoy your evening, my chariot awaits me."

"Have a lovely evening, Audrey," they both say.

As she leaves, Charles says to Pete, "I haven't seen a sparkle in that lady's eyes for a long time. It is good to see. She so deserves it."

"She seems such a genuine person. They have both been so good to Anne and me. Managing to make something so hard a lot easier for us both."

Audrey

As Audrey walks out to the car, she cannot help but notice Miguel's face as he gets out to open her door.

"Audrey, you look beautiful this evening."

"Thank you, Miguel. That is truly kind of you to say."

As they leave the driveway, they are chatting as if they have known each other years.

"Your English is excellent, Miguel. Have you lived abroad?"

"Since I was fourteen my parents insisted that I go to Ireland to practice my English. I was lucky to get the opportunity to do this. For six years, I went to the same family in Dungarvan for the month of July. They were so good to me and it really helped my English. I still go back to Dungarvan every few years to visit the family and the friends I made there. It is such a beautiful place."

"I have been there a few times and I have to agree, it is such a beautiful place. I have a few friends there. They live in Kilgobnet. Have you ever been there?"

"Yes, it was not far from the house of my host family. We would walk in Colligan Woods, such a beautiful place. Clonea Beach has to be one of my favourites. I have to admit, I do prefer it on a winter morning. I find I visit Dungarvan more in the months of October or November, much quieter then. I am due to return for a visit this coming November. I am looking forward to it already."

"That sounds lovely. I suppose the weather is nice for a change for you. Ireland can have four seasons in one day. I think it gives us something to talk about, if nothing else we always have the weather to chat about."

The conversation flows. Miguel drives to a beautiful small restaurant in the hills. He tells Audrey it is a very popular place with the locals. Every dish is made to order so there will be a wait between courses.

The evening flies past. They chat for hours and the food is absolutely amazing. Before Audrey knows it, the coffees have arrived.

Miguel insists on paying. "I invited you Audrey, so that makes you my guest."

"Thank you, Miguel. I have had a lovely evening."

As they are going out to the car, a taxi pulls up, "We will travel back by taxi, Audrey. It wouldn't look good for the chief of police to be caught drink-driving."

"That is true, Miguel!" It had never even crossed Audrey's mind.

As they pull up outside Charles' house, Miguel asks when Audrey will be returning to the island.

"Miguel, I am not sure yet."

"I would like to stay in contact, Audrey. If you would also like that?"

"That would be lovely, Miguel. I would like that. Here is my private phone number, as you only have my work one."

They exchange numbers and as they say goodnight to each other, Miguel leans over and gives Audrey a kiss on the cheek.

"I hope to see you soon, Audrey. Goodnight and thank you for a lovely evening."

Audrey is still standing at the door as the taxi drives away. She really had a lovely evening and Miguel seems a lovely gentleman, but what is she thinking. There could never be anything between them. She promised herself after her marriage break-up that she would never be with anyone again. Nobody would ever control her or treat her badly again. Not that she believes Miguel would ever do any of those things. But people change, don't they? Especially when they have you well hooked in. No, it was a bad idea to give him her number. She doubts if he will phone her anyway.

Just as she opens the door, her phone rings.

"Hello?"

"Hello. I just wanted to check I have the right number in my phone."

"Ok. Well, now you know," she says, trying to be as polite as possible but she knows her tone is different.

"Is everything ok? You don't mind me phoning, do you?"

"No, of course I don't. I was not expecting a call so soon. Sorry about that. It was a surprise, a good one, of course."

"That is good. I hope it won't be too long before we can have another nice evening together. Goodnight again, Audrey."

"Goodnight Miguel."

Boys' Night

While Audrey was out, the boys were also having a good night. Charles did not realise that Pete was a teacher and English literature was his favourite subject. They chatted and drank a few to many beers, ate pizza and generally, sorted out all the wrongs in the worlds.

Pete spoke a bit about life prior to Angela's birth. How things had been. Then of how things had changed. The beer loosened his tongue, but it was a relief to talk about those times with someone who had no preconceived ideas about Charlotte.

"She is a good person, Charles. I wish I could tell her these things. My mother would never understand this. We never speak of Charlotte in front of her as you can feel the atmosphere change, turn icy if we mention her."

"Why do you think that is?"

"She was never really happy with my choice in Charlotte. Always trying to get me together with one of her friends' daughters. A nice quiet girl. You know the type – does everything mammy says and wouldn't say boo to anyone. Not my type at all. I think Charlotte was a bit too confident and strong for my mother. And then after she left, I knew my mother would never forgive her for leaving us. I suppose when you think about it, Charlotte was in a no-win situation."

"I really hope you get to find her, and I will do all I can to help you, Pete. When you find someone you love as much as you both loved each other, you hold on to them with both hands. If I could have even one day back with my wife, I would give the world for it. No money or fame will ever replace what we had together. I miss her every day. I smile, keep writing and get on with things because I promised her this and I always keep my promises."

"I am sorry, Charles. That must be so hard. I know that not knowing was the hardest part for me. Not knowing if Charlotte was alive or not, and if she was, where was she. So, I can only imagine how it is for you. If you ever want to talk, please know I will only be a phone call away."

The boys were chatting away when Audrey came in.

"Well, how did things go?" Charles asks.

"Fine. Can I have a beer, please?"

"Of course. That bad?"

"No, it went brilliant. We have so much in common. We chatted all night. It was just, well, perfect really."

"You say that like it is a bad thing, Audrey."

"That's the problem. Oh, just let's forget about it! How was your boys' evening?"

"You're not getting away that easy. Tell me what is wrong."

"Let it go, Charles. Please."

Charles realises that obviously she doesn't want to talk about things in front of Pete. He forgot himself, as himself and Pete had been chatting so openly.

"Sorry, Audrey. Not my business. We had a good evening, lots of chatting done."

"A few beers were drunk as well, I see."

"Just the odd one or two."

The next morning Charles tries to bring up the subject of Miguel, but Audrey is having none of it.

"I will talk to you another time about it, Charles. I need to sort my own head out first."

After breakfast it's time to go to the airport. They both thank Charles and say their goodbyes.

"Keep in touch, Pete. Chat soon, Audrey."

"Will do. Charles, give me a buzz if you fancy a chat. There is always a room in ours if you feel like a visit to Ireland. No swimming pool, nothing fancy but you will be made very welcome."

"Thank you, Pete. I might just take you up on that offer."

"Take care, Charles. I'm sorry about the drama. Keep in touch." Audrey gives Charles a hug and they get into the car.

The Return Meeting

Pete

P ete says goodbye to Audrey. He noticed she'd been very quiet on the plane.

'I wonder what has happened to this lady to make her panic about liking Miguel. You would imagine she would be happy meeting someone so suited to her. It is obvious they both feel the same way about each other. Oh well, not a lot I can do about that, sadly. Now to get myself ready to tell the bad news to Anne.'

"Goodbye for now, Audrey. Thank you for everything. I really appreciate it."

"No problem. Pete, we are not done yet. I will follow up on Joseph and see where we go from there. I will be in touch as soon as I have any news for you."

They go their separate ways. Pete dreading the breaking of the news and Audrey with her emotions in a heap.

He arrives home well before Anne and Angela are due home. He unpacks and puts on some dinner. He had text Anne to come to his house and she could eat with them.

Spaghetti Bolognese is on the menu, nice and handy for this evening. Pete hears the car pull up outside and goes to welcome them both but to his surprise it is not them. It is his mother. He really isn't up to this visit at the moment. He wanted to have some time with Anne to talk.

"Hello Mother, how did you know I was back?"

"Oh, I knew you would have to get Angela's things ready for school tomorrow. Couldn't wait to see you both. Where is my beautiful grandchild?"

Feck! He has completely forgotten the story he told his mother. "Oh, Anne beat you to it. Herself and Angela are gone for some shopping."

"That's a pity I was really looking forward to seeing her. I will wait until they get back. Is that Bolognese I smell? It is a pity I had dinner. I would have loved some."

"That's a real pity. Well, another day, Mother. The girls won't be back for another hour, so why don't you come tomorrow after school and join us for dinner. You will have more time with Angela."

Joan notices how uncomfortable Pete is but she doesn't care. He deserves it after all the lies he has told her and the upset.

"I don't mind waiting, Pete. Honestly."

"Mother, I would prefer if you didn't stay. You know how you and Anne don't get on. It makes everyone uncomfortable."

"Well, it is not my fault that Anne is such a rude woman. She rubs me up the wrong way. I will go so. I know when I am not wanted. Give Angela a hug from her Granny and tell her I miss her so much."

"Will do. We'll see you tomorrow, ok? I didn't mean to be rude to you."

Joan is not one bit happy. You would have to be blind not to see it.

"Goodbye, son." She puts her most wounded face on, but Pete doesn't even seem to notice or, worse, doesn't care.

Anne

Anne is just coming around the corner when she notices Joan's car parked outside Pete's. She tells Angela that she forgot to get something in the shop. They drive past the house. In the shop, she receives a text from Pete saying not to come back yet. So, they take their time in the shop browsing over which wine to get. Anne's phone beeps with a message, <The coast is clear.>

They arrive back at the house. Pete opens the door and lifts Angela up for a big hug. "I missed you loads, Angela."

"I missed you too, Daddy. But we had a brilliant weekend. Didn't we, Nana?"

"Absolutely brilliant. Angela, do you want to bring your bags upstairs? Put your things away and you can tell Daddy all about it over dinner."

"Ok, I will be down in a few minutes, Daddy." And up the stairs she goes dragging her two small bags with her, Anne brings up her bigger one.

Anne comes down first.

"Sorry for putting you off but my mother was here. And I didn't want her to see you bringing in the bags," Pete says this as he looks anxiously up the stairs.

"It's ok. Don't worry, I have given her a few jobs to do before she comes down. I passed earlier and saw Joan's car, so we went to the shop. I hope you like that wine, took me ages to choose it," she says smiling.

"Thank you, Anne. I have lots to tell you but as I am sure you have guessed it is not good news. I didn't want to text too much in case Angela saw your phone."

"I had a feeling alright. Did you even get to see her, Pete?"

"No, Anne, I didn't. She is not working at the same place. Joseph her boss claims not to know where she is. Both myself and Audrey have our doubts. Audrey and Patrica are going to find out as much about Joseph as they can. We will know more by the end of the week hopefully. It was so disappointing, Anne. I really thought this was it, I was going to see her and bring her home."

"I know, it's so hard."

"I am sorry, Anne. I know this is hard for you too. Especially waiting here for some news but as Audrey says, we have to stay positive."

"You are right, but I was really hoping this was our chance. Do you think this Joseph guy knows where she is?"

"Yes, I do, Anne, but I think he is only trying to protect Charlotte. Audrey says he was very good to Charlotte. It is nice to know she has someone on her side. He spoke of a friend Charlotte has in Ireland. This is the person he said phoned her and told her we were setting her up. That we wanted to get her to sign away all her rights to Angela and that she would never be allowed see her. That's strange, isn't it? I couldn't for the life of me think of anyone. Can you? It would have to be someone quite close to us, as they knew about our connection to Pearse and Patterson's and our plans."

Just as Anne is about to suggest Joan, she hears Angela coming down the stairs. "Shush Pete. Here is Angela."

"Hi pet, dinner will be ready in a few minutes."

Angela

Little did any of them realise that Angela, knowing there was something going on, had been sitting on the stairs listening. Something the adults still forget she can do. She hears everything and the one thing that she remembers clearly is Granny Joan being at Daddy's phone.

Over dinner, she tells him all about her weekend away and all the fun she had. She told her Daddy how Anne had shown her the photos of her mother and told her so much about her. Nana Anne had said it was ok to tell her daddy. Pete was delighted to hear this.

"That's lovely. Thank you, Anne."

"Daddy, when is Granny Joan visiting?"

"I invited her to dinner tomorrow evening, pet. Why, do you miss her?"

Angela is quiet for a minute. She can't show how cross she is at Granny Joan. She thinks Granny Joan might be the friend that talked to her mother.

"Yes, it'll be lovely to see her, but don't leave your phone on the windowsill when she is here, ok?"

"Why do you say that, Angela?"

This is the first time Angela has ever said anything like this.

"Sometimes, I think she imagines it's ringing and picks it up to answer it. But there is nobody there. I told her you don't like people at your phone, but she said you wouldn't mind her checking for you. She said it would be best not to tell you though."

Pete and Anne exchange looks.

"Thank you for telling me, pet. It is best not to keep secrets. Maybe Granny is getting confused, she isn't getting any younger."

"I know, that's what you always say, Daddy. Why do adults keep secrets though and children can't?"

"Sometimes adults think they are doing the right thing and trying to protect their children by keeping secrets."

"I think adults think children are silly and don't notice when someone is keeping a secret. Can I go watch my program now, Daddy?"

"Yes, Angela, you can. Sometimes, I think you are wiser than the lot of us put together, pet."

Angela goes into the sitting room. She puts on the television and the Disney channel. She is glad she told her daddy. She wonders if he might guess that she knows about them looking for her mother. Then she gets caught up in her movie. She loves *The Little Mermaid*. It really is her favourite Disney film.

The Truth

Anne and Pete are sitting in silence, both caught up in their own thoughts. Pete pours them both a glass of wine.

"I'm driving, Pete."

"One glass won't kill you, Anne. What do you make of all that?"

"Well firstly, I think Angela knows we are keeping something from her."

"Really, how?"

"We forget at times that she can hear now, and we didn't know for a long time that she could lip read. She is a very clever girl and has picked up on a lot of things. Things we thought she hadn't noticed."

"I really don't give that child enough credit. She out-wits me all the time. Now back to things like my mother looking at my phone. Well, that's just blown me away. It is hard to imagine she would do that, or to imagine that she might be this friend of Charlotte's. That, I would find really awful. To imagine that she knew where Charlotte has been all these years and was in contact with her all this time! What do you think, Anne? Please don't hold back. I know she is my mother, but I won't be offended if you have something to say about this, something you knew but didn't want to tell me."

"This is hard, Pete. I would have preferred you to find out yourself. We all suspected Joan. We just didn't want to tell you. We've been afraid we would hurt you."

"Oh right, who's we?"

"Audrey, Patrica and myself."

"I think we need to have a meeting, don't you? I need to hear it all. Every single thing. I have been putting a lot of things together. I have also been blind to so much. Joan is my mother, and it is hard to believe she is capa-ble of doing this. On the other hand, I have seen her do things to people that have made me cringe. I just never expected or believed she would stoop this low."

Pete just sits there with tears running down his face. It's all just been a bit too much for him. He needs time to take it all in.

"Pete, are you ok? Do you want me to go? To let you have time to think about what you want to do?"

"Anne, will you make an appointment with Audrey and Patrica for Wednesday, please? We can go together. Hopefully, I will have my head sorted and some plan in place by then. I just need some space at the minute. Anne, thank you again for everything and also for being so kind. I'm sure it would have been easier to tell me all you knew about my mother. I know she has never been kind to you and yet you have shown her more respect and thoughtfulness than she has ever shown to you."

"Pete, I am so sorry. I never really wanted you to know. But now you do, I know you will get your head around it and make the right decision for both you and Angela. I think when you are up to it, you should have a chat with her. You need to explain things to her."

"You're right, Anne. I will. When the time is right. Text me when you have a time for the appointment. After four would be ideal. Chat soon."

"I will. I'll just say goodbye to Angela."

When Anne opens the sitting room door, Angela looks up at her and says, "Well, did you get things sorted?"

"Yes. Angela, I am going home now. Thank you for a lovely weekend. I really enjoyed it. We will do it again soon if you would like."

"Thank you, Nana. I would love that."

"Give your auld Nana a hug."

Angela goes over and gives her Anne the biggest hug she can. "See you soon, Nana. I love you."

"Love you loads, pet."

After Anne leaves, Pete sits at the table with his head in his hands. Could his mother really be capable of this? Has he ever really known her at all? So many questions are running around in his head.

When he looks up, Angela is staring at him.

"Are you ok, Daddy?"

"I am fine, pet, just a lot on my mind."

"About Granny and my mother?"

"What do you mean, Angela?"

"I know you and Nana are looking for my mother. I didn't mean to overhear but I did, and I am really happy. I think Granny Joan has done something to upset you too."

Pete decides to not lie to Angela. She has missed nothing up to now. So, he decides to give her an edited version of things. The last thing he wants is to say anything bad about his mother. That might only upset her.

"You are right, we have been looking for your mother. Things are taking a bit longer than we expected but we will find her. I am glad you know now. I didn't like keeping secrets from you."

"That's ok, Daddy. Is Granny Joan in trouble?"

"No, Angela. Anything Granny Joan did was only because she loves us and wanted to keep us safe."

Pete wishes he could believe his own words. His mother has always been so good to them and he is trying to keep positive about things.

Anne

The following morning Anne phones Pearse and Patterson's. Alex answers, "You just caught me! I am just in the door, Anne. How can I help you?"

"I'm wondering if it would be possible to speak to Audrey or Patrica, please."

"One second and I will check." He puts Anne on hold for a few seconds. "You're in luck Anne. Audrey is in her office, always the early bird. I will put you through to her now."

"Thank you, Alex. Have a lovely day."

"Will do! Chat soon."

"Hi Anne, how can I help?" Audrey picks up Anne's call.

"Pete knows the friend is Joan. Of course, he had to find out himself, and would you believe, it was Angela in her innocence who told him."

"How did he take it, Anne? It can't have been easy for him to believe his mother had anything to do with things."

"He will need some time to get his head around it. He was wondering if we could have a meeting this week – would after four on Wednesday suit?"

"Yes, that's a good idea. I have an opening at four thirty on Wednesday. What do you think he will want to do, Anne?"

"I have no clue, but he is a practical man and whatever he decides, it will have Angela's best interest at heart. Are you going to tell him all you know, Audrey?"

"I will wait and see how he is on Wednesday before I decide. I need to see where he is at with everything first."

"I agree, we will see you on Wednesday, Audrey. And thank you for everything."

"See you then. You are welcome but I hope the next thank you will be when we have found Charlotte."

The Truth Will Out

C harlotte's phone rings. When she sees it is Joseph she answers casually, "Missing me already, Joseph?"

"Of course! All joking aside, I have some news for you."

Joseph had wrestled with his conscience all weekend, putting aside his own personal fears. He decided he could not live with himself if he did not tell Charlotte about the visitors. He had enough to deal with as it is, and this is meant to be the new him. He can only hope his past won't bite him in the backside. That is all he can do.

"Joseph, what happened? Please tell me it is good news."

"That depends on how you take it. I had two visitors the other day."

"The two detectives?"

"Only the one, Audrey. She had a man with her. He introduced himself as Pete, said he was your husband."

"Oh my God! I am glad I moved so quick."

"Maybe not. He seems like a really nice guy, Charlotte. He seemed truly devastated you were not here."

"Really?"

"Yes, really. I told them I hadn't a clue where you are and asked if he was looking for you to sign away all rights to Angela. He really looked amazed at this statement. He said that was never his intention, and where had that come from. I didn't let on that I knew about Joan. I just said a friend of yours from Ireland had phoned and told you the plan. Pete looked genuinely stunned. The only person I feel had some idea about Joan was the detective. Not sure why she seemed relieved that I didn't mention his mother. You have gone quiet. Charlotte, are you still there?"

"Yes, I'm here. Oh Joseph, I don't know who to believe. What else did he say?"

"He told me that your mother, Anne, and himself just want to find you. Not to make you do anything like that. It's just that now Angela is getting older, well, he wants you to know her."

"Why would Joan tell me different, Joseph?"

"I'm not sure. I have been wondering a lot about her motives. You know keeping contact with you all this time, never telling Pete, her own son, anything about this. That seems strange. So many things are not making sense. Charlotte, didn't you tell me that you send cards and presents to Joan to give to Angela?"

"Yes."

"Who does she say they are from?"

"I always presumed she said it was me, but now that you say it out loud, that's not really adding up is it."

"No, Pete couldn't even imagine who in Ireland was keeping in contact with you. You would imagine if his mother was passing your gifts on to Angela, he would have immediately suspected her, wouldn't he?"

"Yes, of course. Oh Joseph, I am so confused! Nothing makes sense anymore. What would you do if you were in my position?"

"Charlotte, only you can make the decisions. I know it's hard, but you need to get your head clear about everything. One way I find helps, is to write down the things you know to be true and what you feel to be untrue. Personally, I would phone Joan. I'd say that Pete was over here. Try gauge her reaction. Then take a bit of time to yourself, take a few days paid leave. You need to be sure that whatever decision you make, is the right one. Give yourself until Monday, ok? Walk the beach – do whatever it takes."

"Thank you, Joseph, and you are right, no more running. The time has come to face things one way or another. I will phone you Monday with some decisions. Hopefully."

"Charlotte, one other thing – please don't be too hard on yourself, ok? It seems to me that others had a part to play in how things went. You and Angela were the vulnerable ones in this situation. Chat Monday but if you want to chat before that, just phone me, ok?"

"Will do. And Joseph, thank you."

When she gets off the phone, Charlotte immediately phones Joan before she loses her bottle. Joan answers very quickly.

"Hello dear, how are you? I didn't expect a call from you today."

"My boss told me that Pete and the private detective were at my old job on Saturday. I was just wondering had you any idea why."

"Really? Pete was in Tenerife? I thought Angela and himself had gone away for the weekend. If I had known, I would have phoned you."

"Right, so you knew nothing of this? That's strange."

"What do you mean?"

"Well, you always seem to know what is going on with Pete. Is he keeping secrets these days, Joan?"

"I don't know what you mean, Charlotte. Pete always keeps me up to date with his life."

"I was just wondering why he never asked you where I am, instead of employing private detectives to find me."

"Why would he ask me, Charlotte?"

"Well, he must know that you have contact with me," asks Charlotte, sure she has cornered Joan.

Silence on the other end of the phone. This could go one way or the other.

Joan

"Why would he know that, dear?" asks Joan sharply. She was really losing patience. She was not sure what has gotten into Charlotte.

"When you give my gifts to Angela, you obviously say they are from me. Surely, it's self-explanatory that we are in contact?" says Charlotte.

Joan is furious. How will she get out of this – think woman, think!

"I told Pete that the gifts came to me by post, oh! Not post, a delivery service, sender unknown," Joan stutters, hoping Charlotte will believe her.

"Oh, that explains things then. Isn't it funny how I never asked you that before? I will say goodbye for now, Joan. Have a nice day."

Now Charlotte knows that Joan has been lying to her all along.

Charlotte

I can't believe how gullible I have been. What am I going to do? I feel Joan will do everything in her power now to blacken me. I will have to be so careful. I am only discovering how dangerous she can be – has been.

I need to get my head straight before I do anything or contact anyone.

Joan

I really had to think on my feet there! I am not too sure what Charlotte is thinking or if she believed me.

I have to get things sorted soon. When Frank is playing bridge on Friday night, I will get rid of all the presents and cards and any other connection to Charlotte. I need to make sure that nobody will believe her and that there is no evidence. I will have a good chat with Alice on Friday morning and see what she thinks. It is great to finally have someone to talk to, especially when she seems to truly understand my intentions.

Wednesday Evening

Anne & Pete

Anne and Pete arrive at the office together. They say nothing until they are sitting across from Audrey and Patrica.

Pete is the first to speak. "How long have you known about my mother's involvement?"

Audrey is delegated to speak. "A few weeks, Pete. We were not sure to what extent."

"Why didn't you mention it to me?"

"We didn't want to upset you at the time. You had a lot going on and we needed proof, real proof, Pete. It would have been a big thing to accuse your mother of anything, let alone without proof. I am not sure you would have believed it at the time."

"I agree. That's probably true. As it is, it took me time to get my head around things even with the evidence so far. My priority is Angela. I never want her to know that her grandmother did this to us. You may as well tell me all you know, and yes, it will be hard to hear, but I need to know."

"Ok, you won't like a lot of it, but we will lay it out for you. Remember no matter what we tell you, everything was done professionally, and the intention was always only to find Charlotte."

Patrica tells him about their neighbour trying to tell Joan she had seen Charlotte that day she left and how Joan put her off. About the Gardaí phoning the house and Joan taking the message and how this had made them suspicious.

Audrey explains how she met his mother at the swimming pool, how they struck up a friendship and started meeting for coffee. She can see the look on Pete's face.

"You're Alice?"

"Yes Pete, it really was the only way I could get to speak to her."

Audrey tactfully tells Pete everything up to date, leaving out the venom Joan used when she spoke of Charlotte. She finishes by telling him of her meeting this Friday with his mother, stating she would cancel it if he would prefer.

There is an uncomfortable silence for a few moments, Pete is blown away by all this. Who is this woman who calls herself his mother? She seems to be two different people. No matter how he feels, he knows what has to be done.

"Audrey, you must go ahead and meet my mother on Friday. She seems to really confide in you, and we need to know what is happening at the minute. Also, we need to find out if she knows where Charlotte is right now."

"If you are sure? Pete, I think you are making a difficult, but right decision."

"Also, can you extend things to a lunch? I will need a few hours to have a good search of the house. There must be some proof there, especially these cards and presents

Charlotte told you about. It is time to check this all out. We need to have everything in place. From what you have told me, my mother will be raging and won't take one bit kindly to being tricked. We need to keep all of this to ourselves until we find Charlotte and then confront my mother."

"Anne, how are you about all of this?"

"I'm relieved that Pete knows the truth, but I agree with him on all counts. We need to find all the proof and go from there."

"I have a suggestion. We can set up a group chat and keep each other connected over the coming days. We need to be kept posted at all times, so we know where we are at with Joan."

"Good idea, Patrica. How have you been getting on with Joseph and his background check?"

"Now, that is a strange one. Joseph opened his first restaurant in Tenerife twelve years ago. But I can find absolutely nothing on him prior to that. It is like he never existed. I have used all my usual contacts, but I keep hitting closed doors."

"That is crazy. He had to exist before then. Have you checked his PPS number? Plus, he would need a NIE number to open up a business in Spain, wouldn't he?"

"Yes, he would. It's all a bit fishy if you ask me. I have searched, and he has only that one restaurant on the island. I am still looking at the other islands in that region. As soon as I know more, I will let you know."

"Trust me, Anne and Pete, Patrica is like a dog with a bone. She will get the information – one way or another," says Audrey solemnly.

"Good, as long as it brings us closer to finding Charlotte. We all know what we need to do. Keep in touch with any information you come across. Would it be ok to meet Friday evening, when we will have more information?" asks Pete.

"I was just going to suggest it, Pete. Say five here?"

"Perfect. Angela is having a sleepover in her friend Emma's house, so I will be free."

"Right. See you all here on Friday and hopefully, we will be a lot wiser than today."

Audrey and Patrica

When Audrey and Patrica are left alone, they are both thinking the same thing.

"That went a lot better than I expected it to, Audrey."

"I know. I really wasn't sure how Pete would take things. I think the fact that he has built up trust in us and knows how we do business, helped. He knows we would not try to cause trouble or lie to him. Tough on him though."

"I admire the way you hid your true feelings for Joan. You really are always the professional. I know if it had been me, I would have blurted it all out!" says Patrica.

"No, you wouldn't have, Patrica. I am sorry for the comment about you being like a dog with a bone. I saw your expression. I definitely didn't mean to upset you."

"Audrey, you're fine. It's just words. You know it is a helpful trait sometimes but well, we both know Margaret would still be here if I wasn't so determined. Something I will never forgive myself for. It will never get easy. I have just learned to live with it."

Friday's Here

Audrey/Alice & Joan

Audrey's phone beeps. It is a message from Patrica. <Chat this evening and best of luck.>

'I will definitely need it,' Audrey thinks to herself. Oh well, here we go. She has her swimming bag ready to go, the only plus in this situation.

When she arrives in the pool, Joan's face lights up as she waves across to her. They both do their lengths and when they are finished, go into the jacuzzi.

"It is so good to see you, Alice. It has been way too long. I am really in need of a good chat. Talking to my Frank is similar to talking to stupid sheep. How have you been?"

'God,' thinks Audrey, 'poor Frank. Imagine he has to live with this awful woman. He deserves a medal at the least.' "All is good, Joan I have been terribly busy. It is good to see you too." She is starting to worry about how easy she lies these days.

They take their time, lolling about in the steam room and sauna.

"Is it breakfast or lunch we are going for?" Joan jokes.

"Are you in a hurry, Joan?"

"No, I don't have to be anywhere."

"Good. I was thinking we could go for a nice stroll and have a lazy lunch. How does that sound?" Audrey will do everything she can to give Pete as much time as possible.

"Sounds lovely."

It is nearly eleven thirty when they leave the leisure centre. They walk over two miles until they arrive at the picturesque riverside restaurant.

"This is a lovely place, Joan. Have you been here before?"

"Of course! Frank and I come here often."

Audrey suspects this is another lie but plays along. "You will know the menu very well then. We deserve a nice treat after all our exercise."

Joan and Frank have only come here once. They found it way too expensive. But the snob in her, doesn't want to let Alice know this. She seems very used to this lifestyle.

They chatter on about minor things, dinners Alice has been attending and how Angela is getting on. Only when they sit down for lunch does Joan start to talk about Charlotte.

"I have been so looking forward to asking your advice on the Charlotte situation. Things have taken an awful change of direction. Would you believe that Pete and Anne – you know, Charlotte's mother?"

"Not personally, but do go on."

"Well, haven't they hired a pair of private detectives – female detectives. Firstly, what kind of women would work at that kind of job? Commoners, I would imagine."

Audrey does her best not to show her feelings of anger at Joan's pure backward snobbery.

"These women found Charlotte and nearly had her coming to a meeting with Pete and Anne! Well of course,

I couldn't have that, now could I? So, I cancelled the solicitors appointment. I told Charlotte that Pete was tricking her into a meeting and he wanted her to sign away all rights to Angela. That of course, did the trick. Charlotte believed every word I told her. She immediately left her apartment and job. It was pure luck that Pete had left his phone on the windowsill that evening."

"Oh, how clever you were, Joan." This really sticks in Audrey's throat, but she has to play along. "Where did she move to, do you know?"

"Would you believe it, she wouldn't tell me! She says she has to sort her head out. Then the other night, I got a strange phone call from her. To be honest, she was quite rude. Especially considering all I have done for her. She asked some unusual questions. I really didn't like them at all. It seems the little lady has decided not to trust me. Would you believe it?"

"Really Joan, why would you think that is?"

"I think that boss of hers had something to do with it, Alice. I know what I have to do, as Pete would never forgive me if he found things out. Frank has some bridge thing this evening, so I am going to dispose of every present, card and anything else that would connect me to her, to that woman. She will not have any proof of my involvement. We know who Pete will believe. He will believe his mother, of course. The one who has been there for him all these years. Although, at the moment, he is being all secretive and aloof with me. But that will settle when he sees sense. Don't you think? I am right. This is the right thing to do, isn't it?"

"Joan, you seem to know what has to be done. Charlotte didn't give you any idea where she is? That is strange, isn't it…"

"I told you, no, not even a clue but I know her boss is behind it. I bet he knows where she is. I might have to give him a call and tell him a nice story. Maybe that Angela is ill, and we need to contact Charlotte. Needs must."

Audrey is blown away with all this information.

This woman is one cold character. At no point has she even imagined anything she is doing might be wrong. That's the hardest part to grasp. Thankfully, Pete decided to do his search today, as this time tomorrow there wouldn't have been a trace of evidence. I really hope he gets what he needs. This woman has to be stopped.

"Are you there, Alice? You seem to have gone away on me."

"Sorry Joan, just thinking of how clever you are. Charlotte has not got a hope of proving anything."

"You see, I knew you would agree with me. I know I am doing the right thing for everyone. We are so lucky to have met, such a like-minded friend."

"Oh, for sure, Joan."

Any trace of guilt on Audrey's part for tricking Joan is long gone. This woman needs to be put in her place for once and for all.

They chatter away, much to Audrey's dismay, but she prolongs the lunch for Pete.

At a quarter to two, she receives a text from Pete.

<all done, thank you>

Audrey breathes a sigh of relief.

 the night. I will have to dash off,
unfortunately. Shopping to be done and a lot of organising. Sometimes that man never thinks of all the work I
will have to do, and all at the last minute! I will leave you
go back on your own. I have to pick up a few bits in the
butchers. It is an incredibly good quality one here."

"Are you sure you don't want me to join you, Alice?
Give you a hand."

"Not at all, Joan! I will be a woman on a mission! But
thank you."

"Ok, if you are sure. I look forward to many more
lunches, dear."

Audrey thinks to herself, 'Over my dead body, Joan.
This is my last meeting with you as Alice.'

Of course, she says different. "Of course. Chat soon."

They pay and go their separate ways, Joan with a
spring in her step.

Joan

Thinking to herself, 'I knew I was doing the right thing.
I only needed a good friend like Alice to agree with me.
Imagine having guests coming from the city for dinner.
How exciting and Alice was complaining! I don't know
what she would do if she was married to my Frank. The
only people he would bring to dinner, if I allowed him,
of course, would be his boring bridge friends. She is very
lucky. I bet her husband is a real gentleman. It is a shame
she doesn't talk about him much.'

272

Audrey

Audrey breathes a sigh of relief once she leaves Joan's company.

That was so hard, but hopefully it gave Pete time to find all he needed. Though, she did get a nice bit of information. A lot of decisions need to be made and made fast, before Joan can do any more damage.

Evidence

Pete & Frank

That morning as soon as Pete dropped Angela to school, he went straight to his parents' house. One thing he is sure of is that his mother wouldn't be home. She is a great woman for routine.

What he did find when he arrived, was definitely something he didn't expect – his father was coming down the stairs with a black bag.

"What are you doing, Dad?"

Looking guilty he replied, "I think I am the one who should be asking the questions. What are you doing here at this hour, son?"

"Hard to explain, Dad. How about we have a cup of tea and a chat?"

"Ok son, kettles just boiled."

They sit with their tea and Pete tells his Dad everything. The scary thing is at no point does his father look shocked.

"Dad, you don't seem surprised by any of this. Did you know what she was doing?"

"No, son, but if I am honest, I always had a feeling she was some way involved. She never liked Charlotte or thought her good enough for you. I am sorry you had to find out what your mother is really like this way. Sadly, I learnt the hard way a long time ago."

"But you never said anything or stood up to her."

"I gave up a long time ago, Pete. I would never have won. She can lie through her teeth and convince people of anything. Now, son, considering we are sharing secrets, I have something to tell you."

He tells Pete about the house and his intention to leave Joan, explaining that he just can't bear being around her anymore.

"The abuse has just gotten out of hand. It's probably my own fault for leaving her away with so much. But I was never one for fighting, you know that, son. Thankfully, you take after me in that way, but your mother... Well, she just seems to thrive on it. She thinks me a weak man, and if not wanting to fight and argue all the time is what that is, well, maybe I am. And now that you have told me all of this, I know I could never bear to be around her after what she has done to you all."

"How long have you been planning this, Dad?"

"I think I have been planning this in my head for years, son. But have only really started doing things these past months. I have bought a lovely little house in a quiet neighbourhood and have been slowly moving my things over this week. My shed is cleared out. The plus about your mother's low tolerance for me is that she hasn't even noticed. I intended telling her and leaving then, but I think a letter will be enough now. I know this must be a shock to you and I am sorry, as you have enough on your plate. But I want a few years of peace, son. God knows, I have earned them."

"You have, Dad. And don't worry about me, I just want you to be happy. I know living with Mother has been hard for you and I have watched how she disrespects you. It was something Charlotte couldn't bear. She would always say you were a gentleman and never deserved how Joan treated you."

"That's good to hear, son. You will come visit, won't you?"

"Try to stop me, Dad. Now I better get moving and try to find these things."

"You won't have to do too much searching. I think I know where to find what you are looking for. Your mother thinks I don't know her hiding places. I never imagined that she was hiding cards and gifts for Angela. I never looked to be honest, Pete. I wasn't sure what she was hiding. Only knew she would savage me if I went to walk into your old bedroom. Let's go up now and see what is there. By the way, if there are gifts and cards from Charlotte, will you give them to Angela?"

"Yes Dad, I will at some stage. I just know Angela needs to know her mother never forgot her. I haven't a clue how I will explain things, but I will think of that when the time comes."

When they arrive in Pete's old bedroom, Frank goes straight to the wardrobe, opens it and takes down the big suitcase, laying it on the bed.

"I could be wrong, but I have a feeling this is hiding place number one."

"Dad, what's with all the bottles in here?"

"Son, that's something else I haven't told you. Your mother is very fond of vodka."

"What? Are you joking me? How has she hidden this, Dad?"

"She only drinks at night when nobody is around. Not sure how many nights I have had to wake her and get her to go to bed. Of course, as you can imagine, I get a lot of abuse. I really am sorry, son. You are not getting a good image of your mother from all this."

"I just wonder who she is, a lot of this is not the mother I have seen. It must be exhausting acting the part of perfect mother, wife and grandmother all the time."

"Son, I know your mother has done very wrong by Charlotte and deceiving everyone but one thing I will say, she loves you and Angela more than words."

"She has a strange way of showing it, Dad. Now, let's open this case."

Frank can't find the words to make Pete understand and maybe it's too soon. He is understandably angry. In time, maybe things will change. He questions why he still protects Joan.

Habit, I suppose.

When they open the case, they both can't believe what they find – bundles of cards for Angela. Lots of wrapped parcels, sixteen beautifully packaged, one for every birthday and Christmas since her mother left. Pete can't stop the tears running down his face.

"Dad, I really hoped I would find nothing. It would have been easier."

"I know, son, me too. There's a drawer over there that I see your mother putting things into." They open the drawer and find letters, all posted from Tenerife, all addressed to Pete.

"Son, I think you should put all these into a bag and take them away, read them later, when you are on your own. The morning is slipping by and we don't want your mother to find us here."

"Your right, Dad. I will get a black bag and put them in the boot of my car. Then I will help you get the rest of your stuff. Have you much more?"

"Well, I wanted to take a few photos and some of the furniture. Your mother won't care, it is all stuff she hated anyway. If you take one load, it will save me having to do two runs."

"Right. Let's get moving and when we are finished, we can go get some lunch together."

The time flies and it is going on a quarter to two by the time they are ready. They get into their cars but just before Pete drives off, he texts Audrey. He has a feeling she isn't enjoying her time with Joan and understandably so – they are so different in every way. Frank has left the letter on the mantlepiece for Joan and Pete doesn't blame him. His father has put up with enough abuse. A letter is all she deserves.

They arrive at Frank's new home. It is a lovely house. They unload everything and when they are done, they go to the little cafe around the corner and have some lunch.

"You know Dad, I can't remember when you and I ever did this. We will be doing this more often in the future."

"I look forward to that, son. To tell the truth, it was my biggest worry about leaving your mother. That she would stop you from visiting. I couldn't bear it if I didn't get to see you and Angela."

"That is one thing that won't happen, Dad. We will have a little housewarming when everything is sorted. Look at the time! I must go soon. I have a meeting with Anne and the detectives shortly. Dad?"

"Yes, son?"

"Be happy. You have earned it and I think I didn't realise how much until today."

"Thank you, son. You deserve to be happy too. I really hope you find Charlotte and can sort things out. I always thought you made a lovely couple."

"See you soon, Dad and it might be an idea to turn off your phone tonight."

"Son, she probably won't even notice I have left until tomorrow when I don't come down for breakfast."

Pete

As they go their separate ways, Pete thinks about his father. How could he not have noticed how unhappy he was? I suppose we only really think of our parents as, well, as parents, not people with needs for peace and love. He wonders will Angela be the same. I suppose so, it is the nature of things. His mother will not know what has happened! She will never believe that his father has left her and had everything so well organised.

Pete is still in awe of him. He is still not sure how he will handle things with his mother, he only knows he needs some time away from her. Driving down the street, he wonders how long it will take for her to notice everything is missing.

Frank

Frank feels sad for Pete. It was a hard way to find out about his mother and what she is capable of. It really has hurt him.

'Maybe I am selfish,' he thinks, 'in being thankful that he has understood my leaving Joan and that he supports me.'

Frank feels a great sense of relief, knowing he will not lose both his son and granddaughter. That would have been unbearable.

Pete

Pete arrives at the office to find, Anne, Audrey and Patrica waiting for him. Alex is even relieved to see him. "Go straight in, Pete, and put them out of their misery, will you? Tea or coffee?"

"I am ok. Thank you, Alex."

He walks into the room and all three ask, "Well, how did it go?"

"Good and bad, I suppose. Firstly, yes, my mother is the friend. She has been in contact with Charlotte all this time."

Anne knows this has really hit Pete. Your mother is the one person you should be able to trust. "Pete, I am really sorry. I know this must be really hard for you."

"Thank you, Anne. It is but to be honest, I am too angry to talk about that at the minute. How did you get on, Audrey? Don't worry, you can tell me everything. It can't be any worse that what I have already found out today. Trust me."

"Ok, if you are sure?" Audrey tells them the whole conversation. She doesn't leave out anything this time. When she comes to what Joan said about disposing of all evidence, she notices Pete's expression.

"Yes Pete, it looks like you got in there just in time. She was going to burn everything tonight when your father is at bridge."

They all look at Pete and are surprised when he starts laughing.

"Oh, today has to have been the craziest day of my life and as you all know, it is been quite crazy up to now."

Anne says, "Are you ok, Pete?" She worries that Pete has been pushed a bit too far with everything.

"Of course, Anne I was just picturing my mother's face when she finds everything is gone and that my Dad has moved out."

"What? Frank moved out? Jesus, Pete! What happened? I never thought he would get the courage. Go Frank! Oh, I'm sorry Pete! I probably shouldn't have said that out loud."

"Anne, you have nothing to be sorry about. You are dead right. It never even entered my head that he would either."

"God! Pete, your world has really been turned upside down."

"It sure has, but through it all, there is only one thing I can't get my head around. That is what to tell Angela. Do I give her the cards and gifts? And if I do, what do I tell her? I know my mother has done wrong on so many levels, but she has been so good to Angela. I don't want to turn Angela against her – more for Angela than my mother."

"You are a good man, Pete, and you are right. Angela has lost enough. I don't want to be the one to tell you what to do but I think she would love to know her mother didn't forget her," says Anne.

"Audrey, Patrica? What do you both think?" asks Pete.

They have both been very quiet up until now.

It is Patrica who speaks first. "Audrey is always better at these things, Pete."

"Thank you, Patrica. I'm not too sure about that. But Pete, I would have to agree with Anne on this. Angela needs to receive the gifts and cards. Regarding what to say and when to do it, now that is the hard part. I always believe the right moment arises when we need it. It is best not to force the matter and to be honest, you really have enough to deal with at the minute."

Patrica turns to him saying, "Pete, it doesn't have to be today or tomorrow, you know. Maybe just let things settle first for the moment. The right words will come at the right time, trust me."

"Thank you, Audrey and Patrica. I know you are right. I need to deal with things myself before I can talk to Angela about things. I would like to read the letters from Charlotte and have as much information as possible before I do anything."

"Makes sense."

They all agree.

"I suppose the next question is where do we go from here?"

Patrica tells them what she knows so far about Charlotte's boss. Which at the moment is not a lot. She is waiting for some contacts to get back to her. It will be Monday or Tuesday before she knows more.

"At least we know that Charlotte has lost her trust in Joan, and that has to be a good thing. At least now when we make progress, there will be no one there to interfere."

There is total agreement, and they call it a day and say their goodbyes.

Audrey's final words are, "Anne and Pete, I know this has been a rough couple of weeks for you both, but we are making progress. Try to take your mind off things as much as possible for the weekend. Do something nice for yourselves. You both need it so much."

"Thank you, we will try our best. You should both do the same," says Anne.

As they leave and reach the street, Pete turns to Anne. "Anne, I am so sorry for this. If it weren't for my mother, we would probably have Charlotte home. I know you must be very angry with her and justifiably so, I hope you still want me on board."

"Pete, don't be silly! We are a team now. What your mother did affected us both, but you and Angela more than me. Yes, I am really angry but only with her. I will go along with whatever you chose to tell Angela. She is always my first priority too. I have coped with your mother all these years, so don't worry, I can keep on doing it."

"Thank you, Anne. Angela is very lucky to have you and one day Charlotte will know this."

"Pete, myself and Charlotte have a lot of the past to deal with before that happens. She has a lot of reasons to be angry with me. I will do my best to give her the chance to deal with them. Hopefully, then we might be able to move forward. That is all I can do. And hope she can forgive me."

They give each other a hug and say goodbye. Pete wishes he could say something to make Anne feel better but what could he say. Anne and Charlotte do have a lot to deal with. She can only hope to get the chance to make amends.

Pete puts his key in the front door. He feels suddenly very lonely. He wishes Angela was here. The house is so quiet. It is nearly eight o'clock by the time he goes into the sitting room to face the box with all of Charlotte's letters. He grabs a sandwich and opens a bottle of red wine. He needs the wine to face this minefield.

As he opens the box, he realises all the letters are in date order. The first one was sent six months after Charlotte had left. They have all been opened already! His mother really has no boundaries. He didn't realise he could feel worse, but he does when he starts reading the letter.

The first letter is a page long. His heart is beating in his chest. He's not sure which emotion is causing it, his anger at Joan or his own excitement at having Charlotte's letter in his possession. He feels both excited and scared about reading the letter.

Just go for it Pete, get reading.

Dear Pete,

Never in all the years did I believe I would ever be writing you a letter like this, but I have to try to explain somehow what happened.

That day I left I was in such a bad place. I now realise I was suffering postnatal depression and badly. This is not an excuse for me leaving but hopefully, it will help you to understand where my head was at.

If I am honest, I became overwhelmed with everything since that day, the one I fell down the stairs when pregnant. It was from then that the doubts started and then when Angela was born and had the problems, I convinced myself it was all my fault. She would have been perfect if I had just taken more care. I know, not very rational thoughts but I was not in my rational mind. As the days passed, it just got worse. I convinced myself that you and Angela would be better off without me. I would only be a burden to you both.

I watched you with her and you were amazing, always so calm and able to handle everything. I just knew you would both be fine. Angela was so lucky to have such an amazing dad. Sadly, the more I watched you, the more inadequate I felt. It is hard to explain but these feelings just became so strong and I doubted myself more and more.

That day you went out and left me on my own, I panicked, petrified of what would happen Angela, if I went near her.

When Joan phoned that day, I was packing my bags. I told her how I was feeling, she agreed with me, telling me leaving was the right thing to do. Well, then I knew it was the right thing to do, and I ran Pete. That guilt will never leave me, especially when I looked in on Angela. I think I wanted somehow to explain but she just stared up at me with her beautiful blue eyes. It was like she knew what I was going to do.

I travelled for a lot of days and ended up here. I hope this letter will explain somehow and that you will see it in your heart to forgive me.

I am sending this to Joan as she said she will know the right time to give it to you, as at the moment you are just too angry and would probably tear it up.

I don't know what else I can say, only that Pete I have loved you from the first day we met. And I do love my beautiful daughter and wish I could have done things differently. The doctor says it is not my fault, it was the depression, and I am hoping she is right. I am in good health now. It took me some time to recover from everything. I just wanted to let you know.

I will say goodbye for now, Pete. Please give Angela a big hug from her mammy and hopefully you will see it in your heart to forgive me some day.

All my love now and always.
Charlotte xx

Large tears fell on to the page as he read. His thoughts were with the Charlotte of eight years ago, all alone and feeling so lost. To think his mother could have stopped her. She had the chance. Why didn't she? What had we done to her to make her do this?

Pete read late into the night. The other letters were short. But all just asked his forgiveness and if one day he would find it in his heart to let her see Angela.

This was all he ever wanted. He had always just wanted to know she truly cared and wanted to come home. But because he never got these letters, he just took it that she didn't and that was what had made him so angry.

He wakes up the following morning on the couch and God, his head hurts! He's not sure if it's the wine or the tears that have caused it. When he looks at the clock, he's amazed to find it's ten thirty. He has to tidy everything away quickly and clean up. He is to meet Andrew and the girls in the park at eleven.

He carefully puts the letters back in their envelopes and decides he will put everything up in the attic for the time being, until he knows what to do next. He has a shower, dresses and takes off to the park. When Andrew sees him, he gives him a strange look. Angela gives him a hug and runs off to play with Emma.

"Rough night, Pete?"

"You could say that. Fancy a boys' night tonight? I'm in need of a good chat, lad."

"Can do, I'll ask Annmarie if she would babysit. I know she won't mind, herself and Emma get on great. If you want, Angela can have another sleepover. I don't think we will hear any complaints on that front."

"Great. Thanks Andrew."

"Is it this Charlotte stuff?"

"Oh, you just wait! You are going to be blown away, trust me."

Andrew gets straight on to Annmarie and as he suspected, she had no problem at all with the arrangement. She says, "Hey Andrew, it's not like you and Pete go out very often. Tell him I look forward to spending time with Angela. Why don't you invite them both for dinner tonight and then you two can head out afterwards?"

"Thanks Annmarie. You are a star."

Andrew tells Pete, and it is all arranged. Andrew's parting shot is, "Might need a shave too, pal."

When Pete and Angela go home to get cleaned up and pack some clean clothes for Angela, he hears his phone ringing.

He had put it on charge that morning as with everything that was going on, he had left the battery run down. He also knew his mother would be on to him about everything and he just wasn't up to speaking to her right now.

Picking up his phone, he sees there are ten missed calls from Joan and one from his dad, also there is a message from Anne.

He chooses to deal with that first. It just read, <Pete, I hope you are doing ok? I am here if you need to talk."

He texts her back, <Thank you Anne. I am doing as well as can be expected. Reading the letters was hard but at least I know now that Charlotte never stopped caring about us. I have arranged to go for a few pints with Andrew tonight and tell him all. Think I need to share this with my friend and let my hair down a bit. I hope you are doing ok? Do something nice for yourself and thank you. Oh, by the way, I've ten missed calls from Joan but am choosing to ignore them today. Chat tomorrow.>

Once he has pressed send, he phones his dad. "Hi Dad, all ok with you?"

"Just wondering the same of you, son. Are you holding up ok?"

"I'm doing ok, Dad. I read the letters last night and wow, they were an eye opener. I never knew my mother could be so cold and calculating. How in God's name did you live with her for so long?"

Dad goes quiet. Then he says, "Not sure, son."

"I've had ten missed calls from her today already. Did you get any?"

"I only turned on my phone in the last few minutes and I have about six missed calls. She left a few voice mails, and I can only imagine what she has to say. So,

I have decided it is best not to listen to them. I deleted them. Son, you know I am here if you need me."

"I do Dad and thank you. I am going out for a pint tonight with Andrew. Angela is having a sleepover. But if you are free tomorrow, why don't we all go out for some dinner somewhere nice?"

"That would be brilliant. We can meet in the hotel out the Dublin Road. They do a nice carvery on Sundays."

"Good stuff. See you there at one thirty."

"Look forward to it, son."

When they are cleaned up, Angela's overnight bag is packed again, it is almost time to go.

"We need to stop at the shop on the way, Angela. I want to bring some flowers and wine to say thank for having us for dinner. Do you want to get something nice for yourself and Emma?"

"Can we get some ice cream, Daddy?"

"Of course. Oh, and I forgot to say, we are going to meet Grandad Frank for dinner tomorrow in that nice hotel. You know, the one where you get that dessert you love."

"Yippee, this is the best weekend ever. Will Granny Joan be there?"

"Not this time, Angela. It will be nice to spend some time with Grandad Frank on our own for a change. We never really get the chance to."

"That's true, Daddy. It will be lovely."

Surprises

Joan

When Joan left Alice, she was delighted with herself. She walked back to collect her car and decided to go get some shopping. She would do something nice for her dinner and get a nice bottle of white wine. Frank always bought the red and she preferred white and of course, a bottle or two of vodka. Not liking her local shops to know her business, she never bought alcohol there. So would drive the extra fifteen miles to the large superstore in the next town. She also liked to browse the shops there. They had all the ones she liked.

It was after four by the time she arrived home after making her purchases. Joan carried in the bags and put them in the kitchen. Something felt wrong to her, but she just couldn't put her finger on it.

After putting away the food and drink, she went upstairs to her room to put away the nice new jacket and trousers she had bought. It was funny the joint account card wouldn't work for her and it was quite embarrassing but thankfully her private account card did. Frank will get a good talking to about that. Even though it is his money in both accounts, she prefers to use the joint account and save her own money. Frank has never questioned her on that. His money was theirs but hers was her own to do what she wanted with. When her parents died, they had left her a very wealthy woman, but Frank does not know how much she received – not to this day and he never will, that is her money.

Looking around the room, she has this feeling there is something not quite right but is not able to put her finger on it. 'Probably only my imagination,' she thinks and goes back downstairs. After all her little jobs are done, and the dinner is on, a nice quiche and a small salad, she pours herself a glass of white wine. Joan has always prided herself in keeping her good figure, not many women of her age can still fit into their wedding dress – not that she would ever want to wear that again, once was enough.

By six she is sitting at the table, her meal and another nice glass of wine in front of her. It is a pity Frank is not here to join me. I seem to eat alone a lot lately. It would be nice to have some company. Then again, he would probably just irritate me if he were here. I will just enjoy the peace and quiet for tonight. Maybe tomorrow we will do something nice together. It is good to keep him sweet every now and then. I don't want to push him too far.

Better not drink too much wine until I have gotten rid of the evidence. Just the one glass with my meal and I can have the rest later.

When everything is cleared away and Joan goes back upstairs. First, she must get the diary she has kept. This is separate from her personal one. She has kept a diary since she was a child. But this is different, it has all the times and dates she has had contact with Charlotte since the day she left. There it is, where she always leaves it, under her mattress. Frank would never have found it as he is never in her bedroom. It has been her bedroom for a long time now. The day Pete and his sister finally moved out, she informed Frank they would no longer be sharing the marital bed. It was only a front they had put up for the kids for all the years and now at last they could have their own rooms with no pretending.

Frank didn't seem too bothered at the time. He had just gone along with it like he always did. "Whatever you say, Joan," he said. He's such a yes-man, never able to stand up to me. I think that is why I lost so much respect for him over the years. I suppose when he did try to stand up to me, I would just explode, and he would back down.

Joan goes into the spare room and walks over to the drawer with the letters. Confident, never for a minute believing anything was not as it should be. As the drawer opens, she notices things had been moved.

'That is strange. I know I didn't leave them like that,' she thinks.

As she moves everything aside, she can feel the panic start to rise in her chest. There are no signs of the letters. Where could they be? Maybe she put them in the next drawer by mistake. Nothing. She hasn't checked for the letters for a long time, there was no need to – sure, who would know they were there?

Trying not to panic, she goes to the wardrobe and breathes a sigh of relief. The suitcase is still there. She lifts it down and notices how light it feels, as she puts it on the bed. She opens it.

"Oh my God!"

She sits on the bed. What is she to do? Everything is gone – all the cards, presents and the letters. Now she is really panicking, maybe the house was broken into.

She jumps up and runs around the house franticly, searching all the rooms but nothing seems disturbed.

In Frank's room, she stops short. His wardrobe is open and empty. The en-suite is also empty of his personal things.

"What is going on?" she says out loud.

She is truly in shock. Where is Frank? Did he find the letters and gifts?

"I will phone him at once, but what am I to say? He must know who they were from… Joan, calm yourself. Think. You need to keep your head and come up with an explanation." Taking deep breaths to steady herself, she mutters, "I will go downstairs and have a glass of wine and calm myself."

Joan pours herself a large glass of wine and sits in the sitting room, taking a few deep breaths. As she is thinking of a reasonable excuse, she notices something on the mantelpiece.

It's a letter.

At this point, she is nearly afraid to read it. She is not sure what to expect but she knows it has to be done.

Lifting the letter, it's obvious to her it is Frank's handwriting on the envelope, he has always had good handwriting. Joan notices her name on the front. Her hands are shaking. This is all alien to her, this lack of control. She has always prided herself on her ability to control every situation. It had always been a big advantage against others. But this is a new feeling, one she really has no memory of feeling. Fear. Pure and simple fear.

There is one page, on which Frank has said it all.

To say dear Joan would make me a hypocrite,

We have not used that term of endearment in many, many years. Once this saddened me but no more.

I have written this letter to you to say I have left. I shall not be living in this house or with you anymore. You have become a woman I cannot connect to, a far cry from the one I married. Now bitterness and anger seem to rule your life.

This will probably come as a relief to you, as I know how much I irritate you.

It is time I was happy, something I do deserve. I will not speak badly of you to our family or friends, but I fear you have done a lot of damage yourself with so many people, especially our son.

May God forgive you for what you have done to him and his family, Joan. I knew you were capable of a lot of things, but this has to be the lowest of all the things you have done.

I will ensure that the money you have received will continue to go into your account as always, which is more than adequate to live on. I am sure you have a lot of savings built up over the years. There is also the sum of money your parents left you. Yes Joan, I knew about this and the amount. You are welcome to it. The house, you can keep and the car. I have put both in your name. But your name has been removed from the joint account, so there's no point in using the card.

Please do not try to contact me. I want to enjoy some peace and quiet for a change. It will be nice to not be someone's verbal punch bag.

Your once upon a time loving husband,

Frank

"I can't believe this! Where did he get the courage to do this?"

Joan drops onto the seat. Her heart is thumping in her chest. What will she do? Frank is gone. Pete knows. Everything is a mess. She slugs back the glass of wine and goes into the kitchen and pours another. Sitting at the kitchen table with her head in her hands, she laments, "Oh what to do!"

"Joan, nothing. You can do nothing today. You will have to deal with things tomorrow."

Pouring herself a large vodka, she drinks and drinks, knowing it won't change things, but it will give her some time. She will come up with a good plan. She just needs to switch off for a little while.

It is bright when she wakes up on the couch. God, how her head hurts.

'Why didn't that man wake me? He left me here all night!' she thought indignantly. Then the reality of the situation hits her. For the first time since she was a kid of seven, she cries heaving sobs. "What am I to do?"

When she looks at the clock it is only eight o'clock in the morning. Looking at the floor she sees that she had started on the second bottle of vodka.

"Oh God, I am going to be sick!"

She barely makes it to the kitchen sink. It seems an eternity before the gagging stops. When it does, she feels totally drained. With the intention of having a shower, she goes upstairs, but only makes it to her bedroom. There she collapses on the bed and is asleep in a matter of seconds.

She awakes several hours later, feeling a bit better, but very fragile. A shower is what is needed and as she steps under the water, the relief is amazing. She has no idea how long she remained in there. Finally, she steps out and dries herself off.

When she returns to her room, she sits on the bed. "Right Joan, enough of this feeling sorry for yourself. Time to get moving. Firstly, phone Frank. Find out what he knows and what Pete knows. Then, go from there. I will have to say that Charlotte swore me to secrecy, that she was blackmailing me. Hence why she sent everything to my house. The rest will flow from there." She nods, convincing herself of her lies.

Frank's phone is turned off. What is that about? He really has a cheek!

Yes, the old Joan is back. She feels back in control now.

Pete is not answering his phone either. She lets it ring out each time. After the tenth attempt, she gives up.

Her head is starting to hurt again, so she makes something to eat, some scrambled eggs and toast will do the job and of course, some paracetamol.

It is after two in the day, when she decides it is time to go to Pete's and face him. She goes upstairs to put on her makeup.

"Joan dear, you are not looking your best," she admonishes her reflection.

This gives her an idea.

After cleaning off her makeup, she rubs her eyes until they are very red. "That's it, Joan. Today is not a day to look composed. You must look like your world has fallen apart. Your husband has just left you. You have also just discovered he has been in touch with Charlotte all this time. It was Frank who had hidden the letters, cards and gifts. Of course, I won't mention that until I know Pete knows about them. How else was he able to put his hands on things?" she talks through her story.

Pete will believe me. He always does. I know his father and himself have no relationship, thankfully, I made sure of that over the years.

Joan arrives at Pete's just ten minutes after they have left for the shops. Pete and Angela decided to go and buy some new shoes for Angela on their way to the supermarket.

Joan notices her hands are shaking. "You can do this, dear. Shaking hands will only add to your distressed state."

As she reaches the door, putting her hand into her pocket, she discovers she has forgotten her key to the house. This irritates her, she was hoping for the element of surprise. Pete would never expect her to call. "Oh well, I must ring the bell so. On to plan b," she mutters to herself.

After ringing the bell three times and getting no answer – the third time she held her finger on it far longer than necessary – she comes to the obvious conclusion that they are not home. "Maybe he's not home… Oh, why didn't I bring my key. I will go around the back and see if the door is open."

Joan has a good peep through the windows to see if anyone is at home but there is no sign of anyone. The back door is locked. She lifts the rock she knows Pete hides the spare key under, but the key is not there. Not sure what to think, Joan decides to try Pete's phone again, and lets it ring out.

Feeling a mix of both fear and anger, she returns to the car and just as she is about to open the door a woman says, "Hello Joan, how are you?"

Great. Just what she needs right now, that nosey busybody neighbour, Mrs Hewitt.

"Hello, Mrs Hewitt. How are you keeping?" This is all she needs, especially when she is not looking her best and is a bit distracted.

"Fine, Joan. I hope you are well. Is everything ok? You look a bit distressed. I hope all is ok with Pete and Angela, the poor things."

"All is good, thank you. It is good to see you, but I am in a terrible rush!" Such a lie, thinks both Joan and Mrs Hewitt.

"I understand. It's just, I do worry about them since Charlotte left, that poor girl. I will always remember the state she was in that day. And you all not knowing if she is dead or alive. I imagine someone somewhere must know where she is and are cruel in not giving the family some peace. Don't you agree?"

"Really, Mrs Hewitt! You seem way too involved in something that is not your business. Now goodbye."

As Mrs Hewitt watches Joan's car drive away, she is content to have upset her. She has never liked Joan. She's just not a nice lady. Besides, she always felt Joan was involved somehow in all of this. One day the truth will out.

Little did she know, it already had.

Joan drove off at a mighty speed.

Where could he be? I might just go home, get my keys and return... Then again, if that nosey woman sees me returning, knowing nobody is home, she will surely tell Pete.

Anne

Anne's weekend is not going great. She is fighting everything in herself not to call on Joan and give her an earful. Friday night was a hard one. She just couldn't stop thinking of Charlotte and what that woman has put her though. I must have been such an awful mother, that she could not confide in me how she was feeling.

On Saturday afternoon she decides to go shopping. She needs to get something for the dinner tomorrow.

"Nana Anne! Nana Anne!"

"Oh, my goodness! What a lovely surprise to see you both! Angela, don't you look pretty!" exclaims Anne. "Hi Pete, how are you?"

"Hi Anne, I'm doing ok. We are just going for a coffee, would you like to join us?"

"I would love it!"

"Nana Anne, look at my new shoes!" says Angela dancing in front of the adults.

"They are fabulous! Aren't you just the luckiest girl?"

"Let's get me some coffee so I can feel lucky!" says Pete leading the way to the café.

"Rough night?" sympathises Anne.

"As good as can be expected. I meant to phone you, Anne. It's just my head is all over the place. How are you doing?" Pete asks, keeping an eye on Angela as she dances ahead to look at the dessert fridge.

"Not too good, to be honest. I have to fight the urge to go see your mother and give her what for, but who am I to criticise anyone? I had as much to do with things as Joan. I should have been there for her Pete. I am so sorry. A lot of this is my fault, I am so sorry…"

Pete can hear she is in a bad place. "Anne, I'm sorry too. Sorry for all of us. We all played a part – though none so much as Joan."

"Come on, let's order some coffee and sugary desserts! I think Angela is going to have trouble deciding," Anne says seeing Angela approach them.

"I feel bad because I would have invited you over for dinner tonight, but we are going to Andrew's for dinner. Angela is having a sleepover there as myself and Andrew are having a boys' night…"

"Pete, you don't need to apologise. You deserve a night out."

Sunday News

Joan

J oan decided to take things into her own hands on Saturday evening. She booked tickets for Tenerife. She had to get to Charlotte first, to make her see sense and go far away. A one-off payment of fifty thousand should do it. Money buys most things and most people, or so her father and mother taught her.

The flight was an early one the next day, six fifteen in the morning. She wouldn't be able to sleep anyway, so the early start made no difference to her.

Charlotte

Charlotte has spent the last few days trying to sort her head out, trying to decide what she was going to do. She meant to let Joseph know, but she still hadn't a clue. Staring aimlessly at the list in front of her – reasons to return, reasons not to.

Reasons to return was winning. The only thing stopping her, was fear and she just couldn't shake it off.

One thing she has realised, is that Joan was not her friend or support but in fact has been the complete opposite of that. It was hard when she realised it was Joan who had instilled all this fear. Why had she trusted Joan, especially when she had known from the beginning that the woman hadn't wanted her near Pete?

Joseph said he would phone at seven this evening, to check how she was doing. She knew she should talk to him, but she had to make sense of everything herself first.

Joseph

Joseph, on the other hand, had decided to go to see Charlotte instead and had taken the ferry across to the island. He wasn't going to take no for an answer. Charlotte needed a friend now more than ever.

Joan

Joan's plane landed on time. She got a taxi to her hotel. After booking in and sorting things in her room, she went down and had some breakfast in the restaurant. She enquired from reception where she might find Cafe de Rosa. She was given directions and told it would be open at twelve noon. This was the place that Charlotte had worked in, somebody there might tell her where she had gone to, especially when she tells them of the emergency. Another story of course. I know this will work. Then I will find out where she is and get things sorted once and for all.

When she arrives at the cafe, Joan calls over the young waitress.

"Good afternoon, how can I help you?"

"I really hope you can help me. A friend of mine used to work here up to a week or so ago and I so need to find her."

"What would this friend's name be?" Joseph had told all the staff not to let on they know anything about Charlotte.

"Charlotte, dear. I really need to find her. You see it is her daughter, she is very ill, and Charlotte needs to know, so she can go see her."

Francesca is taken aback. She never knew Charlotte had a daughter. This woman must be wrong. Joan can see the look of confusion on the girl's face.

"Sorry. I am presuming from your reaction that Charlotte has kept this a secret. It is complicated, you see. Ever since she ran off, leaving her newborn infant. I have been the only person she's trusted, her confidante. I have always kept her updated on how things are. I would not be here except it truly is an emergency, you have to trust me on this."

Francesca is in turmoil. She knows Joseph said not to say anything. But even he would agree with telling this lady where Charlotte is. She seems genuinely like she has Charlotte's best interests at heart. And if it were her daughter, she would want to know. So strange that Charlotte never spoke of her daughter, but I suppose it is just complicated.

"Well, I suppose if it really is an emergency… Joseph has another restaurant. It is in Gran Canaria. He told me not to speak of Charlotte to anyone, but if she needs to go to her daughter…"

"Oh dear, you did the right thing! Have you an address for this restaurant? I will go there immediately and tell Charlotte. Thank you so much. Don't worry, Joseph and Charlotte will be thankful that you told me."

Joan leaves and goes back to her hotel, with the name and address of the restaurant on a piece of paper. She thinks how gullible people are and believed her so easily. Now to get things sorted with that girl once and for all. Time to get her out of our lives. She will jump at the money. People like her always do.

Pete

Pete and Angela were ready to meet Frank and Anne for lunch. He was glad he had asked Anne to join them. He had cleared things with his dad, who was delighted to have her come along.

They had the table booked and when they arrived in the lobby, Frank and Anne were already there, sitting together having a drink.

"You both look very relaxed. I hope you are not driving, Anne?"

"No, I decided to enjoy the nice day and walk down, earn my dinner and I will be able to enjoy a nice glass of wine with my meal. Thank you, Frank, for letting me join you today."

"Your very welcome, Anne. Now, I think our table is ready."

They enjoy a lovely meal and only get to chat openly when Angela goes to the bathroom with Anne.

"Have you heard anything from Mother?" Frank asks Pete.

"No, strangely nothing since the missed calls on Saturday. You?"

"Not a word. That's not her form. I am not sure what to think to be honest. I have a feeling though that she is up to something." Frank knows this is not Joan's usual form. "What do you think it is, son?"

"I really don't know, Dad, but I will find out."

"How did you get on with the letter reading? No worries if you don't want to talk about it."

"It is not that I don't, it is just the timing. I will phone you tomorrow and we can chat properly. That was quick ladies!"

As they are leaving the hotel, Anne catches Pete's eye. "A quick chat? How is the letter reading going? Anything helpful? Any ideas about when you will give Angela the cards and presents?"

"Anne, I will ring you tomorrow and fill you in on the letters. I still haven't a clue how to handle things with Angela. I have decided to leave things for the moment and wait and see. Whatever decision I make, it will always be with Angela's happiness in mind. She has had to deal with way too much for a kid her age."

"I agree totally, Pete. I know you will do the right thing. Chat tomorrow."

Frank

Anne and Frank are walking in the same direction, so they walk together.

"Anne, I am sure Pete has told you about myself and Joan. I would like to explain."

"Yes, Frank, he told me. But you have nothing to explain to me. Though if you need someone to talk to, please know, you can talk to me. As you know there is no love lost between me and Joan. That said, I take no pleasure in any of this and never would. Pete told you about the letters and everything?"

"He did, Anne. I knew Joan was capable of a lot of things but to do what she did to our son… It is just unforgivable. Life is hard enough for everyone without people making it harder."

"My biggest worry is Angela. She loves her Granny Joan. It would devastate her to think Joan was keeping her mother from her. Do you fancy going for a drink and a chat, Frank? Maybe we might come up with a solution for Pete together."

"Let's do that, Anne. We can only try our best to help. The poor lad has had a lot to take in these past weeks."

They stay chatting for hours and at the end of things, they think they have come up with a solution. Hopefully, one to help Pete explain everything to Angela without turning her against Joan. Not that either of them feels Joan deserves it, but as Pete says, Angela has had enough to deal with. They will have to find Charlotte if the plan is to work though.

Angela

Angela knew something was going on.

"The adults think I can't see something is going on," she told Emma the night before. She knew that whatever was going on, Granny Joan had something to do with it. She heard Daddy talking to Grandad and he seemed really angry with her. Also, she thinks that Grandad Frank and Granny Joan are not living in the same house anymore because Daddy had asked him how was his first night in the new house. "I really wish adults wouldn't tell lies. I really wish they would tell me what is going on. I am not even sure if my mammy will ever come home, Emma. What if you only get one wish and I picked the wrong one?"

Emma didn't really know how to answer this. "I don't know, Angela, but I don't think you picked the wrong one. It's good that you can hear again, isn't it?"

"Yes, but I would much rather my mammy was here."

Angela had cried and Emma had just hugged her saying, "Angela, I think your Daddy will find your mother. I just know your wish will come true. It's just taking longer, that's all."

"Do you think so?"

"Yep." Emma did not really know but she didn't want to see Angela so sad.

After they left Frank and Anne, Angela decided she had to ask her Daddy about Grandad and Granny Joan.

"Daddy, is Granddad not living with Granny Joan anymore?"

"Why do you ask that, Angela?" Pete asks as he is buying for time. He didn't expect to have to answer this question quite so soon.

"It's just you asked how his first night went in the new house. I didn't mean to eavesdrop, Daddy."

"It's ok, Angela. Grandad and Granny have decided it is best if they have their own houses. That happens sometimes when people get older."

"Is it because Granny Joan is always so cross with him?"

Pete tries to keep the smile from his face. "Can't hide anything from you, can we? Yes Angela, I think it is because Granny Joan is always cross with him and Grandad Frank wants some quiet now that he is getting older."

"I understand. I love Granny Joan, but she would give you a headache sometimes, wouldn't she?"

Pete just laughs and thinks, 'Out of the mouth of babes.'

"Daddy, why are you cross with her? Did she do something bad to you?"

"Kind of, but I think she meant well. She just got confused. Now how do you fancy going to the park?"

"Yippee!"

Thankfully, the park is a good distraction and Angela stops asking questions. Ones that Pete is just not up to answering. Well, not just yet.

Joan

When Joan gets back to her hotel, she goes straight to the reception.

"What is the quickest way to get to Gran Canaria from here?"

"You can take a flight. It is only thirty minutes."

"Could you book me on a flight for this evening?"

"I will check if there is a flight this evening and if so, I will see if there is a seat available."

"Thank you."

"Yes, there is a flight at six fifteen this evening and there is a seat available. Would you like me to book it for you?"

"Perfect, please book a seat and could you book me into a hotel, one near the Cafe Maria in Maspalomas, please."

"Will I keep your room here for you for tomorrow night?"

"No, thank you. I will return home from there. Thank you for all your help." Joan gives her card to the receptionist. When it is all is sorted, she returns to her room, happy with herself.

Patrica

While this has all being happening, Patrica has been doing a lot of work. Trying to find out all she can about Joseph and where his other restaurant is. But she keeps hitting dead ends. This man just seems to have appeared on the island from nowhere by the looks of things. In the end, she phones Charles and asks for his help. He is delighted to be involved again and is only too happy to do whatever is required.

"Anything I can do, Patrica, just tell me and I will do my best."

"That's great, Charles. It's this man Joseph, you know Charlotte's boss. Can you find out anything for me? There is more to this man than meets the eye."

"Will do, what do you want to know?"

"We need to know if he has another restaurant on the island and anything else you can find out."

"I will go around to Café de Rosa today at lunch time and see what I can find out. The girl working there has taken a liking to me, and she loves to chat."

"You old charmer, Charles! Please phone me if you find anything. Thank you."

"Your very welcome. Fingers crossed my charm keeps working."

They are both laughing as they hang up.

Charles

Charles gets dressed and makes a bit of an effort. He decides to bring his bike today. It was a little gift to himself. He has always loved his bikes but the Triumph Thruxton, well, that is just his favourite. A modern bike but with the characteristics of a classic.

When he arrives at the restaurant, he notices Francesca talking to a mature lady. Whatever they are talking about, it seems serious.

At last the woman leaves and Francesca sees Charles. "Good afternoon, Charles. How are you today?"

"Very good, Francesca. That seemed like a serious conversation, family?"

"God no! She is a friend of a friend. I don't know if you remember Charlotte who used to work here?"

Charles plays dumb. "No, I don't recall her. Was it long ago?"

"No, she only left a few weeks ago. God! Her life is complicated. I thought we were friends, but you know something, she never told me that she had a child in Ireland. Or that she left when she was only an infant."

"That sounds awfully sad. The poor woman. But what did that woman want? If you don't mind me asking."

"Of course, I don't. It would be nice to confide in someone. Joseph says we are not to talk about Charlotte to anyone. I have no idea why. Well, that lady says she is a good friend of Charlotte's, that she has always kept in touch with her. But now she has bad news. Charlotte's daughter is very sick, it seems. And she needs to tell her. She wanted to know where she moved to. Well, as you can imagine, I had no choice. Charlotte needs to see her child, doesn't she?"

"Of course she does, Francesca. Is her friend going to see her?"

"Well, she will have to fly there if she is. Charlotte is in Joseph's other restaurant in Maspalomas on Gran Canaria."

"I didn't know that Joseph had another restaurant there. Does his family live there?"

"I don't think Joseph has any family. He has never mentioned one. He is a very private man, doesn't talk about his private life, to be honest."

"Did Charlotte's friend give you her name?"

"Now that you mention it, no, she only introduced herself as Charlotte's friend. Oh! I better get moving, starting to busy up. The usual, Charles?"

"Yes please, Francesca."

Charles doesn't hang around. He has his coffee and *toastata* – they do the best ones here. As soon as he gets back to the house, he phones Patrica.

"That was fast, Charles! Well, what's the news?"

"Not sure if you are going to like this, Patrica, but it seems a woman claiming to be Charlotte's friend from Ireland is asking for her. You know, the one who says she is the one who has always been there for her."

"Yes, what about her?"

"She was in the restaurant when I arrived, I obviously didn't know this until I spoke to Francesca. Oh firstly, is Angela really sick?"

"No, she is perfectly healthy, as far as I know. Don't tell me that is what she is saying now? God, that woman will stop at nothing."

"Francesca fell for her story and told her where Charlotte is. Luckily, she told me also. Joseph does have another restaurant, but it is not in Tenerife."

"Where is it, Charles?"

"It is in Maspalomas, Gran Canaria and Charlotte is gone to work there. Seems she is living in the apartment above the restaurant."

"Anything else on Joseph?"

"He does not seem to have any family speak of, but Francesca says he is a very private person. A good boss but keeps his private life to himself. Sorry, not much use to you on that one. I will keep looking and see what I come up with."

"Charles, that would be great. Thank you so much. Now I must get going. I have a lot of calls and arrangement to make. Chat soon."

Gran Canaria

Patrica

When Patrica comes off the phone, she immediately phones Audrey.

"Guess who turned up in Tenerife, Audrey?"

She fills her in on everything.

"I am going to book a flight, the first one I can get. Will I book it for two?"

"Yes, please do. Hopefully, we will get one for this evening."

"Give me ten minutes and I will get back to you."

True to her word, ten minutes and all is booked and organised.

"Hi Audrey, we fly at four thirty. I googled the restaurant and booked us into the hotel nearby. I will collect you on my way. See you soon. Oh, by the way, are we going to tell Pete and Anne?"

"Patrica, I think it is best if we keep things to ourselves for now. We can phone when we are positive it is Joan, and that Charlotte is definitely there. I don't want to raise their hopes again. They have enough to be dealing with at the moment."

"Yes, fingers crossed we get some positive results, and that Joan hasn't done more damage by the time we get there. I know one thing, if she is flying to Gran Canaria, her flight is at six fifteen, so she will have a few hours before we arrive. See you shortly."

It is gone nine o'clock by the time they get a taxi to bring them to their hotel. They check in and then go straight to the restaurant. When they arrive, there is no sign of Charlotte or Joan, they sit at the bar, wondering what is going on.

"Do you think we have the right place, Patrica?"

"I am positive, Audrey. Charles emailed me all the details. We will ask the waitress when she comes over."

Joan

Joan arrived at Cafe Maria at eight o'clock. She takes a table and when the waitress brings her a menu she asks, "Could you please tell me if Charlotte is working tonight, dear?"

"Sorry, I don't know a Charlotte. I am new here so maybe she used to work here."

"Oh, that's a pity. I really need to speak to her it is a family emergency you see."

"I will ask my supervisor if she knows her. Give me a few minutes, please."

When Rosario goes into the kitchen, she sees Joseph. "Excuse me, Joseph, but there is a lady outside looking for someone called Charlotte. She says it is a family emergency. Do you know someone with the name? She seems to think she works here."

Joseph

Joseph has a peep out the door. He is thankful that it is not the detectives, at least, but who is this woman?

"Rosario, tell her I will be out in a few minutes, please."

When Rosario returns to the table, she tells Joan that her boss will be with her shortly and takes her order.

Joan smiles, getting her hopes up. She will soon know where Charlotte is and get everything sorted.

Joseph arrives over to the table carrying the glass of red wine that Joan had ordered.

"Good evening, how may I help you?"

"Good evening, my name is Joan. I am a very good friend of Charlotte's. I need to talk to her. Can you help me please?"

"I am sorry. I don't know anyone of that name. I think maybe you have the wrong premises."

Joseph is not going to tell Joan a thing. He doesn't trust her and that was just on what he heard. Now that he has met her, he is convinced that she is not to be trusted in any way.

"That is strange as the waitress in your restaurant Café de Rosa, told me I would find her here."

"Which member of staff was that?"

"Francesca, she seemed very sure that I would find Charlotte here. It is so important, you see. Charlotte's daughter is very sick, and I need to talk to Charlotte. She needs to come home to see her."

"I wish I could help you. Joan, isn't it? I really have no idea of anybody of that name."

"Joseph, isn't it?" Joan says in her nasty manner. "I think it is time you stopped lying, isn't it? Where is she? Stop this pretence. I am not the one you need to protect her from. I only want to help her."

"As I have said, I do not know anyone of that name. I am really sorry. I wish I could be of more help. Enjoy your meal and have a nice evening." Joseph can tell that Joan is savage. It's quite obvious she knows Charlotte is here, but he just doesn't trust a word that comes from her mouth. If Charlotte's daughter were truly sick, her family or the detectives would have contacted him. They know where he is.

What kind of woman would make up a story like that about her own granddaughter? What is going on that she would go to those lengths?

He asks Rosario to keep an eye on Joan and let him know which direction she goes when she is finished her meal.

Joan

Joan knows she has to play things right. That waitress is still watching her. Thankfully, she never let Joseph know that she knows Charlotte is in the apartment above the restaurant. She will go back to the hotel and wait until the morning to call on her, when there is nobody around.

Joseph

In the meantime, Joseph has rung Francesca to see what she told Joan. "Hi Francesca, I believe you had a lady asking after Charlotte today. She arrived here this evening. I did ask you not to talk to anybody about Charlotte. What possessed you?"

"Joseph, I know you told me not to mention anything to anyone. But that lady told me Charlotte had a daughter and that she was very sick. If it were me, I would want to know if my daughter was ill. Charlotte never mentioned a daughter, so I was taken by surprise."

"It's ok, Francesca. You did what anyone would do, but I need to know how much information you gave her."

"I told her that Charlotte had moved to Maspalomas, was working in your restaurant there and living in the apartment above the restaurant. Sorry. I really was only trying to help Joseph. I hope I have not caused trouble for Charlotte. That is the last thing I would want to do."

"Ok Francesca, I will sort things out here. Just don't speak to anyone else about Charlotte please."

"I will not mention a word to anyone, Joseph." When the phone went dead, Francesca decided it was best not to mention that she had spoken to Charles about her. It couldn't do any harm, could it?

When Joan is gone, and Joseph is sure she's not going to call to the apartment. He texts Charlotte telling her he's on his way up to see her.

He arrives at the door ten minutes later. He knocks on the door and Charlotte answers.

"That was fast. I thought you were going back to Tenerife today?"

"Change of plan. You had someone else enquiring after you today, Charlotte. Don't panic. They are gone now, but I don't know for how long."

"Who?"

"Your good friend Joan."

"What is she doing here? Is something wrong at home?"

"I think we need to have a good chat, Charlotte. Joan arrived in Cafe de Rosa yesterday, told a sob story which I can tell you here and now is not true. Poor Francesca believed every word and told her you were here. She knows where you work and live now. Charlotte, I do not trust this woman and I can tell a bad egg when I meet one. Let me tell you, I have met a lot of them in my former life. Do you still trust her?"

"No, Joseph. I have been thinking long and hard and Joan is not my friend. I think I wanted to believe she was on my side, my friend, as she was the only contact I had with home and she said all the right things to keep me sweet."

"Well, that's good. She is not to be trusted and when I tell you the story she is telling, you will trust her even less. I was speaking to her tonight and she says the reason she is looking for you is because your daughter is sick, and you need to come home."

"What? Why would she say that if it wasn't true?"

"Wait now. Calm down. The detectives have my contact details. Don't you think they would have contacted me if it's true? I met your husband, Charlotte, and he doesn't remind me of a man that would keep you away from your sick daughter."

Charlotte is feeling a bit calmer now. Joseph is right but then if he is, why would Joan make up such an awful lie about Angela?

"Charlotte, I really have no clue what is going with your family, but I really don't trust this woman. She seems desperate to me and desperate people are capable of anything. I believe she is clever but not clever enough. I want you to pack a few things and move to my house for a few days. I will do a bit of investigating and see what is really going on. I think it is best that you are out of the way for the time being. Just until we know who to trust."

"I will get some things together and go. I think you are right. Joan is a woman on a mission and not a good one, I don't know how I could have been so blind to have trusted her."

"Stop beating yourself up. She seems like a clever woman, Charlotte. One who will go to any length to get things her way. I will collect you when everything is closed and quiet. I want to go back downstairs and keep an eye out just in case she returns. Don't open the door to anyone please. See you soon."

"Joseph, thank you for being so good to me. You are a good man."

"I am not a good man, Charlotte, but I am trying to make amends."

When Joseph arrived down to the restaurant, he was so busy watching out for Joan that he never noticed the two ladies sitting at the bar. But they both saw him, especially Patrica. The first Audrey knew something was wrong was when Patrica got up from her stool, her breathing was deep – not in panic but temper.

"Patrica, are you alright?"

The only words she utters are, "It is him. It is him."

At that moment, Joseph notices the ladies and goes pale, before he knows what is happening Patrica is right in front of him, her finger in his face. "You! I can't believe it is you after all these years."

Audrey is in shock. "What in God's name is going on? Joseph, is there somewhere private we can go?" she says as she puts her arm around Patrica, noticing that she is shaking like crazy.

"Yes, my office. Follow me," Joseph stutters.

They go into his office. Audrey is practically dragging Patrica. People are looking, obviously wondering what is going on. The staff are trying to pretend nothing is happening, which is not an easy task.

When they are inside, Joseph closes the door and drops into a seat.

"Now will someone please tell me what is going on here," Audrey asks.

Patrica at this point has collapsed into a seat too, all her anger turned to grief. Then nobody says a word for a few minutes, but it is not a comfortable silence by any means.

"Joseph, have you some brandy? I think we all need a glass."

He goes to a shelf behind him which is stocked with bottles of spirits and wine. He gets three glasses from a box on the floor and pours three large brandies. Patrica and himself gulp down theirs.

Audrey is looking at them both in wonder. "What in God's name is going on?" she asks breaking the glacial silence. "Well, is anyone going to tell me what is going on? How do you know each other?"

Patrica is unable to speak. She is just staring at Joseph, as if she has seen a ghost. Joseph is the first of the pair to speak. "I am so sorry, Patrica. I know they are only words. I can't undo what happened but please let me explain."

"Explain? Explain what? Why you killed her?"

"I did not kill her. But yes, I was in the car. As soon as I knew what he intended to do, I tried everything to stop him. I was twenty-two years of age, Patrica. I didn't know what I was involved with until it was too late."

"Shut up with your lies! You knew damn well. You killed her. It does not matter that you were not driving. You were there."

Now it is Audrey who is unable to speak. Not in a million years would she have imagined this scenario.

"Please, I never meant for her to die. I thought we were only to give you a scare. She was to come home and say she had a near miss, that is all. But he was crazy, he had other plans. He told me the only way to really scare people off, is to carry through on a threat. You know like with kids, no idle treats. I tried to stop him. I really did, but he hit me in the face with a gun, I didn't even know he was carrying. When I came around, it was over with and later that night I heard what had happened to you."

"Shut up with your lies!"

"Please believe me! I know I was involved in threatening you. It is not a part of my life I am proud of, believe me. I ran that night and went into hiding. I knew he would hunt me until he found me. I knew too much, you see."

Patrica is just staring at him. To her it is like reliving the nightmare all over again. She is lost for words. Her grief overpowers her.

It is Audrey who finds her voice. "Who is he, Joseph? John? Whatever your name is – who is this man that you worked for?"

"Does it matter? He is dead now." Joseph has tears running down his face. "It was through my older brother that I got involved. Later, when he realised who and what we were really involved with, my brother did everything to get me out. But once you're in, there are only two ways out, my brother went one way and I the other. They murdered him that same night He refused to get involved when he heard what they were intending to do, wouldn't be part of your beating. They just shot him in the head. He had tried to warn me. I discovered the message on my phone the next day. I really had no idea that they intended to murder you both, your survival was not meant to happen, you see."

"When did he find you, Joseph?"

"Three years later. I had gone to New Zealand changed my name and was working hard on the building sites, saving, trying to make a clean start of my life."

"Really, Audrey? Why are you believing a word he says? He murdered my Margaret, beautiful Margaret and his friends left me for dead."

"Patrica, maybe for the first time, you will find out what really happened and maybe, just maybe, you can have some closure. It is no coincidence that we are here, that this case has brought us here. Please just hear him out, if only to know who was behind all that happened."

"Ok."

"I received a letter telling me that my mother had been in an accident. She was in critical condition. I also had a phone call from a neighbour. Of course, that was not their choice. I found out later they had been threatened. A hit and run. Well, I knew it was no coincidence. I was being warned of what was going to happen if I didn't come back. I never replied to the letter or rang my family, but I did travel home. He was the only threat. I knew the boss man wanted none of this brought out in the open. He'd had way too much unwanted attention since your incident. But he could not control this guy. I knew I had one last thing to do so that I could move on. Without going into it, all I can say is I've had no more problems since and am grateful to try to move on with my life. I sustained a scar from him, but it was worth it. The guilt never leaves me. Every day I live with the shame from those times and the things I was part of. Patrica, I truly am sorry and if I can do anything to make amends, please tell me. I will do anything."

They all sit in silence.

Audrey pours another round of large brandies.

It takes a while, but it is Patrica who speaks. "Are you really telling me the truth, Joseph? If you really are, please tell me who this boss is and everything you have on him."

"Yes, I am telling you the truth. I am so very glad that at last I get to say sorry to you. I can get you every piece of information I have on him and send it on to you, but Patrica, be sure about what you are doing. This man will go to any lengths to cover his involvement in anything corrupt. He is evil and doesn't care who gets hurt as long as he comes out on top."

"If I never do anything with it, I will have all the information. I am not willing to endanger anyone again, Joseph. Trust me."

"It will take me a few days to get things together. I have them well hidden. They are my little safety net, just in case. You understand?"

Thankfully, the tension eases a bit and Audrey decides it is time to move forward.

"Right, now that we have that sorted, we need to talk about why we are here."

"I already know that. I had a visit tonight from that good friend of Charlotte's. She seems like a nasty little lady."

"Thought as much. Yes, you are right on that. Joseph, can you tell us where Charlotte is?"

"In her apartment but I am moving her tonight. Is that the right thing to do, or am I wrong about this Joan woman?"

"Oh, you are dead right about her. A lot has happened and now it is your turn to believe us, Joseph. We are genuinely here for Charlotte's good. Her family want her home. Joan is the only one who has been trying to keep her away."

They spend the next half hour explaining everything that has happened, what Joan has been up to and what is going on at home.

"She is trying to pin this on Charlotte? Wow! She makes me look like Father Christmas. Sorry Patrica, bad joke," he grimaces.

"Definitely, Joseph. She is an evil woman."

They decide on a plan and if all goes well, Joan is in for a bit of a shock in the morning.

As they are leaving to go to the apartment, Joseph stops them both, "Patrica, I never expect you to forgive me, but know I truly am so very sorry."

"You're right, Joseph. I don't think I will ever forgive you or anyone involved but your apology is appreciated."

Minutes later Joseph knocks at the door, telling Charlotte it is him. She opens the door, and she stops when she sees Audrey and Patrica. "Joseph? I trusted you. Why are they here?"

"Charlotte, please just listen to what they have to say. You have nothing to lose."

Still unsure, she shows them in. "You may as well take a seat, I suppose."

They sit quietly for a few minutes, then Audrey speaks up, "Charlotte, we are really only here for your own good. We know Joan has told you a lot of untruths over the years. Pete knows all about them now. You know that he knew nothing of his mother's involvement until recently and as you can imagine, it is hard for him to take in what she has done."

"I think I am only finding out myself. Joan has played me for a fool all these years. I really am at a loss to distinguish between what is fact and what is fiction."

"We understand, and we are here to put you right. Look, we have nothing to gain from lying to you. Everything we told you the last time we spoke, is true. Your mother and Pete really do want to see you again. Pete wants you involved in Angela's life."

"I know Joan has told me a lot of lies but can you promise there will be no pressure put on me to sign anything, to waive my rights to Angela?"

"We can promise you that. Hand on heart, Charlotte, none of that was ever going to happen."

After talking for over an hour, they come up with a plan, and it is one Joan won't like one bit.

Charlotte leaves with Joseph to stay in his house that night. They all agree that Joan will be knocking on the apartment door in the morning and the last thing they want is for her to find Charlotte there.

As they are saying their goodbyes, Patrica turns to Joseph and says, "Joseph, please keep her safe. We are trusting you on this."

Charlotte thinks this is a strange comment and when they are alone in the car she turns to Joseph. "That was a strange thing to say. What was it about?"

"My past has caught up with me, Charlotte. And Patrica is a part of it. Tonight, I got to put a few ghosts to rest and hopefully, I will get the chance to make amends."

"Do you want to tell me about it?"

"Not really, Charlotte. It's not a life I am proud of. I would like to leave the past behind me."

"No worries. Joseph, if it's any consolation, I would be lost without your friendship and help."

"Thank you, Charlotte. Now let's get back to the house and get settled."

Audrey & Patrica

Audrey and Patrica go back to the hotel, deciding to have a drink before they go to their rooms.

"Do you think we are doing the right thing, Audrey?"

"I hope so, Patrica. It is for the best. To be honest, I will be glad when it is all behind us."

"I agree."

The next morning, on their way down for breakfast and just as they are about to go into the dining room, Patrica spots Joan.

She grabs Audrey's arm and backs out as quick as possible, not wanting to be seen.

"What is wrong with you?"

"That was close! Audrey, did you not see Joan? Look, sitting over by the window."

"God no! Fair play to you for spotting her. That would have messed up our plans for definite."

Audrey decides it is best for her to go back to her room and wait until the coast is clear. Patrica will text her when Joan has left the hotel.

Thankfully, Joan has never met Patrica and wouldn't know who she is. It's not long before Audrey gets a text saying Joan has left the hotel.

"I bet you she's gone to Charlotte's apartment. You better eat up fast, that won't take long."

They return to their rooms and pack up their few belongings. Patrica checks them out, not taking any chance on Joan seeing Audrey. The taxi arrives and it is just in time. There's Joan on her way back to the hotel and she does not look happy. She notices the taxi driving off, Audrey is looking away from her, out the other window.

"Did she see me?" she asks Patrica.

"I don't think she did, Audrey. Besides, you are the last person she would expect to see here."

"That's true. The sooner we are on that plane and back on Irish soil, the better."

Joan

Joan is definitely not a happy woman. After breakfast she went straight to the apartment and rang the bell. No answer. She tried numerous times but nothing. She would bet that Joseph man has something to do with all of this. She will not give up though and intends to return to the restaurant, prolonging her stay until she sees Charlotte.

'At all cost, Charlotte's trust has to be won back. It won't be easy but once I explain how upset Angela is with all of this, she will come around to my way of thinking. My story will have to be good,' she thinks. Plus, I will have to get her away from her boss. He is influencing her decisions.

As she is returning to her hotel, a taxi is just driving away. For one second, she thinks that one of the women is familiar, then forgets about it.

That evening when Joan returns to the restaurant, one of the waitresses approaches her. She tells her that Joseph wondered if she could wait around until Thursday. He has had a change of heart and says he will have news for her. He will fill her in on everything Thursday.

Joan is delighted with herself, thinking, 'Who says perseverance doesn't pay off? I think I will make this a little holiday for myself and enjoy the sunshine. I really do need a break after all the stress I have been under.'

When she arrives back to the hotel, she books herself on a couple of outings. She has a lovely couple of days in the sunshine. All too fast, Thursday comes around and it is time to meet up with Joseph.

Back on Irish Soil

M eanwhile, a lot has been happening in Ireland
while Joan is in Gran Canaria. When they landed,
Patrica phoned Pete and Anne, making an appointment
with them for Tuesday evening at four thirty. They both
agree to be there, even though Patrica didn't give them
any more information.

Pete and Anne

As soon as they got the chance, they were on the phone
to each other.

"What do you think, Anne?"

"I have no idea, maybe they have more bad news for
us. I really don't think I can bear any more disappoint-
ments."

"Me neither."

"Oh, by the way, have you heard anything from your
mother?"

"Not a word, which is not like her. I thought she
would be on to me day and night. Not sure what to think
really. Dad hasn't heard anything either."

"That is strange. Maybe you should call around to her,
see if she is ok?"

"No, Anne. I would be afraid of what I might say to
her at the minute. I have been reading the letters from

Charlotte and it is becoming quite clear that my mother was keeping her away from us all this time."

"I guessed as much and that is terrible, but somewhere deep inside, I really think she was trying to protect you in some crazy strange way."

"I am not sure what to think, Anne. I only know I need to get everything clear in my own head before I talk to her. To truly know what has been happening, I need to talk to Charlotte, to know what my mother was telling her. It is so frustrating to have gotten so close to finding her and nothing."

"I know. I feel the same, Pete. We can only hope that Audrey and Patrica have some positive news for us Tuesday."

Tuesday's Appointment

T uesday arrives at last. Pete and Anne meet outside
and walk into the office together.

"Good evening folks. I hope you are both doing well.
Audrey said to send you in as soon as you both arrived,"
Alex greets them as usual.

"Thank you, Alex."

When they walk into the office, Audrey is sitting at
her desk and there is no sign of Patrica.

"Hi Anne and Pete, please take a seat."

"No Patrica today, Audrey?"

"Not yet, Anne, but she will be joining us shortly."

"You look very serious, Audrey. Please don't tell us it
is more bad news."

"On the contrary, we have found Charlotte and had
the chance to explain everything to her. She wants to
meet you both. How do you feel about meeting her and
when would you think you would be ready?"

Both Anne and Pete can't contain their excitement.

Where is she? Does she really want to meet? We are
ready whenever she is! When will she come here? The
questions are flying at Audrey from both Pete and Anne.

"Slow down. Firstly, Charlotte is in Ireland. She wants
to meet you both but needed to be sure it wasn't too
soon. Will I call her in?"

"You mean she is here? Now? Oh God! I am nervous… What will I say to her?" Pete wrings his hands.

"Pete, it will be ok. Let's just meet each other again first. Everything else will happen as it needs to."

Audrey picks up the office phone and tells Patrica to come in. A few seconds later the door opens. Patrica and Charlotte walk in.

"Hi Mam, Hi Pete…"

Then they all blurt out together, "I am so sorry!"

Anne runs to her and throws her arms around Charlotte. "I am so sorry, Charlotte! I have let you down so badly. Please forgive me."

Charlotte hugs her mother, not something she is used to, but it's nice all the same. The truth is her mother was never one for hugs. She's not sure what has changed but she's not complaining.

She looks over at Pete. He is just standing there. Then she notices the tears running down his face. She really feels for him but somewhere inside, she also has this awful feeling of anger.

"Hi Charlotte, it is really good to see you," he says quietly.

"You too Pete."

Audrey and Patrica can feel the tension and realise it is time to sit down and do some talking.

"I know this is really hard for everyone, it's not going to be like in the movies. A lot has happened and lots of talking has to be done. But today is the start, now Charlotte needs a few things cleared up understandably. Do you both mind if she speaks first?"

Both Anne and Pete nod their heads giving her the go ahead.

"Go ahead, Charlotte. This is the time to get clarity."

Charlotte is sitting on the chair, picking at her nails. This is not easy. She knew it never would be but didn't expect it to be this hard. She takes a deep breath turns to Pete and asks the question that is worrying her the most.

"Can I see Angela, please?"

"Of course you can, Charlotte, and you can be the one to give her all the gifts and cards."

"You mean she never received them?"

"No. My mother kept them from her, those and the letters. I only got them last week when my mother was out of the house."

"Pete, if Charlotte gives Angela the cards and gifts, what will she tell her? I know your mother has done so many horrible, damaging things. But Angela loves her, and I know your mother loves Angela. You need to come up with an excuse. I really think Angela would be devastated."

"I agree with Mam, Angela will have enough to deal with. Why don't I tell her that I had them sent to a post box in Ireland hoping one day to be able to give them to her myself."

"You would do that? After all my mother has done? Why?"

"Not for you mother, trust me, for Angela."

"When do you want to meet her?"

"As soon as I can. I know we will have to take things slowly. It's going to be a lot for her to take in."

"How about Thursday afternoon in the park?"

"Are you sure?"

'Yes, it will give me time to talk to Angela and prepare her.'

"That sounds good to me. I agree. We'll need some time and space to adjust to things."

"Charlotte, where are you going to stay while you are here?" asks Anne.

"Audrey has kindly let me stay in her house, Mam."

"Why don't you come home with me? That is, if you feel it would be ok?" Anne asks hesitantly.

"That would be lovely, Mam. Are you sure?"

"Of course, we will have plenty of time to talk, or not – whichever you want."

"Audrey, do you mind if I get my things and stay with Mam? I really am grateful to you for letting me stay at yours. Grateful to you both for persevering with things. You didn't give up on us."

"I am only delighted that you will be staying at your mother's, and that things are working out."

Pete and Charlotte arrange a time to meet up in the park and Pete leaves.

As he is leaving, Audrey asks to talk to him privately. She is a bit worried about him. They go into the other office.

"Pete, how are you feeling? This is a lot, and it wasn't what you imagined, was it?"

"I don't know what I was expecting. I suppose as you said, a bit of me thought it would be like in the movies. Where everyone hugs, all is forgiven, and they all live happily ever after. Naïve of me, I suppose."

"Nothing wrong with that, Pete, but that's not what it is like in reality, sadly. Things need time, and lots of talking. But I do believe they will work out ok for you both. It may take time, but anyone can see you both still love each other very much. You just got a bit lost, needed your family to support you and help you both through but sadly that didn't happen."

"I know you are right. As for Joan, thankfully I haven't heard a word from her since Saturday mornings' barrage of missed calls."

"You wouldn't have. She was in Tenerife and then flew to Gran Canaria."

"You are joking me? Where is she now?"

"Still in Gran Canaria, waiting to see Joseph on Thursday. We wanted to keep her out of the way until you had met up. We wanted to give you some time with no interference."

"God, that woman will stop at nothing, will she? I swear if I never see her again, it will be too soon."

"Pete, whatever happens, you have to remember she is not only your mother but Angela's grandmother. You need to be sure you mean those words before you make any decisions."

"I know, Audrey, but at the moment I need to be angry with her. I spent too long being shut down, not allowing myself to feel anything after Charlotte left."

"I agree, Pete. But try to not let it eat you up. I have a suggestion for you. I put it to Charlotte, and she agrees, but only if you want."

"What is it Audrey?"

"Would you think of going to someone to talk? A mediator. They would help to keep you both focused and maybe help get through this difficult time."

"I can't see why not. I think it might be good idea. There is such a lot to talk about and sort out. Do you know somebody?"

"I do and he is an excellent mediator. I can give you his number and you can make an appointment. I will phone him and tell him I am sending you both his way. He is always terribly busy but owes me a little favour."

"Thank you so much. Audrey, you and Patrica have been amazing to us all. We must owe you a lot of money at this stage, why won't you let us pay?"

"You know, Pete, money isn't everything. Sometimes it is just nice to be able to bring people back together. Most of our cases are about getting proof of adultery which usually pulls people apart, so it was refreshing to be part of reuniting people."

"When thing settle, we can all go out for a nice slap up meal together. Though, it might be a while down the road."

"Sounds good to me, Pete. I know Patrica would also be only too delighted."

Pete is happier and more optimistic as he walks away. This is thanks to Audrey, and Audrey feels happier knowing he is ok.

Anne & Charlotte

Anne and Charlotte follow Audrey to her house. There is not a lot of chat for a while. They are both a bit awkward.

Charlotte collects her bags and thanks Audrey again, leaves and goes out to Anne's car.

It is Anne that speaks first, as they drive away. "Charlotte, I am sorry for not being there for you, but I hope you will let me be there from now on. I understand that it won't be easy, and the chances are, I will still make a lot of mistakes. Just know this, I love you and will keep trying to improve on my mothering skills."

Charlotte looks at her mother. She has never, as long as she can remember, been told she was loved by her mother.

"That's the first time you have said that to me, Mam. I love you too. I want to clear the air and move forward. It is going to be very strange for us all, but we are back together and that will make things a lot easier."

With the ice broken, Anne tells Charlotte everything that happened since the search began, a lot of which has Charlotte sitting open-mouthed.

Over the coming days, Charlotte tells her mother her story, from the pregnancy onwards. There were times Joan was lucky she wasn't nearby, as Anne would have loved to have slapped her and not only once or twice.

Pete

Pete arrives at Andrew and Emma's house to collect Angela. When he rings the bell, it's Annmarie who answers. It seems she is spending more time here than in her own house. Which is a good thing. It really is good to see Andrew so happy.

"Hi Annmarie, I am here to collect Angela. Thank you so much for collecting her today. I really appreciate it."

"No worries. She is a lovely girl. Herself and Emma are such good friends, aren't they? Come in, they are out the back garden playing. Sorry, no homework done yet."

"No worries, we can do it after dinner."

Pete and Angela are in the car after saying their good-byes, when Angela says to her father, "Daddy, are you ok? You look different?"

"I am, Angela. All is good. Now let's go home and have some dinner. What do you fancy? Think it's a take-out night. I'm feeling a bit lazy tonight."

Pete is just too whacked after the day to cook and Angela loves her nuggets and chips.

"Brilliant but it is only Tuesday, Daddy. We usually get takeout on Fridays."

"I know but I just fancy a big dirty burger tonight."

Pete is still not sure how he is going to tell Angela about her mother or how she will take it.

He waits until after dinner when they have cleaned up. Angela is washed and in her pyjamas. They sit on the couch together. He has decided to pave the way first and see how the land lies.

"Angela, Nana Anne said you talked a lot about your mother when you were away. I was wondering why you hardly mention her to me."

"I just don't want to make you sad, Daddy, that's all. You always get sad when anyone mentions her."

"Do I? If I do, it's not that I mean to, it's just that I miss her. Do you understand? If you want to ask any questions about her, you know you can."

"Really, any question?"

"Yes, of course. What do you want to know?"

They chat for a long time about Charlotte. When he tucks Angela into bed, he feels a lot easier about everything. Pete has decided not to mention the meeting until tomorrow after school. Two nights of waiting will just be too long for Angela. He can only hope it goes well. Another decision he has made, is to give Angela the cards and gifts when he tells her about her mother. He knows it's not what they had arranged but he wants Angela to know that her mother was always thinking of her. Hopefully, it will help to break the ice.

After dinner Wednesday night he sits Angela down. He is really hoping things will go well.

"Angela, I have something to tell you. I am not sure how you will feel about it, but I hope you think it is a good thing."

"You found her, didn't you, Daddy?"

"What do you mean? Found who?"

"I have known for a long time that you and Nana Anne where looking for my mother."

"How? Who told you?" Pete is blown away. He hopes his mother had nothing to do with this.

"I overheard you talking to Nana Anne one day. Please tell me you found her?"

"We did, Angela. She wants to meet you, if …."

Pete never gets to finish the sentence. Angela jumps up and throws her arms around his neck. When she steps back, she is smiling from ear to ear.

"Of course I do! Oh Daddy, when can we see her?"

"How about tomorrow?"

"That would be brilliant! My second wish has come true. I just knew it would."

"That was your second wish, Angela?"

"Yes, that is why I couldn't tell you. I was so scared it would ruin my wish."

"I have something to show you, Angela." With that he takes out the cards and presents from Charlotte and gives them to Angela.

Pete has decided to tell Angela the truth. No more secrets. There have been enough of them.

"Your mother never forgot you. She sent a gift and card to Granny Joan's every birthday and Christmas. But Granny Joan never gave them to you. I think she was trying to protect you in some strange way. I hope you won't be cross with her."

"I am not cross with her. She loves us, but sometimes she does do silly things, Daddy. Are you cross with her?"

"I am a bit, but for different reasons. We will sort them out at some stage. Now open your gifts and cards." Pete has put them in order and as he watches Angela open each card and gift, he realises he is relieved she is not cross with his mother. Then again, it is Angela, and she is too kind for that.

Angela reads the messages in each card and then hands them to her father to read. By the time everything has been read and looked at, both Pete and Angela have tears running down their faces. They cuddle up on the sofa quietly thinking about what was written.

It's Angela who talks first, "Daddy, she must have been so sad and lonely."

"I know, Angela, but hopefully not anymore."

Pete wakes bright and early Thursday morning, even though he has not had much sleep and looking at Angela, it doesn't seem like she slept much either. Pete told Angela they were taking the day off from school because they were meeting Charlotte at twelve thirty in the park. After breakfast they go for their usual walk and when they arrive at the fairy tree, they tie on the ribbons that Angela wanted to give the fairies. These are to thank them for making all their wishes come true. She even put one on for Emma, a nice yellow one, her favourite colour.

She whispers, "Thank you fairies, for making all my lovely wishes come true, especially for bringing my Mammy home."

At twelve fifteen, Pete calls Angela, "It's time to go. Are you ready?"

They get into the car and just as they are driving away Angela says, " Daddy, do you think she will like me?"

"Angela, she will love you the same way we all do. You are so loved and so special. Never forget that, ok?"

She nods and smiles, but she is still worried.

As they step out of the car and go towards the park, Pete sees Charlotte and like the old days, his heart skips a beat.

Charlotte sees them immediately.

Before he can say a word, Angela says to him as she walks ahead, "That is her, isn't it?"

"Yes Angela, that is your Mammy."

Pete stands back and leaves her to it but is surprised when she walks over to her mother and puts her arms out to her. Charlotte takes her in her arms and they just hug each other. Pete has no idea what is being said, but that's ok. This is their moment.

"Hello Mammy, I wished for you to come home and now you are here."

"Hello Angela, I have missed you so much. I am so sorry. I should have come back a lot sooner."

"You never forgot me."

"Never. Not for one second."

When they move apart, Pete can see that they both are crying, but smiling at the same time.

They talk for about an hour and it's Pete who suggests lunch. They all go to the local cafe, the one Pete and Charlotte loved back in the day.

When Angela goes to the bathroom, it is the first chance Pete and Charlotte get to talk. "Charlotte, before Angela gets back, I need to say one or two things please."

"Ok Pete."

"Firstly, I am sorry I wasn't there for you. I really didn't know what to do. Secondly, I am so sorry about my mother and the things she did to you."

"Pete, she did them to you too. You had no control over that."

"I know. One more thing. I told Angela that it was my mother who kept your cards and gifts from her. She is an amazing kid, she was not angry. I think she knows my mother better than all of us. We have so much to talk about... Did Audrey speak to you about the mediation?"

"Yes, and I am happy to go ahead with it, if you are?"

"I am, Charlotte. God, I have missed you so much."

"It will take time, Pete. I have missed you so much too. I really hope we can make things ok, that we can move forward somehow."

"I hope you will be able to forgive me. This is my mobile number. Maybe we could meet for a chat, just the two of us? Here's Angela."

They go back to eating when Angela sits down.

"I was just telling your Mammy, that you received her cards and presents, Angela."

"I am sorry, Mammy. Granny Joan should have given them to me, but I think she thought she was protecting me. I hope you are not too cross with her."

"It is ok, Angela. I understand."

She is so cross with Joan, but she has promised herself she would not say a bad word about her in front of or to Angela. The poor kid has been through enough.

The Plan

J oan never knew that Charlotte was to meet the detectives, Audrey and Patrica, in the airport. Charlotte had decided it was time to face up to everyone and get things sorted once and for all.

Patrica phones Pete and Anne, making an appointment for them for the Tuesday at four thirty. Charlotte has agreed to meet them but had to wait until Audrey had explained everything to her mother and Pete.

When Audrey was sure everything had gone well, she phoned Joseph to tell him he could go ahead with meeting Joan on the Thursday. She told him that Charlotte would be meeting her daughter at twelve thirty on Thursday. Joseph was only too delighted to ensure Joan had stayed in the area for a few more days. The staff had told Joan that Joseph said he would see her on Thursday and that twelve thirty would be a good time.

"I shouldn't be really telling you this, but Joseph has some news for you."

Joseph had told Maria to build up a bit of a bond and trust with Joan. Maria had no problem doing this after he had told her the story.

"I won't say a word, dear. You can trust me."

Not once in those few days did she see Charlotte, but maybe today she would. Hopefully, that will be the news Joseph has for her. She was running out of patience to be honest.

She was at the restaurant at twelve fifteen, but Joseph didn't turn up until twelve thirty, just like that waitress had said he would.

"Good afternoon, Joseph. Well, what news have you for me? Where is Charlotte? I hoped she would be with you."

"I have news about Charlotte alright and I hate to disappoint you, but you won't be seeing her here today."

"Well then, what is this news?"

"You see, Charlotte returned to Ireland with the two detectives. Audrey phoned me to say things went really well in Ireland. Would you believe it, she is meeting her daughter today!" Joseph looks at his watch and then looks at Joan "Actually, they are together right now. Isn't that just fantastic news?"

Joan is silent. She just cannot believe what is happening. Joseph is loving this, the shock on her face and then the realisation that she has been made a fool of by both him and Charlotte.

"You kept me here with the promise of news, when all the time you were making sure I wasn't at home to stop this fiasco from happening. Do you know what you have done, you stupid man!"

"Yes Joan, we all do. We stopped you from depriving your own son of his wife, your granddaughter of her mother and Charlotte's mother of her daughter. You must be one of the cruellest people I have ever met. And trust me, I have met some evil ones in my life but you, you beat them all."

Joan raises her hand to slap Joseph, but he is too quick, he grabs her hand. "Joan, I would not try that again. Now, I think it is time you left my restaurant."

He walks away and can feel the rage coming from Joan, but she knows better than to go any further.

Joan leaves. She is furious and returns to her room at the hotel. When she has cooled down, she phones reception to get her flight booked for tomorrow morning. Then she goes to the supermarket down the street and buys herself a bottle of vodka. Back in her room, she pours herself a glass and doesn't stop until the bottle is empty. Her last thoughts were very miserable ones, as she passed out in a drunken stupor.

Joseph returns to his office to phone Audrey and tell her the news.

"Thank you, Joseph. I would love to have seen her face I bet she was livid."

"That she was! She even went to give me a slap in the face. Audrey, before you go, I have a question."

"Ask away, Joseph."

"Do you think they will be ok? You know, Charlotte, Pete and Angela?"

"I do. You could see when they met that their love is still there. It will just take time and a lot of work."

"That's good to hear. I hope Joan will give them a chance. You know, let them be."

"Now that Pete knows everything, he will keep her in line. She won't get a chance to cause any trouble, trust me on that. Thanks again, Joseph. I will keep you posted on things and I am sure Charlotte will be in touch. Take good care."

"Thank you for that. I appreciate it. Take care, Audrey."

One Year Later

Pete

I am so looking forward to this holiday. It will be our first as a family. It has been a strange time, but it is so good to be together again. The mediator was the best thing for us, helping us to move forward. At times it was so hard, when Charlotte spoke about the day she left and all that followed… the loneliness. I still have not forgiven my mother for all she has done but Charlotte always said we should not exclude her from Angela's life.

I still remember my mother's face that day she arrived at the front door, ready to tell me what a mistake I was making.

She got a right shock when I would not let her into the house. I took her by the arm, guided her out onto the street, out of view of the house. In a quiet voice, I told her everything I knew – about the letters and gifts. She had tried everything to blame Charlotte, telling me she was a devious dangerous woman. I just looked at her, put my hand up and said, "Stop Mother. You have lost your husband, a good man who only did his best for his family and you are so close to losing your son and granddaughter. Trust me, only for Angela you would be gone out of my life. The only devious dangerous person in all of this is you. I will not let you cause any more problems.

Do you hear me? If you go near Charlotte or her mother, that will be it. This is no empty threat, Mother. I need some time before I can see you again. I am still in shock that you did all those things, and I am not sure if I will ever forgive you."

"But Pete, you have to understand, I was only protecting my family. She was never good enough for you!"

"Mother, I'd leave now if I were you, before you do more damage and really lose us."

"Pete, you would never take Angela away from me! You know I love you both so much…"

"I used to think that, Mother, but I am not so sure. It's best if you leave now and trust me, if you cause any trouble, I will cut you completely out of our lives."

She was not a happy woman that day, but she did as I asked. In time, she was gradually allowed back into our lives. Knowing better than to ever say a bad word about Charlotte or her mother. It must be agony for her, but I don't really care. The sad thing is, I really don't think she sees that she did anything wrong. I have done a lot of reading up on narcissists and I am convinced that my mother is one. Sadly, she will never believe she is at fault in anything, it will always be someone else's fault. All I can do is keep an eye on her when she is around, I have told Angela that she is to tell me if Granny Joan says anything she doesn't like. Thankfully, to date, nothing seems to have been said.

It was so sad when we lost Anne. I had only just truly gotten to know her, only started getting to know all that she had been through. She really did have a hard life. No wonder she was so closed down for so long. I was so happy that herself and Charlotte got to have that time together to heal the past. She gave her daughter an amazing gift – closure. Charlotte was able to grieve her mother, with the past left where it should be, in the past.

Dad is doing great. He seems happy out these days. He is turning into a right chef and dating Mary. He says they are just friends, who enjoy the same interests, especially bridge. A bit of company for each other. No matter what, it is refreshing to see him so relaxed and happy. We meet for lunch every second Saturday, just the two of us. It is nice spending time together. He is such a good man. Not once has he said a negative word about my mother and always asks me how she is keeping. Sadly, I can't say the same about my mother, even if I mention his name around her, she glares and says, "Do not speak of that man, after what he did to me." It should be the other way around but that's life, I suppose.

Audrey and Patrica are doing well. I really think Angela is good for Patrica. She is always a happier person when she is around her. Angela even said to me once that Patrica isn't as sad as she used to be.

Audrey told me that Patrica is in a new relationship. It is early days, but they are hopeful. She says it is thanks to Angela. My nine-year-old is such an amazing young woman. But I always knew that, from the first day I held her in my arms.

Joseph is there waiting for us. He gives Charlotte a big hug and you can see the emotion between them. It doesn't bother me. I am just so thankful that she had

Joseph through those tough times, and it is thanks to him that we have her back.

We climb into the car and I reiterate Josephs words, "Let the holiday begin!"

Charlotte

The plane has landed. It is the first time I have returned to Tenerife since everything happened and what a year it has been. It took a lot of work to get where we are today. The mediator was great. I suppose the thing that stood to us, was that myself and Pete were still in love, so we had a good base to work from.

A lot of talking had to be done and it wasn't always plain sailing, but we worked through things together. Myself and my mother also went through so much, and I was so glad we got to clear the air before she passed away two months ago. She had discovered she had cancer, two months before she started the search with Pete. Nobody knew. I found out from her doctor that she had turned down any treatment, wanting to be in good health for as long as possible. We spent a lot of time together, going through old photos, chatting, just being together. Mam spoke a lot about her childhood and her time with my father. She really did have it tough. I read somewhere once that to really understand your parents behaviour, you need to know their story. And I now know that is so true, since she told me about my own dad and his family life. We both agreed that it explained a lot about him, but it still was not possible for me to truly forgive his behaviour to his family. I am just grateful that we had that time together. Pete has been amazing through it all. To be honest, he always was. He is much more aware, and we talk through everything. He kept his word about his mother. We did not exclude her from Angela's life. Not that Joan appreciates this, it's just that Pete takes no nonsense anymore.

When she arrived back from Gran Canaria, she went straight to Pete's house demanding an explanation. Using her bully tactics as usual but Pete later told me he had made things clear to her from the outset and that I need not worry about her coming near me.

Angela and I took time also. She was better than me. I suppose kids adapt faster. I had so much guilt, especially when I realised how much I had missed out on. That I wasn't there to hold her hand through the appointments, not there to meet doctors. Pete says it is in the past and the mediator agrees, saying guilt is such a wasted emotion. We should now focus on moving forward. It's taking me time, but I am trying. I have my bad days, but I talk to Pete about them and he reassures me. Angela is an amazing child. She is years ahead of her age. I suppose it's all she has gone through. I am so very proud to be her mother.

She brought me to the fairy tree a few months after my return, telling me the story of her wishes. It is lovely to imagine that I was a wish come true for her. I made my own wish that day while there and it looks – fingers crossed – looks like it's coming true. I'll tell Pete and Angela on holidays.

It will be lovely to meet everyone again. I haven't seen Joseph since I left but we have spoken over the phone. It sounds like himself and Maria are becoming an item. I am so happy for him. He is such a lovely man. He says that Patrica and himself have spoken a few times and at last, he is letting some of his ghosts rest. He never told me what they were but that is his business, and I am glad he is moving forward.

We will be here for a fortnight, staying in Joseph's house. He insisted. We intend to enjoy every minute.

Audrey and Patrica have also kept in touch. They are meeting us here, but will only be staying for a few days, due to work commitments. They will be staying in their friend Charles' house, and we intend to meet up over the coming days. It is nice to say we have become good friends. They were both so upset when they heard my mothers' news and visited her regularly in her final weeks. They have been so good to us all. Angela and Patrica get on so well. I think Angela is one of the few people Patrica can really connect with.

Frank is like a new man and has started to date his friend Mary from his bridge club. Joan was not a happy camper on hearing that! I really wish she would keep her opinion to herself though.

There's Joseph! He has come to collect us from the airport.

It's an emotional moment when we meet. We hug, then Joseph moves back saying, "Now, everyone into the car. Let the holiday begin!"

Angela

It is so exciting! It's our first holiday together. Mammy and Daddy are so happy. It was strange at first, especially after Mammy moved into our house. It has always been just me and Daddy, but Emma really helped. It was the same when Annmarie moved in with them. Before it had always been just her and her dad. Emma said it took a while but that after a few weeks she realised how good it was. It was nice not to worry about her dad anymore, knowing there was someone to take care of him.

Emma was so right. Daddy has Mammy now to mind him and they are both there to mind me. Things are more fun with the three of us together and Daddy's so happy.

Granny Joan seems crosser these days. She pretends to smile but her eyes never do. They always look cross. I never told her that I knew she kept my cards and presents. I think it's best not to. It is not the same with her and Daddy. He told me that if she says anything I don't like, especially about Nana Anne and Mammy, I am supposed to tell him straight away.

I don't though. Sometimes she says nasty things, but I really don't think she means to. It's just the way she is. Emma agrees with me that it's best not to tell Daddy because it will only cause a row.

I brought Mammy to see the fairy tree. She made a wish that day. I hope it is the same as the one I made. It would be lovely to have a little brother or sister one day. Emma wished for her Daddy and Annmarie to get married and they did. She is waiting for her new brother or sister to come. She says it should be here next month.

Grandad Frank is great fun these days. He loves his new house, and his friend Mary is lovely. She is always smiling and laughing, even at Grandad's not very funny jokes. I am glad he has a new friend. I wonder, is she his best friend like Emma's mine? I hope so.

It is lovely when we meet up with Patrica and Audrey. Granny Joan was not too happy when she met Audrey. It was so funny. She looked like a goldfish and kept calling her Alice. I am not sure why she keeps calling her the wrong name, maybe it is because she is getting old. Audrey found it very funny though. Granny Joan never said anything else about Audrey but it's obvious she doesn't like her.

Patrica is not as sad anymore. I brought her to the fairy tree, telling her to make a wish like myself and Emma.

She didn't say much but when she made her wish, she started to cry and cry. It was ages before she stopped. I just held her hand and when she stopped crying, she thanked me for bringing her to my special place. Her friend that was always by her side is gone now, and Patrica smiles more. Daddy says that she has a new friend. I was so happy when he told me.

We are meeting Audrey and Patrica here on this holiday. Mammy says it is where she first met them. She is going to show me where she worked and lived when she was here. I am going to meet her friend Joseph. She says he was so good to her when she lived in Tenerife.

It is so exciting!

When we walk out into the arrivals hall, Joseph is there to meet us. I like him already. Himself and Mammy hug, she has to stretch to reach, because he is so tall.

He tells us to get into the car, saying, "Let the holiday begin!" with a big smile on his face. That's when I tell him I have decided to call him the BFG. He laughs at this, "What does that stand for, Angela?"

"The Big Friendly Giant. It's a book by Roald Dahl. You will have to read it to me, Joseph. Then you will understand."

Joan

All off on a family holiday, like nothing has ever happened. I didn't even get an invite. Not that I would have went. Tenerife if you don't mind, as if that is a normal thing to do – go back to the place your wife absconded to nine years ago.

The way Pete goes on, it is as though I am the lucky one just to be allowed into their lives. It wasn't me who ran off to Tenerife when the going got tough. But I bite my tongue, or else I won't be allowed to see Angela. He has forbidden me from saying one negative word about Charlotte, especially to Angela, but sometimes I do slip up – by accident, of course. Angela never says a word to him about it. She is such a good little girl, but things are just not the same anymore. She is all about her mother.

As for Alice, or should I say Audrey, that private detective. She made a right fool out of me. When I think back on the things I told her – she even has recordings. She told me that if I give Pete and Charlotte any problems, she will play them to Pete. Threatening me, if you don't mind. But it would be best if he never heard those things, I would be cast out for good. I have to keep my head down and my mouth shut if I want to see my granddaughter. All I ever wanted was to protect my family and this is how I get paid in return.

Anne's passing was of no real loss to me. I wonder if Pete will be as upset when I go. She was such an interfering woman, but I overheard Pete and Charlotte saying she left them a nice inheritance. Who would have thought! They both spoke of how it would not make up for the loss of Anne. You would swear she was some kind of saint! A few years ago, neither of them had a good word to say about her.

I met Frank for the first time since he left, last week in town. He was walking along with another woman, if you don't mind.

He did stop to speak to me, but I was not having any of it. I just walked past him like he didn't exist. They both started laughing and kept walking. The cheek! He did look ten years younger and a lot happier, I have to admit. This only added to my irritation, not just with him but with all of them.

I am no longer the person my family look to. If anything, I feel completely out of control. Pete was not happy when he had to collect me from hospital before Christmas, when I had a little bang in the car. I don't know what all the fuss is about, nobody was hurt. But the judge put me off the road and I had to pay a hefty fine. I had to go to counselling to help me with my 'drink problem'. Pete insisted.

So, I am not drinking now... Well, not openly. Just a few glasses before bed. How else would I sleep?

I do get quite lonely at times. People would say it is of my own making. Just what I deserve but I am still not sure why I should be penalised for wanting to protect those I love. As I said, it wasn't me who ran away when the going got tough, now was it?

Frank

Who would have imagined that life could change so much in one year? I have never been so happy and at peace. It is lovely having my own little house, never worrying if I leave a cup in the sink or the toilet seat up. No more shouting, being attacked for unknown reasons – all that is behind me.

Watching Pete, Charlotte and Angela becoming a family again, that has to be the best part. I was glad that Pete let his mother be part of their lives. I have to admit, a little part of me pitied Joan, even though I know she doesn't deserve it. It must be agony for her to keep her mouth quiet and not interfere. She will never see that she did anything wrong. The counsellor I attended for a few sessions explained to me that Joan is a narcissist. After she explained what this was, things started to make a lot of sense. You see, Joan had me convinced that it was my fault that she behaved the way she did. I provoked her. Even though I had left the house and don't live with her anymore, it's still taking time to adjust.

Mary suggested that I go for a bit of counselling to try move on. It was the best thing I could have done. I never realised how much Joan's behaviour impacted on me, how my self-esteem was so low, always thinking I was a fool… It's so hard to live with that and many other untruths Joan had convinced me of. But after eight counselling sessions, I realised it was not my fault. I had been bullied and manipulated all the years. This is not saying I am perfect, I have plenty of flaws, but I was not the man she portrayed me to be. I realise now that the fear of losing my children was the only reason why I stayed so long.

I saw it happen to my friend John, when his marriage ended, even though the kids were grown up and had their own lives. Their mother had slowly poisoned them against him. She was always the victim and played the part so well that she eventually convinced them. They spent less and less time with him. He was penalised for just wanting to be happy and at peace. I was terrified that was how it would be for me, but the funny thing is, Joan made sure of the opposite with her interfering and deviousness.

We met her in town the other day. It was the first time I saw her since I had left. I was so glad that Mary was with me. Would you believe it, I almost panicked! Never had I realised that I'd lived for all those years, just waiting for Joan to erupt. Mary was great. She just squeezed my arm when Joan pretended she didn't see us. When we were past, Mary looked at me and we broke out laughing.

"God Frank, I hope you don't mind me saying this, but she is a scary looking lady."

"I know. It's sad really. She is so poisoned with anger and bitterness. Is it mad after all she put me through, to just wish that she would find some happiness or joy in her life?"

"That's not mad. It just shows the good man you are. Now, let's go have a coffee and big, bold slice of chocolate cake."

Mary is such a good friend, and we have lots in common. I hope one day we will be more that friends, but I am just happy to have her in my life.

I got a lovely text message from Pete. They are having a lovely time in Tenerife. It's twenty-eight degrees. I am looking forward to seeing them when they get back, but I am delighted they went on holiday. Anne was so happy to see them back together. I am sure she is watching over them.

One thing Anne's passing assured me of – life is so precious, it is for living, not in the past or in the future, but right now, in this moment.

Anne

The day the doctor told me it was cancer and terminal, I didn't know how I would cope. He told me there was treatment available if I wanted to go down that road. When I asked how long, he said he didn't know. He always felt it was down to the individual. I could last a year or more. We discussed the treatment and it seemed to me that it would only prolong things by a few months. It would be very severe, and it would make me very unwell. My decision was that I would rather have the time left to be of quality. After all, it was my choice and I choose to live as full a life as I could, while I could.

I booked into a lovely cottage in Clare for a few days, needing time to digest everything. A lot of walks on the beach were had and a lot of tears shed. It was at then I decided to find my daughter, wanting to make my peace with her. Also, I worried for Angela. It was so important for her to have her mother in her life.

By the time I returned home, the decision had been made. It's time to put my life in order. Nobody was told about my illness. I had decided to pretend, even to myself, that all was ok. I just blocked it from my thoughts, but deep down knew it was the reason I had started the search.

That same day I told Pete my plans and he said he wanted to be a part of it, I put things in motion. It was a hard few months, but oh, it was worth it.

The day Charlotte came into the Pearse and Patterson's office was one of the best days in my life.

At last, I had my daughter back. She was so thin and scared. I had to hug her. I could feel the stiffness in her body. Understandably, it is not like I had ever hugged her or showed her much affection.

It took some time, but thanks to her understanding, forgiving nature, we got there. That trait is one Angela has received from her mother for sure.

I was over the moon when herself and Pete got back together. They make such an amazing couple. They both worked so hard to reconcile everything. Of course, it was because they love each other so much.

Angela, well, she just embraced having her mother home. My mind was at peace at last. They were going to be ok.

My health started to deteriorate. I had gotten over a year. I was lucky to have had the time to get all my affairs in order.

It all happened very quickly. Within a few weeks, I was bedbound and on morphine. I got to say my goodbyes and my beautiful daughter was by my side as I passed.

Over those weeks, I was happy to let the past go. It was such a lovely feeling knowing that at last, I could rest in peace.

The End

Acknowledgement

I am so very lucky to have the support of my wonderful partner Jack, my daughter Rachel and son Stephen. A big thank you to them.

To all those people who encouraged me in any way, and to Bernie for her help with final naming of the book over an inspiring glass of wine, I would like to say a big thank you.

Please Review

Dear Reader,

If you enjoyed reading this book, would you kindly post a short review on Amazon, Goodreads or what ever platform you purchased the book from? Your feedback will make all the difference in spreading the word about my book. It would mean so much to me also as most potential readers do judge a book by what others have to say. Thank you in advance for your kindness.

Siobhan